I, Death

Chapter One

I ASKED YOU, HAVE you ever seen yourself in an article, a character in a book, a person on stage, and thought, "That is me! That is who I am."

Even if you are not named, your life stands before you in the mind of another's imagination, and it is either enlightening, frustrating, or terrifying. When I read that book, when I saw myself in the mind of another who had foretold of my existence, I was at first disturbed. But then anger grew, for the author had downplayed the way I was able to bring devastation to the world. With just a small amount of willpower, I could cause a person to commit suicide, tear apart their lives, and with greater urgency, I could…I could…

Well, let me show you exactly what I can do if you push me to anger.

The one thing that the author got right was the way in which I was killed.

Death comes for Death…I can almost write the obituary and headline myself. And yet I was not dead. It takes more than being hit over the head by a solid, heavy blunt instrument to kill me.

You know that Stones classic, of course; everyone does. They sing the words with deep affection and full gusto of voice; they want you to literally have sympathy for the entity downstairs. Yet no one really ever has sympathy for Death, not even the comic writers.

I stared at the book for a long while, an old, well-thumbed, disintegrating volume, almost weightless in the palm of my hand, and I felt my anger grow.

On the television, a man dressed in a sharp blue suit with a matching flawless tie was expressing his doubts on one of humanity's greatest achievements: the manned mission to Mars.

"Humankind, surely, we are not naïve enough to believe that we can survive in such harsh conditions as the red planet coldly harbours. It is preposterous to insist that we keep spending tax dollars on selling a fantasy to the public." He drawled these words as if he were a Southern Baptist preacher conversing with God and the angels on one side of the church and urging his mortal congregation on the other to acknowledge that they were too dumb to ask questions or raise objections to his holier-than-thou stance.

I dislike these types of preachers. I wanted him to choke on his words…but my attention was not focused enough to send him to his own devils and gods. And he had a point.

We have screwed up our own home, and now we want to vandalise the neighbour's garden.

The mission to Mars had been the talk of everyone for weeks, and it only heightened as the spacecraft and its twelve intrepid explorers drew closer to fame, fortune, and living immortality. It was everywhere: on satellite, in the papers, on the internet. It dominated conversations the length and breadth of the country and the wider world. You could not walk around a village green without someone stopping to engage you in conversation; you could not mind your own business in a bookshop without a tug on the arm and a beaming, supercilious face looking at you in expectation of another morsel of information being pushed out into the ether. I began to hate it.

It was the sense of false hope that drove me to think of the expedition to the barren planet in ways that would result in the first chink of concern that the news anchors described as *"a glitch that would rectify itself."*

The book worried me. Written years before I was born, it was almost like a prophecy. I was no devil, just an ordinary man— admittedly one who believed himself cursed—but the book made me sound as if I was more than human, as if I were the spawn of something beyond human conception.

"Ground Control, how are the figures looking your end?"

It was the captain, a robust and insanely competent woman from Stockholm, to whom the voice belonged.

I tore myself away from the book for a minute and glanced at the small bottle of Scotch on the table to the right of me. One-handed, I unscrewed the cap, poured a measure into one of the two empty glasses I had set out, and then just as easily replaced the top back on the bottle. I raised the glass to the television and saluted the team as they raced towards infamy.

I resolved to ask my guest, when they arrived, what they thought of the book that had worried me. They had obviously thought the resemblance between me and the monster within was worth exploring. After all, if you had given a biography on Christ to a person with delusions of grandeur, you'd expect some sort of response.

"That's superb."

Again, I raised my glass but then set it down on the table, the glass almost touching its unused neighbour.

I looked at the cover of the book. A disturbing green title that screamed out late-sixties fascination with the macabre and hinted at disease and scum-like filters. A hideous mask contorted in what appeared to be pain was painted ludicrously onto the dust jacket, garish, lurid, as provocative as they came in that heady period of English Literature dominated by the cartoon-like. The face was that of the Gorgon, and there the similarities ended.

"Give our love to our family and friends," is what she intended to say, what she had almost turned into her sign-off for the cameras and audiences at home, but she was cut off by a loud, threatening bang between 'family' and 'friends'.

I heard it, the world heard it. Despite it being almost two hundred and fifty million miles away, everyone who was watching the feed via the media of their choice heard it as clearly as if it happened right next to the chair they were sitting in. They heard it in the crowded pubs of the East End; they heard it in the curry houses in Manchester as the small black-and-white television spoke softly in the background of the hot and sweaty kitchen; they heard it while they made love with the television on in the background; they heard it as they shopped, as they played, as they worked. It was a sound that the human race would never forget.

It was not the bang of a part rupturing on board the vessel, nor of a dropped spanner reverberating around the metal capsule. It came from outside, a single thud, a jolt, small but powerful...and the screen went blank.

It stayed blank for several hours, by which time, I was on the floor, blood slowly pouring from an open wound. In my mind's eye, I subconsciously saw a group of people standing over me, one of them staring at my eyes and declaring me to be in a coma.

The television was still on; nobody had thought to turn it off.

"What do you think made that noise then, Mam?"

"No idea, Barry. Could be anything!"

If I wasn't in a coma, I would have been...well, miffed doesn't quite fit the feeling of ill will I was harbouring in my deep unconsciousness. Perhaps provoked is a better description. Incited, overlooked...I never did like that feeling. But what was I to do? I was as close to purgatory as I had ever been, limbo for the living, and yet I could see them crowding around the television watching the next step in human history, while on the floor lay the victim of an attempted murder...some people's priorities are often lacking in decorum.

"So, that is the situation. The crew are said to be in good spirits, and checks have been made. So far there is no indication of what the noise was that we all heard. Within the next day or so, as the craft draws closer to Mars, the landing craft will be deployed and then the real work begins..."

IAN D. HALL

I rather enjoyed the word 'we'. It was meant to place emphasis on the act of union, that humanity stands together in pride and hope, as well as adversity. It didn't work.

I heard the television being turned off; the silence became deafening. I miss the days when I was small, and the box of unearthly delight would pop and make a fizzing sound as the connection was cut. Now it just goes silent, not a pop or a wheeze, not a single measure of complaint at its life being cut short. In a way, I was glad; at some point one of those dreadful celebrity programmes would have reared its ugly head and my subconscious would have been subjected to more torture than it could stand.

"There are two glasses out, look. Here on the table. One has had alcohol in it for certain—whisky by the smell." The person's voice paused, and the giveaway sound of a glass being picked up and sniffed filled the room. "And this one is empty, not been used at all."

I could tell the voice was female, but I couldn't see her. My head was tilted in such a way that her face was out of sight, but the memory of her perfume lingered long after I was taken from the apartment to the local hospital.

She sounded familiar, though. Perhaps I had met her at a book signing, or maybe in one of my infrequent trips to the morgue where I would gather up information to use in one of my less-than-bestselling books.

I should say, I am not sure who attempted to kill me. I have a suspicion, but then it could just as easily be my ex, a critic, or a relative of anyone who believes my assertion that I am the bringer of death. The assailant, though, might have done me a favour; for in a few days' time, the world and its wife might have come barging through my front door brandishing weapons of various depths and magnitudes as they learned of my part in the greatest space disaster of our age.

Chapter Two

IT'S BEEN...HOW LONG? I really couldn't tell you. Time works differently when you're in a coma and all that you have are your thoughts. I can make an educated guess, though. The crew is still alive—well, not all of them.

See, even when I'm not able to see the action, I can influence certain events, and they'd thoughtfully placed a television in the corner of the room, high on a wall so that it could look down upon me as an agent would on a first-time would-be author that they couldn't coax or bribe into bed. The television stood out in a world dominated by wires, by cables, switches, and machines that made small beeping noises. It was the only electrical item in the room that seemed unnatural. I should be thankful they tuned it to the news channel, not a daytime magazine show filled with an audience screeching in unison, howling like monkeys as they peed on the tigers below.

I have a fourteen-hour gap in this...memory. I don't know what you would call the actual ability of recollection when you are out cold on a hospital bed and not expected to wake up. I overheard the doctor, a chap called Wasteacre, I think, talking to a woman in a long, brown trench coat, her short, brown hair just touching the edge of the jacket collar. I couldn't her face, but I heard her introduce herself as Detective Inspector Bridge.

Apparently, I had to have an immediate operation on my brain when I was brought into the hospital, and she had been waiting for me ever since. I would say that it showed care, compassion for my situation, but really, I deduce she wanted to ask a series of questions that might point her in the direction of my attacker and that she could say at her next review that she had earned the promotion. Cynical? Absolutely. I've made my living on such statements of outlandish outrage and pessimism.

Time in your own head can be a frightening prospect—hard enough when you're awake and fully in control of your faculties. When you're in a coma, when the world goes on around you as your body, your mind is being operated upon and you are left truly alone, that is torture.

It was in those hours after the operation that memories resurfaced.

Let me introduce you to the moment when I began to think I was capable of harm, when my aunt's words fell on my ears as though she had physically assaulted me with the back of one of her thick pudding-shaped hands.

I was not yet a teenager, and I had walked sullenly to school, ignoring the calls of those who might have casually called me a friend. It was a damp British day. The last remaining seconds of a soaking wet summer had faded into the wreck of an autumn determined to be grim and fiercely unattractive. The leaves were sickly yellow, as if a rampant case of jaundice had been brought out into the open and caused an epidemic of bitterness to lay on the floor in floral tribute to the dying of the year. Each step taken was filled with the possibility of skidding and taking a tumble. I watched in earnest as women in heels gingerly made their way across uneven pavements and through unseen rivets that held the grating in place as they crossed the market square...victims of their fashion.

I was sullen because, and not for the first time, my aunt, who I had the misfortune to live with since the death of my parents several years before, had called me evil, a devil, a calculating evil spirit, and said that if I came home, I might just find all my belongings in the front yard and on fire.

I wasn't intending to go home. There are only so many times you can take being called names before you start to believe it, before you start to act like it. As it turned out, I had no home to go to that night anyway.

Once past the Market Square, it was normally a bus ride out to the school I attended, a fifteen-minute journey in which ancient squabbles were reignited, where the girls stoked dirty rumours and the boys were more than pleased to live up to them. It was fifteen minutes of quick romances, of fist fights and drama… of cigarettes smoked as if the habit had taken twenty years to develop and not the six weeks since they first caught the smell of burning tobacco as it growled and crawled into the air past the hedges that separated the sports block and the pristine computer science room.

I didn't like catching the bus. It reeked of false masculine bravado and unearned dominance of desperation and the previous evening's family abuse. It was the damnation that not even a can of body spray could disguise. Only those who didn't want to walk in the rain, those who felt the need to be seen and heard, caught one of the buses, from which they would hurl abuse, cans and lit cigarettes at passers-by and carve their initials into the upholstery. They were the ones who ruled the world early in the morning and in the late afternoon.

I knew my aunt was not joking when she exploded in a foul-mouthed tirade of everything that was wrong in her life, and how much I was to blame for it. I knew she was not joking, because she never did. She was the meanest woman to have walked this Earth—at least, that was what I always believed until I was forced to bounce from house to house as part of the foster-care system.

Before I was able to storm out of my aunt's front garden, its tidy borders and maddening neatly trimmed grass that was not permitted to grow over two inches in length or be anything other than deepest green, I almost tripped over a can of petrol my aunt had put out in readiness to fill the tank of the small petrol-driven mower she had bought herself out of my trust fund.

IAN D. HALL

I was about to leave it in its overturned position when I heard her screech.

"Oi, you put that can back where you found it. It's bad enough I found your stash of disgusting porn, you dirty little pervert, but kicking stuff over in the hope that I'll trip over it and break my neck—well, that just proves you're the devil. No wonder your parents died, you little shit!"

Now, before I continue—after all, it's not like I have got places to be—I didn't knock the can over on purpose, and I didn't have porn. It was a health and sports magazine, which I'd borrowed because it had an article on supplements I wanted to read for a biology class. And who in their right mind says to a child, or to anyone, that you were the shame of your parents' life, that they died because you lived. I'll tell you who. Only the distressingly wicked.

What I did do, and I admit that my words that day were thrown back at her with typical teenage spite, was loudly retort, "Shut up and mow your lawn, you stupid mare. Perhaps you'll run over a wire somewhere and electrocute yourself."

It was heartless, and if I had a chance, I would take it back, apologise and beg for forgiveness. If I had a chance.

People should not throw objects at people.

If they miss, it creates litter, a potential stumbling block for another to trip over. If they hit, well, the damage can be… revealing.

My aunt threw her shoe at me. It missed. The action, though, made me more determined to get out of her sight with not even a sorry aimed in her direction. In fact, I flipped a middle finger at her and sloped off sullenly to school. Her red shoe was still beside the gate when I later returned to the disaster that had taken hold.

She must have hobbled after me, as I heard the metal petrol can grating on the stones as it was picked up, and I lengthened my stride so that I would be out of shot by the time she threw it at me. She muttered a few choice words, the sort that would've made a sailor blush and had a psychologist signing her up for a full course of anger management, but I didn't stop to respond.

Over the years since, I've perfected my sullen slouch and resting bitch face. As a man, the former is easy to achieve, the latter, not so much…especially as a teen. You're supposed to want the greater public to be scared of you, to love you, to feel as though you could hurt them with a smile or mend their heart with a well-aimed piece of sarcasm…in short, they're not supposed to know where they stand with you from one minute to the next.

Sullen I was, sullen I remained. Hostile, bad-tempered, but never morose, never miserable. People have always assumed that I covet misery; nothing could be further from the truth. It is just that misery of the human experience is one that follows us all, and I have managed to find a way to use it as a tool, as a divining rod to punish the conceited, the vain, and the arrogantly proud.

I passed a park on my way to school.

The memory of the morning, the storm that had broken out between my only remaining relative and myself raging in my head as I took smaller and smaller steps, the trudge another teenage reflection that I had perfected.

My mind was…I guess, in a whirl, thoughts flickered between the before and what was to come. I knew by the time I got through the day and arrived back at my aunt's house, everything of mine would be ash. I found myself thinking ahead, what was the point of staying there? She was using my inheritance to gratify her own needs.

I don't know to this day if it was wish fulfilment or if the smack to the head drew out some latent ability, but as I lay here, for all purposes dead to the world except for the machines keeping me alive, I begin to see that it was both, that the world I came to distrust, to sneer at, in some cases openly despise, was born out of anger at injustice, and fate had, as it often does, chosen a champion in the darkness.

IAN D. HALL

Chapter Three

SHE IS SEATED on a plastic chair that is a deeply offensive shade of yellow and looks distressingly uncomfortable. Her hair has come undone from the tight-bunched medium-length ponytail that was prominently positioned when I could only see her from the back and now flows around her, straggled and unkempt, as dishevelled as a summer dress discovered on a cold tiled floor long after the washing machine has completed its cycle and the sun has sunk. Lifeless, unloved, forgotten.

Though she looks better than I felt when the wooden boomerang hit me with a painful crack on the side of my head.

To this day, I have an indentation in my temple where it struck with unrelenting and unapologetic ferocity. The hairline crack in my skull is testament to the strength that the lad had hurled it, the way I fell to the ground, lost in dark thoughts about my aunt, thus did not brace for the fall and broke my nose as the concrete pavement met me with glee in its stony heart. If it were to happen today, someone would call an ambulance—admittedly, it might have taken several hours to reach me, thanks to the monstrous cuts in public health, by which time the crowd would've become bored by the spectacle and, having shared my misfortune with the world, put away their camera phones and carried on with their day—but as I groggily clambered back to my feet, I saw only two lads staring at me, horror etched deeply into their faces.

Wearing the same uniform as mine but taller than me by at least six inches, they seemed caught between coming to my aid or running as quickly as possible away, hoping, quite correctly, that I would not recognise them again.

I was holding aloft the offending weapon, and the weight of it caught me by surprise. It wasn't plywood or one of those softer woods that catch the air perfectly. No, this was a substantial piece of timber, at least a foot from tip to tip and so heavy my wrist bent under the strain of holding it.

"What the hell?"

Those three words were all I could find to say to them, and I regret deeply not having the guts nor the guile at that age to have taken either one on in a fight. Alas, because my mind was spinning and the blow was causing me to see oddly, I could not remember what they looked like later when I had the wherewithal to exact my revenge.

As I held the evidence of the assault high above me, a man in his late forties walked past and sniggered outwardly.

"What?" I demanded, surprising myself with the ferocity of my question. The man was also surprised, but he recovered quickly—far quicker than I.

He flung his arms out wide as an assertion of dominance, an unspoken challenge to me to take him on. I had voiced my anger, so of course, in his mind, I wanted a fight.

I hadn't been able to focus on the faces of the two lads who had been mucking about with the boomerang, but this man had stepped into my personal space without thinking it would be a problem, that being a mere boy, I would step back, cower, stammer an apology for my outspoken verbal attack on his right to open mockery.

If my aunt had not filled my morning mood with unnecessary drama, if I had not felt the shattering blow of wood on skull and fast-bruised skin, if this cynically endowed man who thought it was funny to inflict further humiliation on a twelve-year-old by laughing in his face and being a jerk about it, I might have got to school unmolested. I might even have had a good day.

And maybe, my aunt would not have gone through with destroying all that I had left.

"What?" he repeated, mimicking my tone, mocking me with his expression. "Poor baby got hurt by a stick, did he?"

His chest puffed out as if he was a toad caught in the middle of an inhale, and his eyes went a funny creamy white. His arms, open to their fullest extent, were orangutan-like, almost unseemly disproportionate to his body. Even his neck was scrawny, ill-fitting, giving him the appearance of a doll that had been screwed together by two left hands wrapped in thick rubber gloves.

I don't know what he expected, and I wasn't sure what I was meant to do. Throw a punch? Kick him quickly in the reproductive area and hope that I could run quicker than he did after the pain and shock wore off? I felt small, awkward, intimidated; alarm and fear started to dine on my heart. I felt danger at the confrontation, and yet I was angrier than I had ever been in my entire life. That dichotomy of emotions, of preteen browbeaten anxiety coupled with a force of unknowing power, drove me closer to him until my forehead almost rested on his stubbled chin, and I stared intently upwards.

He had a significant height advantage on me, and those arms could have crushed me without a bead of sweat breaking. He had the air of a man who would think nothing of entering one of the town's more salubrious bars, urging the biggest bar fly to come at him with a bottle and enjoy the attention it garnered. What could I do?

I fixed my eyes on him and stared deeply into those white-glazed eyes, but the more I glared at him, the more I saw they were the eyes not of a man willing to act insanely, but one of the long-term effects of the diabetes coursing through his body. He was ill, and as much as I wanted to walk away and just let him be on his way, I found I could not back down. I had to stand up for myself.

The two lads had found their courage once more and quickly moved on, their nerve restored enough to hightail it to school, leaving me with their heavy wooden boomerang, which I still held in my hand high above my head. I slowly lowered it. The man's eyes never moved, yet underneath that milky appearance, I saw my initial fear reflected in what remained of his sight, and I drew confidence from it.

I dropped the boomerang to my side and let it hang loose, my fingers barely gripping it. What I was thinking…it was simple. *Just walk away, old man. Just walk away and you might live another day.*

My head hurt. The more I inwardly implored the man to turn away, the more I felt a stab of pain cascade across my brow, and it was becoming a battle of wills. After all I had gone through that morning, I would not be defeated.

In any other world, at any other time, he would have hit me and once more I would have fallen to the floor, a nose that was surely already broken taking more damage and abuse. I would have looked a right state in school that day and was tempted to allow it to happen—school somehow had lost its appeal in the last hour—but I could a glimpse of that fist clenching, and…

***

For weeks, I flinched at the sound of a police car siren. If anxiety was part of my genetic make-up, then hearing on the grapevine about a boy who could bring on an illness in a grown man was certainly one way to push me further into the shadows of myself.

I had been fortunate.

The man couldn't give a description of the face he saw, only the intense eyes, dark eyes, terrifying eyes that turned black, and the two lads who had been messing around in the park, far too close to the pavement and the road with an object that could shatter glass and destroy lives…well, they never came forward to cast doubt over any defence I might have offered to weary policemen and detectives with grudges towards society or to the Home Office for tying their hands in binding red tape.

I didn't touch the man, never laid a finger on him, but he reacted as if I had. He staggered backwards, first one short step, then another, and then he attempted to turn. It was as if he had

IAN D. HALL

taken on the role of a punch-drunk boxer and his legs wouldn't coordinate with his mind, a misfire of communication that saw him reel and wobble down towards the crossing fifty yards away where, quite by chance, he fell at the feet of a woman walking one of those miniature dogs that yap consistently.

He didn't die.

He was, though, quite unwell for a while and sent his time in the hospital rambling about seeing the devil. I know because one day, in an act of contrition and fascination, I walked to Avoncross's hospital on the hill and hung around by the nurses' station in pretence of waiting for a relative to turn up for visiting hours.

That's the thing with appearing indistinct. You can sit on a chair for a while and be invisible. This would become impossible as I aged, as my pre-teenager stage was replaced by a growth spurt and a career where I was on dust jackets and people inserted my name in reviews and dropped the colour of my eyes into conversation.

Back then, I was small and scrawny and fitted in because I wasn't seen. That knock to the head changed that, but that would only really kick in once the hormones started to surge.

I sat there watching nurses, falling in love with those who smiled, avoiding eye contact with the more austere ones who passed me by, their shoes clicking in time to the heart monitors and the beeps of machines out of the realms of science fiction. A dystopian revision of *The Wizard of Oz* where Dorothy kicked her heels together on bleach-clean walkways. *There's no place like hell, there's no place like hell.*

He started to scream. That delusional witch who threatened Dorothy's dog, Elphaba Thropp, could not have screeched it with more conviction.

"The devil! The devil is here! He walks amongst us! Nurse, Nurse! Please keep him away!"

Alarms sounded. Voices rose in concern. I overheard one nurse, all tightly bunched hair and obsessively clean fingernails, remark without a shred of respect for patient confidentiality that he'd been so quiet of late.

I took advantage of the melee and said to anyone who cared to listen that I was upset over the shouting man's words, and that I would come back later with my mum.

Nobody paid me heed. The invisible have this advantage over the rest: they can, and do, get away with saying anything.

The last I heard, the man who had stopped men in the street, who had sniggered at my misfortune, who had allowed himself to become distressed enough to fall ill, was transferred to a facility somewhere in the Oxfordshire countryside.

I occasionally send flowers to him. I don't leave a name. The card is always blank.

Chapter Four

I WONDER WHAT THIS is that has been handed to you.

Is it by any chance one of my journals?

You will learn a great deal about me in there, Detective Bridge. But not as much as I could tell you if you were able to hear me, if you could understand the thoughts in my head…these dark thoughts that cause people to die and catastrophes to happen. Or did you think that many disasters could have been avoided, human errors explained by an admission of hatred for the world and all who ignore its dying pulse?

You haven't noticed, though, have you, your own power?

I can tell we are similar creatures, Detective Bridge. We just have different ways of expressing them. I am darkness. I am the bringer of Death. You are the bringer of Justice, driven by the thrill of the chase, so consumed by it that you are oblivious to the way Doctor Wasteacre and others conduct themselves around you, exuding typical male sexual aggression in the belief that it shows vulnerability and passion. Not that your pheromones are wasted on only the male of the species; from my bed, I have spied a couple of female nurses turn their head more than once in your direction, and I suspect that if truth be known, half your colleagues have fantasised about taking you to their bed.

But you don't notice, do you? Turned on by your work, no room for a little laughter—or is it more than that? Perhaps a lover broke your heart and stilled your soul. Or perhaps you realised that sex is not your thing, and if so, I find myself congratulating you, for you have found a path that would have suited me more.

I certainly think my ex-wife might be alive had we not been consumed by desires and faults.

That journal will only tell you so much.

Let me continue, Detective. Allow me to linger in the memory of that first day, the one that changed how I saw myself. Close the journal, put down your Dictaphone, shut out the television for a while. After all, those astronauts aren't going anywhere, are they? Except maybe to their graves.

I arrived at school in a foul mood and with a headache that was making me feel sick. I was late. It happens, but it is not every day that you face a detention for having been attacked with a boomerang. Thankfully, the trudge of my walk up the hill towards the downs took me over the bridge, where I paused to watch a train disappear into the tunnel and resurface, slowing to a snail's pace as it drew into Avoncross station. My school was just beyond the bridge in Merebrook, a district named for the lesser of the rivers that meet in the city, merging with its siblings then separating once more before it rolls towards Southampton, the Solent, and the sea.

The reason I stopped for a moment on the bridge was not only to watch the train magically enter the world of the underneath and the darkness of the city, but also because I felt a sharp, searing pain as I heard the squeal of the train's brakes as. It was as if the vibration, the echo of metal on metal on metal, aroused something deep in my head, and whilst it was fleeting, it forced me to rest against the old brick bridge that had stood long before there were trains, when Merebrook was no more than a river passing through marshes and bog land.

Some years from this point, a train derailment would see the start of the city's downfall; for me, on the bridge that day, it was part of a reveal that would turn me into the living embodiment of Death.

I excused myself as I walked breathlessly into the school's computer science lab. The teacher was a kindly man who had done much to keep many a student on the straight and narrow, often arguing for leniency when the child's actions would normally necessitate a harsher punishment. He was respected, and he responded in kind even when confronted by a latecomer.

Without pausing from his instruction to the class, he nodded and directed me to a free computer. Shoving my bag under the desk, I logged in while he droned on. *A special guest… a test…*

The visitor took over the presentation, but my attention was lost to the screaming of my headache. The more I looked at the screen, the more intense the pain felt, yet I could not take my eyes from the invisible flickering and electronic power, as if it was calling to me, imploring me, damning me, daring me to destroy the image on the screen.

It was a polite clearing of the throat by the class teacher that sidelined my attention from the screen to the last faltering words of the visitor.

"Don't forget, while this is a test, it's also a bit of fun. It will not reflect on your history with the school. No conclusions will be drawn. It's only being used in a national experiment. When the buzzer goes, you may start. You have the maximum of one hundred attempts, and…" He genuinely paused when he said this as if it was a momentous gift he was offering. "Anyone who solves it once will get one pound. Complete it five times and I will give that person a crisp, brand-new, ten-pound note. Any more than that, you will have the chance to be measured against the national average, and the one with the most will receive the opportunity to visit London and spend time in our offices as a consultant on a range of new children's games."

He couldn't have sounded any less sincere or enthusiastic. Still, the promise of a ten-pound note was enough to motivate most of the class into participating. The screen sprang to life with no buffering, no advertisements, wasting no time in capturing the class's attention. A simple counter in the corner ticked away the seconds, accompanied by a blinking cursor. It was rudimentary, basic, yet an immediate hit.

I find myself playing it even now, during breaks from writing, when words refuse to flow, and it takes a swig of prune juice to clear the mental blockage. It serves as a distraction—an infuriating, enraging, annoying, blood-boiling amusement that I have yet to conquer.

The pre-teens destined to shape the future, to become the pioneers of the computer game's limitless advance, eagerly jumped into the experiment. Almost without exception, they failed on their first attempt. The beep of failure unified them, amplifying their groans throughout the room. The second attempt was equally swift, as they all hit a mine with a single click on an 'x'. The sound echoed like a klaxon, reverberating around the room, until one child stumbled upon a blank space, followed by another, and then, unlikely as it seemed, a third. The revelation of hidden mines behind each grey panel was enticing, promising riches that overwhelmed each kid as neurons fired, pushing them into a relentless battle they wouldn't abandon.

Amidst the clamour, I remained a lone voice, a solitary peace activist in a battlefield of fervour. While others signed up, I silently protested, a conscientious objector awaiting an end to the madness. In amongst the whizz-bangs and the exploding shells, I felt as though, I could almost hear the haunting strains of 'Silent Night' waft across the no-man's-land of the computer science lab and into the ears of every up-arrow, down-arrow, left-and-right-dash-weary soldier.

My resolve lasted a mere thirty seconds before I was conscripted and the generals forced my fingers onto the keyboard.

The teacher leaned in, whispering words of encouragement, sensing my unease.

"You seem out of sorts today. Are you okay?"

I could have cried off. I was being offered a way out of the war to come. I was injured. *I'm not fit for duty, Sir. Permission to go to the medical officer's room, Sir, where I shall present a chit and confine myself to quarters for a week.*

Instead, fearing the stigma of cowardice, I muttered without conviction my intention to stay.

His touch, though friendly, was a little more than I liked, but as I said, he was one of the good guys, never an ounce of malice. Nevertheless, the touch was there, and it nudged me forward.

A good five minutes had passed since the pandemonium of selection started, but just as I was about to press an 'x' for the first time, a siren pierced the air—a relic of the Cold War, an anecdote of horror that thankfully, so far, has not come to pass.

I was the only one who felt it seep into the dark chambers of my heart. Every neuron seemed to fire at once as my brain found it could not distinguish between the reality of the game—of trying to avoid clicking on a predetermined pattern of pixels—and that of hiding in a cellar as the world above was incinerated. I felt the heat of the explosion, the walls closing in, the very air catching light and my bones becoming ash and dust as I pressed 'x', hitting a mine on my first attempt.

Did I want to play again?

The screen reloaded, and I pressed x once more, hoping for an empty square or a clue to the mine's location. Direct hit.

Undeterred, I persisted.

Third attempt.

Fourth attempt.

Fifth.

Sixth.

Seventh.

Somewhere behind me, a squeal of delight accompanied another siren's violent shrill. Today's lucky winner, a pound in her pocket, a beaming smile from the man in the suit and a pat on the back that lingered far too long. The girl didn't notice, but I did, my concentration momentarily captured by a blot of red in the corner of my eye. I saw the hand pause over the girl's bra fastening before it was swiftly snatched away.

I returned my focus to the game. An eighth, ninth, tenth attempt, and each time I hit the target on the first go.

Others around me were groaning as they found fifty blank spaces or clues to the closest mine, some almost clearing the screen before striking the mine.

I was told a couple of weeks later that I had performed the worst of all the group in that session, the worst in the area overall during the trial. One girl in our class went home with five pounds that day, her bra remaining safely fastened, but she was the only one whom fortune had favoured with a smile.

My own session came to an abrupt halt when a gentle knock at the classroom door sent the teacher scurrying to answer it. The door creaked as it opened, the sound carrying a greater sense of dread than the machine's noise as a message was quickly passed on. I had turned around—we all had—and for the moment, there was no clicking on the x-marks that seemed to be permanently against me. Instead, there was interest, surface tension, and a finger beckoning me to join the conspiracy at the door.

I followed the direction and peered out into the corridor, the barest chink of light revealing the headmaster and a policeman.

I was about to protest, and then admit to my part in the man's possible death, until I saw the headmaster's sickly smile and beady, narrow eyes crinkle in supposed concern as he guided me away from the classroom. He had sad news to impart.

Chapter Five

S HE HAD BURNED alive.
"That's what the policeman told me," he said, trying to meet my gaze, bending down so we were eye to eye; equals. He wanted to show for the record, for my supposedly 'impressionable' memory, that he cared about the feelings of a young boy being told, for the second time, that he was alone.

A petrol can, kicked over and forgotten, and a sharp stone that had somehow punctured the aged seal, so that when my aunt struck a match near the small pile of belongings she had gathered to make a point, the petrol ignited and the can exploded, showering her in burning liquid.

The headmaster made all the right noises, his pencil moustache contorting in what appeared to be genuine sympathy. His nodding gestures of concern followed a script, a handbook likely crafted by the Department of Education—Chapter One; Subsection Five: How to appear sincere when delivering bad news to a student.

I don't think the policeman was fooled any more than I was.

I spent a good half-hour in that office. The headmaster, having exhausted his repertoire of comforting nods, kept glancing at his leather-strapped watch, comparing it to the ornamental wall clock that hung above a faded colour photograph in a wooden frame, depicting a young man receiving a degree. The words beneath it were too small, too intricate, to decipher.

There was another secret knock at the door, a code to be broken at some stage, and Mrs. Cordage, the headmaster's secretary, burst into the room, austere in her skirt suit, not a crease to be seen, not a strand of hair escaping the tightly pinned bun I'd once seen her brush into place with the stamina of a hedgehog traversing an overgrown patch of grass while pursued by a predator.

She smiled at me, a shark amidst a school of fish, a piranha circling its prey. Despite everything that had happened, I smiled back, welcoming her insincere sympathy. It brought a tinge of red to my eye, seeing her for what she was—a disease in human skin, a virus that needed to be eradicated. Little did I know, I would confront her again in such a fashion a few years later.

Neither the policeman nor the headmaster noticed our exchange, but she did. I could almost feel her heart freeze, turn to ice, as she interrupted with the reason for her intrusion, handing me my school bag, which had been retrieved from the computer science room.

Before anyone could thank her, she hurried away, her two-inch heels barely grazing the floor, as if the devil himself was pursuing her, and in a way, I was!

Those heels…and that one red shoe by the garden gate. Some find the symbolism of the mismatched pair arousing, but I find it disturbing. I felt as if I had stumbled onto the set of *The Wizard of Oz*, but one of subversion, where Margaret Hamilton lived on a while longer, and Dorothy, that beautiful spirit embodied by Judy Garland, perished at Glinda's hands, set alight by a vengeful munchkin harbouring a grudge for lack of work in the porn trade.

Still, that one red shoe was enough to break my heart.

I held firm.

A policewoman took my hand and called me brave. I loved her for that. It wasn't true, but I thanked her anyway without looking at her face.

Inevitably, I learned that despite the house belonging to me, I could not stay there on my own. Would it shock you, Detective Inspector Bridge, to learn that it hurt me more than losing an aunt? One offered security, the other a whip; one held the lingering presence of my parents, the other the smell of acetone and barbed criticism.

Ian D. Hall

But for the moment, my focus was on the ash-covered remains. It was as if she had spontaneously combusted, all that pent-up hate and bile erupting within her. No one wants to be beholden to an ungrateful child, it is better for the sanity if you walk away from their actions, but she was paid to be my guardian. The least she could do was give me hope. And now, I thought, I had that hope.

It was to be cruelly dashed.

For only one night, I had the chance to live and breathe freely. Then, at half past nine the next morning, there was a knock on the front door. The policewoman who had stayed with me overnight and fallen asleep on the job, appeared in the hallway, still in her wrinkled uniform as I descended the stairs.

For the first time in quite some time, I felt the urge to hug someone, to put my arms around this woman who was perhaps less than ten years older than me, but who, even in first light of day and with her hair shaped by the grooves of the sofa, looked both dishevelled and authoritative—a sight unlike anything I had seen before.

I told her to take it easy, that I would make her a cup of tea and toast if she wanted, once I'd seen who was at the door. This was now my house, after all.

Imagine my shock…

"I am sorry, your aunt borrowed heavily against this property and even took money from the various savings that had been left for you for when you reached the age of majority."

The policewoman stood to the side of the kitchen, both hands wrapped around the mug of tea I had poured for her, her eyes noncommittal but observing everything that was happening, listening to revelations of fraud unfold.

My mind could not comprehend the solicitor's words. I was twelve, I had no understanding of what the grey-haired older gentleman was saying, his apologies floating around me like metal ducks at the funfair, my grasp of his language failing to hit the target directly.

"It seems she found a way to exploit a junior member of staff, who, I assure you, will be dealt with by the full force of law. But that does mean, I am afraid, that in terms of this house and in concern of your age, the best course of action is to place it on the market and what remains from the debt accrued will be placed into the trust fund that your aunt depleted."

I noticed he'd tidied up her actions, made it seem almost genteel, as if she had made a simple and honest mistake, a doddery old woman conned out of her life savings being comforted by a grizzled old detective who vowed to hunt down the bastard and string him up by his… and he would stop there, suddenly mindful of his audience and the old lady smiling up at him.

I was not afforded that luxury. I had a young female police officer, and in my naivety—an early warning perhaps of the sexism that threatened to flourish—I found myself acknowledging that she would not be able to help me, that she was simply there as a youth worker, a babysitter.

What it boiled down to was that my aunt had monetarily raped me. She had taken all that my parents had put aside for me in the event of their deaths and left me with twenty thousand—still a considerable amount but barely enough to see me beyond my twenty-first birthday.

I felt my temple throb, a reminder of the impact of the heavy wooden boomerang, and rubbed the side of my head. I saw the room darken as I grew angry. It was only the soft touch of the policewoman's hand on my shoulder that stopped me from causing a scene.

Still, I cursed aloud when I heard some of the places where my aunt had spent the money, the cheques she had casually written for the cathedral trust, headed by Mrs. Diane Ratoon. I had been introduced to the god-fearing woman the summer before last and hated her immediately. It was the look in her eyes as she weighed me, judged me without a single question passing her lips. I had to sit there in a shirt, a good pair of trousers, and tie forced into place by my aunt, as this self-righteous woman sneered at me, made comments about my upbringing, and said I should be grateful to be in such highly valued company as her and the woman who had stolen from me.

I didn't get her meaning at the time, but with the benefit of public scandal reaching my ears in later life, with the knowledge that Avoncross has darker secrets that breathe in mouldy corners and live in nightmares, I find it hard to reconcile her supposed Christianity and faith with that of wishing me to be buggered by a prominent former and disgraced Member of Parliament.

I have met and enjoyed the company of many people for whom faith is a healer, but never before, or since, have I met anyone as disturbed and truly evil in their bigotry as Diane Ratoon.

I would like to tell you that I was the one who killed her, but it seems that nature found a way to bring her soul to justice. Instead, I will just tell you for now that the last time she saw me, I left her under no illusion of how much I hated her. Religion, if it gives you peace, then, no matter the God, so be it; but don't claim to have the moral high ground when you are nothing but a thief, a bigot, a liar, and a friend of a man to whom young teenage boys were regularly 'gifted' too.

The look on her face when she saw just how revenge is delivered by the gods when you smite their name…well, I have never forgotten it, and I enjoyed it immensely.

Chapter Six

I HAD LOST THE house.

One silver lining had presented itself via the solicitor's lips, although it didn't thrill me at all.

It seems my parents, specifically my father, having perhaps envisioned what his sister was capable of, had set aside a fund that would pay for an education away from Avoncross. A modest private school in London, one that would see me become a boarder full-time if the need arose, at which, in the event of my aunt dying whilst I had not reached an age when I could legally look after myself, would remain there until I was eighteen.

Of course, my father, despite being a wise fellow, could not really have foreseen my aunt's treachery. It was meant to be a last-ditch survival plan, no other relatives to call upon, grandparents on both sides having passed long before I was born, no godparents who might be coerced into guardianship, no old friend who could be cajoled into taking pity on the offspring of a dear colleague. My parents had been vaguely insular all their lives, and I was a product of that inward-looking union.

I didn't get a say.

I could have run away, simple enough to do. I knew a few kids who had done it, but life was not easy for the broken teen in Avoncross. Too many one-way streets and lost closes, not enough wide avenues from which to see the whole picture. Ask the policewoman if you ever find her; I'm sure she must have seen the fleeting temptation in my eyes when the solicitor spelled it out for me.

A single to the coast, enough money to get to France and perhaps a bit beyond, but what then? Find myself a job treading grapes, squashing them to death as they leaked wine in the barrel? A fine trade indeed, but not one I wished to enter.

Or I could head north, aim for Liverpool and its docks, lie about my age and sign on as a noble merchant seaman discovering new lands and cold waters... But there it was: my age. I was barely old enough to handle the responsibility of pouring a cup of tea without splashing it on the good rug. And what did I know about sailing anyway? What inkling could I muster to save myself and a crew in a thunderstorm that threatened to sink the vessel?

I was taken to my new home and school by a representative of the solicitor's office, a stern, unyielding older man with a grey-flavoured moustache that resembled that of a walrus in its pomp on the ice surrounded by the unfathomable waters and grim prospects of starvation.

It was an unhappy, uneventful train journey. There was no conversation. There was no answering of questions. No reassuring gestures. Only the occasional clearing of the throat gave any indication that the man was alive and not some partially animated tailor's dummy. The only time he moved was when he lightly touched his moustache to stop the tail-end hairs he had missed that morning from entering his mouth.

From Avoncross, through Wiltshire, the small edifice of life that was Andover and Basingstoke and onwards towards the steaming capital, I watched from across the divide of seats as his small end hairs turned inwards every mile or so, tickling his narrow, unremarkable lips. He would raise his left hand and gently, with his thumb and little finger, sweep them back out again, then, just as methodically, lower his spindly hand to his lap where it joined forces with its partner for another mile and a half, until the need arose once more.

Although raised in Avoncross, I had never really had much to do with the army units that surrounded our genteel city as if protecting a monument to religious pageantry, some long-lost relic of military secrecy. Thus, for the remainder of my time at that infernal hell hole, I did not realise that the man opposite me on the train was a retired captain in Her Majesty's Army, retained by the solicitors in Avoncross to handle potentially difficult clients.

That was it. I was a nuisance, a problem to deal with. Nothing had changed; my aunt had seen me through the eyes of her religious bigotry, a sinner who refused to repent; the school branded me a delinquent as I refused to bow down and be the model student. I was not evil, but apparently, I was a foul soul, a malevolence to be kept at arm's length.

I lost interest in the man's grooming habits, but his eyes never left their fixed position of staring intently at me. Those eyes, almost glass-like in their appearance, were the windows to an empty space, soulless and black.

I bet nobody ever heard him scream.

As, the train and its several carriages juddered along as it approached London's Waterloo Station, I came to—*enjoy* would be too sentimental a phrase to describe my feelings for the station's interior—*admire* its pomposity and ability to be so grand yet feel so dirty, so polluted at the same time. A quite incredible feat; at least in terms of architecture. In humans, it is quite ordinary, mundane, sickeningly commonplace.

I had never seen a station so full. Every square foot seemed to heave with the heartening masses, the complex emotions that emanated off them enough to make me feel ill, and it was a struggle to walk with my nondescript, cumbersome suitcase by my side as we weaved through passengers and reactions, past coarse language and nightmare-inducing announcements and deliveries. We fought our way past a group of women singing in the name of Jesus as they raised their voices to the heavens, past the large clock that governed time and train departures. A couple of bored-rigid but short-sighted sparrow-eyed policemen stood guard close by, missing the pickpocket who delved lightly, fingers supple and temperate of touch, to remove the stuffed wallet from the taller one of the two.

Piss stains pocked the floor, years of cumulative expressions of drunk passengers relieving themselves in unseen corners. Ground-in particles of food added to the mosaic, imprinted for eternity, or at least until such time as the railway decided to make certain stations more welcome to the overseas visitor with their foreign investment.

We headed towards the exit, so the sign informed with stark unfamiliarity, towards the bus stops and the theatre.

My silent companion stopped briefly to pick up a paper, the *Evening Standard*, from one of the kiosks, and I had a moment to look around me and see a true theatre in action, the players, the chorus, usherettes with their wares on sale as stockings were rolled up in private, knickers loosened and each potential customer given a secret sign of intention. Male and female prostitutes of a golden age, lacking security in a period of boom, delivered by a despicable woman inside London's own private fiefdom.

That was the thing, it was all... so big. My world had been one of sleepy streets, of narrow lanes and out-of-the-way alley shops, where the fair descended upon the Market Square once a year to sell candy floss and stomach-wrenching burgers, the dark night alight with a faint neon haze and the joyous screams of teenagers and children at their annual brush with the outside world, beyond the hills, beyond the control and reach of the church, before, once more, the town cloaked itself from view.

The town had secrets. Behind every closed door and dark-curtained window, there were enigmas, but no surprises.

My marvel at the expanse wasn't too last long, as no sooner had I settled my gaze on a man in a tailored dark uniform who was gesticulating wildly and with a certain amount of pain on his greying brow while he and a member of railway staff almost came to blows over a misplaced ticket... than the solicitor had informed me of my status as ward of court.

To be yanked, not just beckoned or verbally instructed, but to be hauled with no dignity almost off your feet by a firm-gripped hand is not a pleasant way to be reminded of your place. As I grappled my suitcase, catching my knuckles against the heavy straps and glimmering oversized buckle, the suddenness of the experience was enough for me to yell out, unsure if I was being attacked, struck by some unknown assailant who saw me as an easy mark.

Nobody noticed, or if they did then they didn't care. A scream in London is as a whisper to the rest of the world, unnoticed in the maelstrom and cacophony of noise.

I managed to twist in such a manner that I was no longer teetering on the backs of my heels. Imagine my shock when my assailant turned out to be the man who, for the last couple of hours, had been keeping a beady eye on me.

I was so angry. I felt the words tumble out of my mouth, several months' worth of bitterness and hostility taking the opportunity to express themselves in ways that as a child I would have been ashamed of but in the last few days had realised I had missed out on all the fun.

This older man, straight-backed and narrow-minded, took it all with ease. Now that I know he had been in the military, it does not surprise me in the least that he was almost at attention as I spoke down to him while having to crane my neck upwards. He showed no retribution, not outwardly anyway, of this low-level act of insubordination.

I fairly exhausted myself in the short time that my...rant...was served to the uptight and overly composed former military man, the proverbial water of a duck's back. Not a sign of agitation, his marshalled outward shell undented, I was a gnat pressing against the hide of a robust elephant. Nothing could dissuade him from his superior attitude. I resented him, the embodiment of my condition, my new place in the universe. Oh, how I stared at him,

Ian D. Hall

with the kind of passion that one holds only for those we truly find contemptible.

"I did ask you to get a move on," he said dryly.

Those were the first words he had spoken to me. They would be the last.

There had been no prior command to leave this strange and wonderful place of exotic electrical vibe, of rush and foreboding, of newspapers from distant cities, of events taking place worldwide that appear so small, so insignificant at the time but which, when connected to random other moments, are to be seen as the decline of civilisation in progress. This was the world flowing in every direction, look the wrong way and you miss everything.

He turned on his heels and marched onwards, the newspaper he'd purchased held stiffly between his arm and his chest, a surrogate for the swagger stick he was obviously missing.

Outside, the sun began to beat down on the streets of Waterloo. Someone hollered for a taxi; chatter rebounded off every building, large and uncomfortable, a conflict of sound that was even louder than in the station; a fist fight rampaged on the other side of the road; still, my train guardian ignored me.

I shouted his name. I wanted to throw my suitcase to the floor at the unjustness that had been handed to me. Petulant? Absolutely. But what else was being a pre-teen about if not to show how distorted the feelings of anger and detachment could be, how volatile they were in the hands of someone with nothing left to lose.

Again, he ignored me, instead intent on ensuring that he had caught the eye of a taxi driver, who signalled that he would turn around and collect us.

This time, I screamed and yelled with all my might. This was the howl of intolerant juvenilia, of wanting attention, of needing courtesy and thought…some kindness. I just wanted a reaction.

I got it.

"Now look here." He spoke with an even greater degree of authority but with an undertone of someone being pushed to the limit. "I am not your nanny, I am not a tutor, a babysitter, your confidante or a surrogate father figure. I am paid to deliver you into the possession of the headmaster at your new school. That is my job, my reason for being in your company today, and in…" He paused momentarily and looked at the watch on his wrist. "…one hour and fifteen minutes, I shall enjoy a half pint of London Pride before heading back to Avoncross. Now if you get into the—"

He didn't finish his sentence.

He crumpled onto the pavement of Waterloo Road, his head at an odd angle, one of his eyes hanging limply on his cheek, a small piece of metal sticking out of it. The taxi had overshot the turn and the driver had lost control when he realised he was going to hit a cyclist.

The military man would not get to press his lips against a half-pint dimpled glass of warm beer. He was dead, killed by accident. Yet as all around him exploded into fuss and calamity, I could only wonder why his face had turned white before the collision, that moustache stretched around an agonising silent scream, as though he had looked Death in the eye.

Chapter Seven

MY FIVE YEARS at the academy were boringly idyllic. I was lonely and had no friends, but if the initial days burned slowly, the rest became a feast of fire through which Time stomped with relentless zeal.

Do I have an issue with authority figures?

Surely, we all do, don't we? Why else do many of us vote if not to deliver a verdict on the current incumbent?

I have heard you all, at one time or another, complain loudly about traffic wardens, Her Majesty's Police Force, the Royal Family, each member being preceded by 'parasite this' and… well, heaven forbid some of the names various members of that institution have been called, but I see your point, I hear your anger.

Across the world, it is a right to take issue with authority. We are individuals, after all, and if we kneel willingly before all who have supposed influence over us, then our lives will be forever tainted, controlled by fear.

I am not a people pleaser. However, I wanted my time at the academy to go quickly, to be rid of the shell without leaving a mark against my name. My father had set aside the money, the foresight to leave me an out if the worst happened, and I intended to use it.

Of course, if you are reading my journals, dear Detective, then you know that I had a couple of run-ins during my time. A refusal to wear a tie for a while, purely because of a burn-like mark that appeared on my neck during my fourteenth year, and the time when I found myself going up against one of the biggest, most sadistic, fearsome bullies it was ever my misfortune to come against in my life, Mr. William Evan Tew.

The moment I first heard his name, I felt a shiver in my spine. For two years, I pretty much avoided him, his interests lying in the older boys who would represent the academy in his passions of rugby and mathematics. In my third year, my luck ran out, and I first butted heads with him when he substituted the carefree Mrs. Engel, who had done much to encourage her English and drama classes by the discarding of blazers during her lessons in summer, and by her own decree allowing the top three buttons of her ever-starched blouse to reveal the pleasures underneath.

Every boy in the class, at any one time, would have run into hell for her just because she sparked their passions, and because of this, she inspired groups of hungry boys to take literature seriously, to dispense with the idea of becoming a politician, entering the forces as an officer with a cut-glass accent, or going into battle on the stock exchange, inflated egos drawn, sabres rattling, a few million quid squandered, all in a day's work.

But then, suddenly, she was gone. Hell had claimed her, and none of us were brave enough to rescue her.

She did return at the start of the following term, her normal disposition weakened, shallowed, hollowed out, and whilst the boys still loved her, the desire in her had been curtailed and cut short, her eyes heavy with a sadness that hid a terrible agony, a pain which she alleviated by occasionally, absent-mindedly, rubbing her stomach as if massaging something that was no longer there.

For three miserable months, whilst Mrs. Engel was missing from my life, our English class was taken over, invaded, by the despotic figure of Mr. William Evan Tew.

If my train companion had the bearing of ex-military, Mr. Tew was the perfect example of a teacher those at the end of World War Two given prime positions in schools as a thank-you for their efforts in freeing Europe from the forces of evil. Of course, such old men do not always make the finest examples of the profession, but he had stuck it out. Year after miserable year, he became more embittered. I speculated one evening during some free time with a couple of acquaintances that he had lived for the war, and when peace was signed, when the Nazis were supposedly beaten and Hitler had taken his life, Tew's his purpose was gone.

The authorities, perhaps noting the man's passion for rules, regulations, and the ever-growing streak of manic depression that was masked by a failing heart and admiration for all things dictatorial, placed him into the education system, which would see his sadistic tendencies flourish and might give the students reasons to ape his furious zeal for the flag—a flag he proudly pinned to his regimental tie. The dragon and the dragon, double the fire. He was a fierce Welshman, a man who made me cry in frustration.

That was merely a prelude to the following year when he became not only my housemaster but my tormentor.

I had no natural inclination towards the sciences. I was in awe of those who could make the new computers bend to their will and create art. I was awful at maths, terrible at technical drawing, but held my own in history, English, languages, and music. I was the personification of a new breed of teenager, rallying against conformity in this age of plastic suits. I recited poetry with charm. I found a natural love for the violin and the saxophone and played them both with a modesty of intrigue. My thirst for knowledge of Tudor Britain and the language of Chaucer held me in front of my fellow prisoners inside the academy. Yet in that short term where Mrs. Engels was dealing with her own furious pain, Mr. Tew did his best to undermine my passion for the humanities. He called me a fool, a waste of space, claimed the army would make a man of me. This, though, as I said, was the prelude, only the beginning.

I didn't go back to Avoncross; I had no reason to. I occasionally received a letter from an old friend, a girl who had beaten the system that final day in class, informing me that she was being coached privately in the evenings in some sort of extracurricular activity involving programming. Those were odd letters, for they were not signed, which left me concerned about what she believed she knew about those last few days in the town.

I stayed as a boarder throughout my time at the academy, only venturing off grounds to watch Queens Park Rangers in the depth of winter, the downtrodden beauty of Shepherd's Bush appealing to my romantic nature, and in summer for one week every year, a tradition I have carried on, spending time watching England play various opposition at The Oval.

Did I miss my hometown? Surprisingly, not as much as I thought I would. This was now my keep, my castle, my defence. Nothing could destroy me...until Mr. Tew became my housemaster.

It started off with ridicule, then progressed to insults, and then, towards the end of September, downright abuse.

Let me tell you, Detective. There is nothing I hate more than an authority figure who not only gives you a hard time but also finds a way to make you a laughingstock, a figure to despise because you cannot help but show feelings. These days we attack the fury of such insanity, and we are guided by those who drop the word 'snowflake' into the conversation as if that makes it any better. For snowflake, read sissy.

The day began with sport, or as our academy preferred, three hours of gruelling rugby training.

That is for everybody else; for me, the day began in the comfort of an indifferently warm classroom rather than the chill and frost of a September morning brutally careering into another human body and half snatching at necks and testicles in naked aggression. I allowed the sound of a saxophone to sway my heart and a lethargic drum to wilt under the pressure of the heavy-handed gorilla who didn't enjoy rugby as much as he did beating smaller pupils up and smashing their faces into the ragged cold pitch.

Three hours of music tuition, a blessing in the guise of avoiding broken ribs and studs on kneecaps.

Three hours without a toilet break. Three hours that aligned with the rugby team's drill sessions and year-on-year mass fight.

Did you ever find yourself needing the toilet so badly at school that you were happy to miss out on the line that led directly to the food hall at first sitting? That line consisted of rugby players, freshly showered, unceasing muscles craving nutrition, noses broken, heads smashed, all full of bluster and bravado, and you think to yourself… *Damn, I am glad to miss the scrum for overcooked kidney and pan-fried onions.*

That was my mistake, to get caught out of line. If only… if only I had been three minutes early. If only I had held on for another twenty minutes. If only Tew had not been on lunch duty. If only he had been shot and killed in the war. If only I had the courage to shout down and stand my ground when encountering a bully. That came later, unfortunately not in time to deal with Mr. Tew. Not on this occasion anyway.

Imagine the scene: a large dining room full of lads, chunks of meat dressed in pressed, starched shirts and knotted ties, bruises covered by finely ironed trousers, shoes so polished that you could see the bright lights of past students' decaying relevance to society in them.

As I scampered towards the toilet, my bladder straining under the pressure, the noise from the dining room was akin to a full-blown orchestra of five-year-olds picking up an instrument for the first time, the din of misogynist banter twanging the snare of the drum, the squeaky deflections of the timid a screeching scrape of the bow as high-pitched voices of pre-adolescent boys went up against the muscle of sixteen-year-olds. This was soon drowned by a couple of toilets being flushed, the weird noises emanating from the third cubicle—always occupied by Mr. Ferris, who was rumoured to pleasure himself to pictures of the head boy in each year in his annexe room—and the sound of my overworked bladder as it gushed out a lake of urine accompanied by the imagined renditions of Blues guitarist, Robert Johnson.

All was quiet, all was noiseless. I was lost in my own bliss and fury; all I heard was the sound of a muted saxophone in my head and my desperate wish to one day hear my own interpretation of those notes.

Lost in my thoughts, I washed my hands, I dried them, I smiled. It was a grin of purity, for in that moment, I knew I had seen a future, playing jazz and blues.

I carried that smile all the way to the now deathly silent and still dining room. No one paid me any attention as I sat on one of the long wooden seats, large enough for twenty young men, a rugby team and management, or one giant ego about to be brought down to Earth by a simple remark.

I reached for the water jug, its metallic fading paint still having the purpose to shine as it offered its goods to all boys whose thirst was earned.

What made me look inside the jug instead of pouring it straight into my glass I shall never know; but there, inside, was the disgusting sight of someone else's display of contempt for cleanliness.

"Bugger me. Someone's flobbed in the bloody jug!"

A small utterance of outrage and resentment towards the unknown beast who thought it was clever to spread disease, it was barely audible. It was not like I had stood up, waved my arms in the air, created a disturbance or a scene. Yet looking around that room, where boys and teachers alike studiously pursing their lips as they chewed, I realised my error.

I had not heard the order for absolute silence dictated by my new tormentor.

"What part of complete silence do you not understand, boy?"

His words were slammed into the air, each syllable accompanied by the thud of the end of the knife hitting the table in perfect time. He looked directly at me. Even if I was innocent, if I had kept perfectly quiet with head bowed, he would have still picked on me. It had been coming.

I started to stutter, to panic over my words. This was a conflict I was unprepared for. The war may have been in the back of my mind, I had been aware that it would someday erupt, but I had done nothing to formulate my response once the enemy declared their intentions of total and complete subservience.

I decided not to antagonise…much.

"I'm sorry, Sir. I only mentioned that someone had spat in the water. I didn't mean to cause a problem."

"I thought I had expressed myself quite clearly, boy. No talking means no talking. Or am I to believe that you are above the instructions set before you, that you are too good to follow orders when given to you by a senior member of the school?" Each word was a primed grenade ready to explode in my face.

There was no foxhole to jump into, no gun in my holster to draw and fight it out in the murky air and diseased mud of no-man's-land; this was only going to end in me surrendering. A capitulation.

"No, Sir." The words stuck in my throat. An unhappiness welled within me, and I felt the hot sting of immature tears start to roll down from my eyes and onto my anger-blushed cheeks.

"On the table…now, boy. Do not make me tell you again. Stand on the table to show every boy in this room how pathetic you are!"

He motioned to the boy next to me to pour out a glass of water from the tainted jug. To the lad's credit, he paused, looked at me with a sense of camaraderie, of empathy, for he, like every other boy in the large dining room, understood what was going to happen next.

Tew carried on talking but was now raised to his full, unbearable height, his towering frame giving his voice more depth, more seniority, more hate towards me.

"Drink the damned water."

What is the price of refusal in such a situation? I wish with all my heart that I had been brave in that moment. I wish I had the wit, the temerity, the sheer guts to say no, or even to deploy that wonderful Anglo-Saxon phrase of displeasure and incredulity. Would you think more of me if I had? However, I was not able to summon the courage so brazenly at that point. I drank the glass's contents down and swallowed. I wanted to be sick.

"You will stay standing until everybody has eaten their lunch, in SILENCE, and then I think you require further punishment. Something that will give you a backbone. You will report to the playing field a week today in full kit, and you will play rugby. And every time you drop the ball will be another five minutes that you stand on the table at every lunchtime next week."

He drew breath. Long and hard his lungs worked. He was old, but he was of stern stuff.

"Is that understood?"

I nodded and whimpered a feeble sounding yes. Satisfied, he turned sharply on his heels and marched with a measure of glee in his step back to his seat.

I could not contain the tears, each one an embarrassment I wanted to avenge.

Chapter Eight

Mr. Tew was as good as his sadistic word.

For two months, I was forced out onto the rugby field and compelled to take part in a game I had no wish to play. Each week, I dropped the ball more than a dozen times, each lunchtime, I stood on the table for the duration and went hungry for the rest of the day, my tormentor delivering a sermon on the waste of a generation not willing to take one for the team.

For two months, I was deliberately hit, punched, kicked. My ribs were permanently bruised, my knee had been wrenched so badly that to this day I still walk with a slight limp. And still, the sadistic Mr. Tew kept me on that pitch.

My life was, without exaggeration, a misery.

On more than one occasion, I contemplated suicide.

Many would have taken it in their stride, perhaps hit out in retaliation—got in a few swift kicks of their own, pulled down hard on another player's testicles whilst in the scrum—and gained their teammates' respect for doing so. I refused to stoop to that level, not because I didn't want to become one of the lads; because I didn't know where allowing my anger to grow further would take me.

In that eighth week, I finally took a blow to the head.

I had been kicked and punched eight ways till Sunday but had avoided having anything connect with my head.

As I lay on the damp, muddy ground, I dug deep and pushed the anger down. My knee was enraged and inflamed, the pain on a par to that caused by the wooden boomerang that hit me on the temple a couple of years earlier. Just as I was thanking my lucky stars it was only my knee this time, a foot swung towards me. I raised my hands to my face protectively but was too slow.

I cannot tell you what happened next. I can only give you the account of one of the lads who was on the field at the time and who visited me a couple of days later in the hospital close to the school.

I had been knocked unconscious; that much I could have worked out for myself, thanks to suddenly waking up with a nurse's concerned face hovering above mine. Apparently, there had been a huge uproar on the pitch when two lads, bigger, beefier, no nonsense in their stance, turned against Mr. Tew and threatened to punch him. Courage comes with age, it seems.

Tew, in turn, had insisted it was an unfortunate accident, that as he attempted to intervene, he had slipped and his foot had caught me on the head. It was a mere tap, an insignificant blow that any other boy on the field would have laughed off. It only proved my weakness as a man, he claimed with ever increasing defence in his voice.

The headmaster had hoped to brush it under the table, to mollify me by assuring me my punishment would be over if I took the matter no further.

This I learned second-hand, for after a week, I was still in the hospital not only nursing a dislocated knee but also a small fracture in my neck.

The lad who had come to see told me that many of the pupils, the sporty and arty alike, had protested enough that Mr. Tew was put on leave pending an inquiry, which would not take place until I returned.

That might have been the end of it. I could have gone into the school, shook his hand in front of the headmaster and seen out my days in a comfortable haze, safe in the knowledge that I would never again be picked for rugby.

I would have done it too...had it not been for two conversations that took place, within hours of each other, ten days after the initial accident.

The first was with a doctor, a grave man with eyebrows that had a life of their own, shaggy caterpillars that somehow had learned to dance of their own accord. He placed a tender hand on mine and, with a sizeable amount of sympathy, informed me that the damage to my neck was such that it would eventually heal, but that he advised against me taking part in any physical contact sport again—and that a saxophone hanging around my neck would not be the best of ideas in the future.

Imagine finding something you love and being told that for the sake of someone's ego, for the want of just being human enough to let a grudge go, you are denied ever doing it again. I would always love the sound of a saxophone; I would travel to hundreds of concerts to hear one being played as sweetly as an angel's love ballad to their beloved, but I would never again lift one myself, never perform the kind of sweet ode that might make another fall in love with me.

If that hurt, then a surprise visitor, as they say, floored me.

Mrs. Engel had been a shell of a woman since she returned to the school. The once-enormous heart, the larger-than-life figure whom every boy admired, had been replaced by a skulking shadow who clung to the walls as she drifted silently from room to room. Like a character from Cluedo, she became a two-dimensional interpretation of a human being, a faceless caricature, a moveable piece that could not break out of its pattern. The picture on the box, her character, was there for all to see—the woman in the schoolmistress outfit with her hair tied in a bun and a twinkle in her eyes—but all that was left was the small plastic token, wiped clean of fun and free thought; a misplaced figurine.

Yet this woman, who burned with a secret so awful she had detached herself from her from the adoring crowd who hung themselves on her every action, deed and word, was sitting beside me when I woke from a troubled and fierce sleep.

I don't know how long she had been there, I never thought to ask, but hers was the first face I saw after the bandages were removed, liberating me from the nightmares that had been my constant companion for what seemed an eternity, though I think, looking back, that is when they truly began, brought on by being pumped with painkillers and palliative care.

She was holding my hand, soothing noises coming from a mouth that betrayed her sorrow.

Through eyes blinded by gossamer, the flimsy web of silk from a spider caught in a light breeze, I saw her pain, and it caused me to at first blush, then fear the anger I could feel rising from my stomach.

Since her return, she had worn enough clothes to fill a wardrobe. Her daily attire was excessive, and even off duty, when I had seen her wandering the high street, aimless and half forgotten, she wore big thick jumpers that covered her upper torso, veiling her sex.

Now, for a moment, she was uncovered, or at least her forearms were. I could see the telltale lines of self-abuse on both wrists, deep scores barely beginning to fade. In the crease of her right elbow there were cigarette burns, angry, unforgiving scorch marks on what was once pale, beautiful marble skin. On the left side of her neck there was a deep-seated bruise, profoundly engrained, the aftereffects of a man's sickening dominance over a woman. There was little sign of bruising on the other side, a giant hand capable of holding a woman, a hand so filled with rage that it didn't require the help of its mate to complete the objective of destruction.

It is only men that make women so timid, so devoid of emotion. We are all guilty of it at some time in our life, though in my line of work, I have come across a few women who are just as violent as any man, just as calculating, as evil. But for the most part, it is men who dominate in such a fashion.

My young mind raced.

IAN D. HALL

She spoke of how the other lads were missing me, an exaggeration I wished I could believe. I had few real friends, even fewer that I have kept in touch with, and only then because they have me on a retainer to sort out their minds, but underneath, the unspoken plea was evident.

She was showing me these wounds, and no doubt under her clothes there were many more that neither she nor I wished to see, because she somehow instinctively knew that I could help her. Had she seen something in me, a force, a projection, a manifestation of ill-intent, thus had sought me out to avenge her?

There are numerous ways to analyse my reasoning at that moment. The young lad desperate to be the hero for the wronged older woman; the blurring of lines between teacher and student; the mother figure I had lost and never regained. Trust me, I have gone through every scenario, trying to make sense of how she had seen that I was beginning to glean my own power; that to know me, to cross me, was to bring about your own death. I was the Grim Reaper in the flesh, and I wanted vengeance for her.

The reflection of my alter ego being born…it blazed in her eyes, and I didn't have to ask the identity of the man was who had done this too her. She provided the clues herself by telling me how much she hated Mr. Tew for what he had inflicted upon me.

The constant drip of his name, the way she instinctively held her breath for the barest microsecond before she let it pass her lips, spitting it out, a frustration that could not be scratched away, no matter how many times she cut herself and watched the blood slowly ooze towards her palm.

Tew…Tew…Tew…Tew.

In her fear, she had become obsessive, and I was the only one who could stop it. But not from a hospital bed.

It was not until the new year, when those first grey mists swirled like phantoms and stank of stagnation, the taste of decay and entropy in each droplet that clawed its way into the mouth, prising open the opportunity for chaos to ensue, that I found myself on the sidelines of the pitch where I had felt at my most vulnerable.

An important fixture between two fierce and equally matched rivals was taking place. The referee had been caught in early morning traffic as London dragged itself to a standstill.

Away from the river, a safer distance but no less cold, the visibility was a little better, not by much, but enough for the match to go ahead as long as someone stepped in to referee the game. Of course, Mr. Tew insisted that he shoulder the responsibility. He had his various certificates, he was an upstanding member of the community, and would be fair and impartial to both sides. Despite being the head coach of our rugby team, he swore he would oversee a decent game.

I watched from the sidelines, not giving a damn about the score or the possession; my quarry was Mr. Tew. I didn't know if I would catch his eye, if he would ever dare to look my way, but I wanted him to know I was watching him, following his every move...but how to get him to confess to his crime? For I was sure that was what Mrs. Engel wanted. He had to pay. Why had he done it, though? That part had not been explained.

At that point in my life, it was not enough to sway me from my course of action, especially as he had killed any hope of my future as a musician.

The first half of the game was without incident, a dull response in keeping with the weather—that January mist, I'll never forget it. I've never seen anything like it before or since, and I used to live quite close to the main river in Avoncross where the air would get so murky and wet it stung the eyes...

It was only in the second half that it livened up. One of the lads on the opposing school team was questioning a decision; the intricacy of it would have gone over my head even if I could have heard it being explained, but the words were muted, muffled by the dense atmosphere. However, one word somehow broke through, a solitary flare rising from a smoke-filled battlefield.

"Cheat."

I smiled. I wanted to punch the air and hug the young man who had given his opinion with force. I peered into the gloom and finally made out our teacher, the referee of the match, giving the young dissenter his marching orders and signal for a scrum.

The mist suddenly seemed to part, at least enough so that as Mr. Tew bent down to observe the path of the ball, he saw me staring at him.

I have never seen my face when I am angry; I have not witnessed the madness in my eyes. I can feel it burn, I feel the intensity and the strength of concentration. Most of all, I feel the hatred I have for... I would say *victim* but that suggests some sort of innocence on their part; perhaps *prey* might be a finer name for them.

Was that how I truly felt? The romantic in me wants to say no, that I was merely acting out of vengeance to a bully's actions. Yet the realist argues that it is reasonable that those who had caused me pain or to feel belittled deserve retaliation, to pay for their crimes. What had been no more than a spark of injustice had been magnified by the rape of a woman I had come to admire by a despicable man, an aggressive tormenter, a tyrant in uniform.

I stared so hard at that man, my eyes felt like they were popping out of the sockets as I mentally unleashed hell on him, forcing my will into his brain. I watched him tremble, his face turn red, purple hues appearing as veins seemed to stretch and burst. His eyes bulged and drooped in one swift moment. He was still bent over, directly facing me, fear stretching his mouth into a soundless sneer as he collapsed onto the field of play and the ruck fell upon him. He was dead before he hit the cold mud and mist-moist grass, but nobody realised until all the players had removed themselves from the towering heap of bodies.

I turned away, a strange sensation flowing over me, one of pride... I didn't particularly enjoy the commotion it caused my heart to feel it. The mist pulled in again once more, and I swore I saw Mrs. Engel being swallowed up by it. I was conflicted, so

I let her appearance, or at least the shape of her, fall away into my subconscious as the uproar behind me took hold and gathered strength... I enjoyed that; strike one for vengeance.

Do you now see, Detective, why that journalist called me Doctor Death?

Chapter Nine

LET ME TELL you about Faith Croy'ance.

You know the story, I suspect, well enough.

A star of her quality, despite her youthful age, does not die without leaving a lasting impression on the public, or even a ripple of sadness in the aisles on a matinee performance. I am glad she passed away in an era before social media. For her to be fawned over in such a manner as today's generation show with their claps and emojis and over-sentimental status updates when they have no idea of the person behind the art...it would have tarnished her. She would have been aggrieved to be remembered in such a way.

To die a mysterious death, an accident of course, was pain enough, but she went out in such a way that it left all in the theatre that evening with her last moment on Earth forever etched in their memory.

Faith Croy'ance was born in Solihull, a result of mixed heritages colliding, and never finding her true self until she was thrust to the front of the stage in a school production of *Romeo and Juliet*. Back then, she was plain Faith Tuttle, fourteen years of age, crippled with shyness, few friends. Her relationship with her mother was...like a tornado destroying a fledgling community during the days of Pioneer America, every shred of belief she might have had in herself torn apart by a woman who resented her existence, the consequence of a one-night stand with a soldier visiting the local area and leaving her with a memory she struggled to feed and clothe. Finally tiring of her offspring's lack of personality and dependence, Faith's mother left her at home one heavy, sweat-driven August morning and turned up a few days later on a beach in Southern Spain.

That was how Doreen Tuttle, daughter of Edna and Lionel Tuttle, became an overnight celebrity, a life model for the disenchanted and disenfranchised of greed-wrought Britain. You can have it all if you are prepared to be seen as a contemptible being, not fit to be part of a society that gives a damn.

After her mother left, Faith was passed around an ever-declining list of relatives, all of whom soon understood why Doreen had left her home alone and showed no sign of ever returning.

I first met Faith when she was nineteen. Initially, she was recommended to me by a sizeable studio who wanted the aspiring actress to undergo therapy. Faith had worked hard. She was adored by the press, her name and her face behind many fashion brands, and she was touted in certain sections of the press as the new Liz Taylor, the latest incarnation of Lauren Becall, the up-to-the-minute heroine adventuress who espoused glamour and had a future so bright that she could have named her price and been guaranteed top billing in any film she so desired. Yet despite guaranteed stardom, she remained, in private, fixated on the past, refusing to ever fully believe that she deserved the adulation and the praise.

Thus, I met her as Faith Croy'ance, but it was Ms. Tuttle who revealed herself in our thrice-weekly sessions.

"Are you comfortable?" I asked her on her fourth visit. I had not yet been able to afford the location that befitted my patients, and I was painfully aware that I had only been given this opportunity because one of my old schoolhouse friends had convinced the director and producer that I was worth every penny if they wanted the actress to truly shine in their upcoming remake of a 1940s Noir.

My office was sparse, but it was filled with possibility. I liked to think that my clients and referrals saw it that way—empty but room for growth. I wish I had coined that at the time; imagine the kudos on a business card.

She answered with a solitary nod of the head.

Three days before our first meeting, I had been invited to the studio and introduced by my friend to the director and producer by name. They wanted me to see their star from the wings, out of sight so she could not see me as I witnessed her in character and in what they insisted was her glory.

I watched several run-throughs, each one captured with elegance and precision. She was a natural. And that was the problem: it was her lie that was the truth of her performance to the camera. She was confident, the camera loved her, she was indeed a woman upon which the industry would shine a beacon— think Grace Kelly, Faye Dunaway, the startling fragility of Yvette Mimieux, the sublime radiance of Dorothy Dandridge, and you have this incredible talent from Solihull, a slight Midlands accent giving her an endearing homely edge, a star.

And yet…

"How did the shoot go today?"

If she had given a shrug, it would have at least been a sign of indifference I could have worked with. If she had affected grandiosity, I could have brought her down to earth. But I was thirty years old, fresh out of university and into practice. It was a challenge finding a way through to someone so in need of reassurance yet not willing to engage in any form of honest interaction.

"That scene where you had to slap the woman playing your character's mother, did that upset you?"

"It was okay, I guess…I mean it was difficult to really let go. The director asked me to punch her, but who does that to their mother?" Her reply was honest, but it wasn't the truth.

"Well, didn't you ever want to slap your mother for the way she treated you? She abandoned you, Faith. Surely, that is an image you, as an actor, can utilise. Isn't that what your profession calls method?"

I expected to get a rise out of her, a fierce defence of her mother's actions or a rage-filled attack on the woman for leaving her to fend for herself and turning her into a burden for a multitude of people who didn't care. What I didn't expect was indifference, resignation, an apathy that was deep-rooted, not planted beneath the surface, but bottomless. Even with the glare of a camera's loving lens on her, she felt unimportant, meaningless, an easily disposed of triviality.

I changed tack.

"That first time, at school, that must have been special, right? To be told that you could take one of the lead roles?"

There it was, a glimmer. A sparkle in the back of the eye. She had felt alive at that moment, and it showed as she allowed herself to blush in my presence.

Over the course of the next two months, she blossomed… well, okay, truth be told, she allowed herself to take control bit by bit. She still had a deep-seated self-loathing, but she could at least now see herself as an injured party. She was the one abandoned; she had not driven those people away.

The film was a huge success. She won a couple of awards, and whilst I declined to attend the premiere, despite her pleading, I did catch the film the following week, on my own, in a cinema out of town.

To have the world at your feet at nineteen, to have people come up to you in the street and pour their heart to you, love you, give you their complete attention…you either thrive in that moment or you shrink back, fall, and lose control.

And that is what she did. She fell.

For the next three months, I visited her in a facility outside of Oxford. I even went on weekends, staying in a small hotel in a town not two miles from where she slept at night. I hasten to add that she was in no danger, she was quite safe; even with the surrounding adverse publicity that the facility had in later years, they took good care of my patient.

For a while, she was unresponsive. I began to think that the performance she had put in on the film was akin to a high, and she had given so much to the role that she had simply burned herself out. I was not far from the truth, and over the next decade, I came to see that truth for all it entailed.

The studio, her representatives, her agents, and I had weaved a tale that she was taking a back seat for a while, that as a young woman, she wanted to explore other options in relative quiet before choosing her next role. This was to be the go-to statement for several years, and it worked. Slowly, she would regain her identity and come to trust me and others again. If I didn't know better, I'd call it a 'reboot', her senses shutting down and then reawakening when the time was right.

I wish I had understood long beforehand that the mental abuse she suffered through her mother's actions was only part of the issue, but the psychological aspect was merely the tipping point. It was the physical abuse that had left her teetering on the edge.

It all tumbled out in one of our sessions. I witnessed her shed several layers of hidden trauma and felt overwhelmed by what had been done to her. Not just sorry, not just apologetic, but overcome with grief, compassion and empathy filling my heart to a place where I wanted to crawl into a bottle and drown myself in her sorrow.

I didn't of course. That would have helped no one, least of all my other patients, for whom I was just as concerned as they went about their own trials and destructions.

It is that easy, though. Feeling complete empathy for another soul can drive you as insane as you may believe others to be. You can take on their struggle, immerse yourself in their pain, and as I had with Mrs. Engel, so too was I beginning to feel the burning anger well up and engulf my soul.

After around five years of knowing Faith, of treating her and losing some clients who found my focus on their problems slowly diminishing, a producer from Hollywood rang me out of the blue to make an appointment to see me.

I hadn't heard from Faith for a couple of months at this point, which was nothing new, nothing out of the ordinary. She spent a short while in the facility after every major film to rest and recuperate. She gathered strength, and I would visit her often and treat her the best I could. As far as I knew, she was filming in Brazil, a romantic epic or some such movie, which paid well and had her name above all others on the posters.

The producer was in London the following week and wanted to discuss Faith's life with me. I was intrigued but told him in no uncertain terms that what was discussed in the privacy of our sessions was confidential, that I could not, and would not, discuss her private life with anyone. He told me that was fine, that he wanted to talk to me, not listen, find out what I could offer.

Something in that manner, the self-assured nature of the ambitious American, has always bothered me.

He was as good as his word. I found him patiently waiting outside my office door when I was showing another client out. He was facing the wall when I saw him, peering at the handwritten description of the painting outside my office door. He half turned as he heard me say goodbye to my client, and without a missing heartbeat or offering an introduction, he said with annoying confidence, "Quite the picture you have there—a fascinating modern interpretation of the Greek myth."

He turned to look at it once more, and I joined him, standing by his side, just a few inches separating us as the piece of art I had purchased from a young student from one of the art colleges close by became our topic of conversation for a few minutes.

It was a dark, vibrant but ultimately disturbing piece, all blues and greens that bore the patterning of oxidisation. The depth of the colour drew the eyes around the body of Perseus as he stood heroically over the headless body of his foe, holding the severed head aloft in front of him, her stone-faced eyes turned upwards but somehow still appearing to look directly at the artistic voyeur, the slight tint of pearl sloe black found in each serpent strand of hair being the only other colour on show.

The artist's name is lost to me now, unless I look closely at the information card below. I don't do that often.

"Excellent use of colour. Almost corrosive. It wants to show decay, and yet the vibrancy of the artist's intention is transparent. They want you to stare at the scene so that the Gorgon woman might feel your presence, snap back to life, and turn you to stone... Feels a bit like ELO to me!"

I allowed myself a wry smile. Music was a passion of mine, even the contemporary, and I found the former Birmingham band a cut above much of what many would consider 'elite'. But to compare the painting, even the tragic tale of one of the lost sisters to a three-minute track was a little beyond me. I simply smiled at the picture for a moment and then took a step back, stretching out my hand in as friendly a manner as I could exhibit. He reciprocated, but with a lot more gust in his handshake.

"Linus Rugren. It is indeed a pleasure to meet the man who put our girl Faith on the map." He almost bellowed the words, his bluster matching his suit for lack of meek respect to the senses.

"Won't you please come in, Mr. Rugren?"

"Oh, Linus please. We may be gentlemen, but we can dispense with formalities, can't we?"

I wanted to say no, to admonish him. I had grown used to being referred to by my title and surname only. I had no one in my life that called me by first name. Like the artist who had created the artwork that hung outside of my office, I had almost forgotten it.

I allowed it by not confirming my acceptance. The sooner this brash, overconfident man was out of my sight the better, and if it meant acceding to his pride and manner, then so be it.

"What kind of name is—"

I stopped him in tracks. The less he was familiar, the more I could cajole him along before reaffirming what I had told him a few days earlier down the telephone.

"As I said, Mr..." I caught his eyebrow raising in friendship that was not asked for. "Linus, I cannot tell you anything about Faith's life. You surely understand the ethics of my profession, don't you? You have therapists in Hollywood?"

"Sure, of course. The whole damn town is full of them. I often think that for every neurotic actor there are two shrinks, one for comfort, and the other to disagree with the first's opinion. Now, if there were two bartenders for every actor on screen, I'd make a fortune opening rehabilitation centres and AA rooms from Santa Monica all the way to Vegas." He roared at his own joke.

I affected a laugh that required little effort on his part to understand my unhidden contempt. Still, Linus Rugren ignored it, and his smile grew wider. He must have thought we were getting along famously.

"But seriously, it is Faith that I have come to talk to you about." He held up his hand to stop me interrupting him again. "Hear me out. If at the end you wish to give me further insight to allay my suspicions...my fears, then all well and good. Do you hear a loud, urgent beeping?"

No...wait, he didn't say that. Why would I tell you that? Ridiculous!

He opened his mouth, but it's not his voice I hear. It is far off and...female. Light panic starts to spread and that urgent beeping, well, it is now in full desperate mode. I don't know what's going on. I think I'm dying.

Chapter Ten

DETECTIVE INSPECTOR BRIDGE slumped heavily in relief onto the chair in the corner of the hospital room.

It had all happened so quickly.

Absent-mindedly, she rubbed her left arm and felt the bruise that was already forming. The kick she had taken from the person dressed in hospital scrubs would leave a reminder for some time of the on-duty police officers' near-failure to protect the man in their care.

The doctors and nurses on hand, who had rushed to the aid of Ingrid Bridge and Officer Torlay, had caught the would-be murderer squeezing the plastic IV line and kicking the youthful officer in the face. It caught the perpetrator off guard and gave an opening for Torlay to reach for the Taser and shoot his attacker in the stomach.

Bridge watched the would-be assassin be taken away, the blue scrubs now carrying an unsavoury smell as bodily fluids seeped through. They were escorted to a recovery room, where they would soon face brief questioning and cautioning before being taken to the local station for thorough interrogation—a problem for another hour. For now, her concern lay with the man who had survived two attempts on his life.

"What is so special about you?" she asked aloud, knowing she wouldn't receive a reply, at least not directly, not from him, not from the horse's mouth, so to speak. The stack of personal notebooks, however, had been enlightening—so far. Were they merely ramblings, fabricated lies, or cryptic musings from an unleashed imagination? Could he truly believe he caused others' deaths by mere will? It bordered on insanity, and he didn't seem the type to warrant such a judgement, but who knew? He appeared persuasive, respected in his field, evidenced by his papers and endorsements.

No physical clues to the identity of the original attacker were found inside the house—not a fingerprint nor a loose strand of hair. Apart from the victim, one could be forgiven for suspecting he had inflicted the injuries upon himself. Impossible, of course.

The detective sighed. Her arm throbbed, her mind ached from the extensive reading of the past twenty-four hours, and now she had a suspect to question. Could it be, she hoped, that both attacks were perpetrated by the same individual? The thought thrilled her briefly. Yet instinct, the nagging doubt of a seasoned police officer, smothered the hope before it could take hold.

There were others to interview, a plethora of names mentioned in his notebooks. A couple stood out, not as suspects, but as potential sources of information, if they were still alive. The policewoman in Avoncross was one. She must recall details about the young boy orphaned and the mysterious death of his aunt. The teacher—Engels or Engles—could confirm or deny certain facts. And then there was the man who visited him, the producer. What became of the actress? Bridge wasn't a film enthusiast, but she was sure she'd remember someone with a name like Faith Croy'ance.

The television, previously switched off by a nurse during the doctor's examination, flickered back to life. The sound was barely audible, but the images conveyed the dire situation: the mission to Mars was facing disaster.

She turned her head away from the screen, regret filling her gaze as she surveyed the empty bed where the enigmatic man had lain for over two hours. Though assured of his eventual recovery from this second attempt on his life, the possibility lingered that he might remain in a coma upon his return to his private room. She whispered to herself with a hint of reproach, "More security in the hospital. No one in or out without my knowledge."

IAN D. HALL

Bridge delved into her jacket pocket and took out a notepad and pencil. On a clean, unmarked page, she listed the names of those she intended to chase up, to see of what they remembered of the man who believed he held the power to mete out death to those he deemed deserving.

Pausing as she circled the actor's name, she swiftly added the woman's mother. It troubled her deeply that a mother could abandon her child in the manner described in the man's notes. How hard would it be to find this errant parent, someone last seen some twenty years ago? Was she even alive?

Too many names to sift through. Bridge disliked cases with too many leads, where facts remained indistinct, cluttered by an excess of information. A meaty but neat investigation was her preference. This one, she sensed, would be arduous, prolonged—a series of days stretching into an uncertain future, where any prospect of nurturing relationships would be indefinitely postponed. Bridge grimaced at the thought. *Good thing I'm not invested enough in anyone to face that problem,* she thought cynically to herself.

Officer Torlay returned to the patient-less room, his demeanour almost defeated, offering a weak greeting to his superior. He had borne the brunt of the assault by the unknown assailant, and Bridge felt a pang of guilt for her internal complaints about her own injury. It looked as though Officer Torlay had taken one for the team. His face bore numerous cuts and bruises, including a deep, nasty gash just above his left eye that had been stitched. His ear looked as though he had been playing rugby against a team made up of Victorian barbers and pirate cutthroats. He was also hobbling and told Bridge the doctor had said he was lucky he wasn't in crutches.

"Oh, and the clown who messed up my weekend—big match coming up with the local kids—is awake and responsive. You won't believe who it is." The officer grinned, his expression quickly contorting with the discomfort of his wounds.

"How many stitches in total, Torlay?"

"Fifteen on the face, four more at the back of the ear. The bugger could have torn it off!"

Bridge let the colourful language slide. If she had found herself in danger of losing an ear, she would have screamed the hospital roof down and then given the perpetrator a good, hard slap.

"Who is this mysterious fiend then? Don't keep me in suspense."

Torlay had never wanted to smile so much in all his life. This was a big deal, even more than the birth of a child, his wedding day, or the Christmas when his brother finally located all the missing stickers for his 2000 football annual.

"Drusilla Pero, the artist, sculptor, painter, poet, activist… although I've never understood what half of these so-called activists do except moan and complain for the sake of it."

"Not sure I know her," Bridge said. "And if it's about art, I'm surprise to hear you do!"

Torlay was hurt by the insinuation. "What, because I'm a six-foot copper with muscles with a pedigree in every sport known to humanity, who drinks with the lads, and has had two run-ins with top brass because I like to fight scumbag dealers, you think I don't know about art? That's a little concerning, Ma'am."

Bridge had worked alongside Torlay for over a decade. He was a good man and fiercely loyal but prone to sarcasm, and she had learned over the years to not take him too seriously. Chances were he was winding her up, so she raised an eyebrow and said nothing.

Despite his stitches, Torlay couldn't help but laugh. "Yeah, okay, I heard her tell the nurse her name as I was passing by the door, and then I looked her up. Good stuff, though. She's done some cracking paintings of characters from Greek mythology, really dark, a little sexy…if you like that sort of thing. Certainly catches the eye. On her homepage, there's a picture of her with a painting called *The Death of Medusa*, and guess who she's standing next to? Yep, you got it. I can tell by your stunned expression. Our victim. She tried to kill the man who bought her painting."

Bridge *was* stunned—not at the reveal, but at Torlay's enthusiasm, and she had to wonder if he'd taken a shine to the artist. He tended to do that on cases involving a good-looking woman, which was a shame. Otherwise he was an officer of excellent standing and professionalism.

"Has anyone checked on the whereabouts of that piece of art?" she asked. "Is it still at his office, does he even still have one? It wasn't at his home. We would have found such an object, surely?"

"I can check, Ma'am. I think Boase and Parsons are still there," Torlay replied before turning on his heel and slowly limping out of the room, his mobile phone already in hand.

Far too efficient, Bridge thought. Torlay was loyal, yes; capable, resourceful, effective even, when dealing with certain elements of the underworld and criminal activity near Waterloo. But to show such initiative in what was a matter of low interest to him? *Perhaps he's finally eyeing a promotion... Yeah, and I'm ready to believe any party is worth my vote!*

She wished she had voiced her thoughts, but he was already gone, no doubt hoping to elicit sympathy elsewhere.

Detective Inspector Ingrid Bridge eased herself from her seat and stood tall. She made a mental note not to show any pain to the assailant. *Let her think that she barely even touched me*, Bridge resolved with a steely determination her father would have admired.

Names and places crowded her already overworked mind. What was it about this particular case? She had attended scenes of violence many times, and this one didn't even rate in the top ten. If not for the notebooks left on the desk—neatly stacked as if he wanted someone to notice them and take in the words written— she might have dismissed it as a burglary gone wrong, a lover's quarrel twisted by accusation, or even an accident.

She longed for simplicity, for clarity. In a time where everything seemed to teeter on the edge of confusion, where cathedrals could fall and rumours of children found catatonic in woods circulated, where strange events near water, filled the front page of every newspaper and were the source of gossip in the station canteen and in her local pub, all she wanted was to get on with her job of convicting rapists and count down the years until retirement. If it left time for the occasional game at The Valley and walk her dogs, then so be it. But she didn't need further confusion added to her day.

As she was about to walk out of the patient-less hospital room, the television increased in volume without warning. The news was still focused on the astronauts and their spiralling descent towards Mars. Bridge said a small, silent prayer for the souls on board and departed.

The commentary continued long after the room was empty.

"Just to recap, one of the astronauts on the ship has been confirmed dead. The fire, which quickly overcame them, has been extinguished, but unfortunately, Flight Engineer Thomskilyvan died. His captain, Licett Nyholm, spoke of her admiration for her friend and crewmate, calling him 'One of the most heroic men she had ever had the honour of working alongside.'"

The volume dropped to its normal volume again, yet there was nobody there operating the remote control. Indeed, nobody entered the room until the victim returned, by which time, it was almost too late.

IAN D. HALL

Chapter Eleven

THE INITIAL INTERVIEW was a waste of time. Drusilla Pero neither confirmed nor denied her name; she refused to speak to anyone until she was inside the police station with her lawyer present. Bridge didn't expect anything less.

That didn't stop Bridge from feeling angry as she approached the office of the man she had become determined to save. Having never seen his face outside of a photograph, the bandages covering his injuries left everything to the imagination, and she found herself fixating on his blank, closed eyes.

She located Officer Parsons on the steps of the building that housed his and several other offices. A small community of therapists of various kinds worked side by side in the building, which was partially obscured by the tall skyline south of the river and by the leafy green vines and foliage that crept up the left side of the three-storey structure.

"Where's Officer Boase?" Bridge snapped uncharacteristically.

If her mood bothered Nathaniel Parsons, he didn't let it show. She remembered when he first was introduced to her, his first day on the job, in the middle of a terror alert near Waterloo Station. He was calmness personified, making everyone feel as though he had been part of the team for years, not just the three hours since he walked in, fresh-suited and hopeful. In just one year, he had already impressed those higher up the pay scale than Ingrid Bridge.

"I'm sorry, Parsons. We have a woman in custody who is being a right terror. She nearly killed our victim in his bed!"

"Not a problem, Ma'am. I came out to escort you. There's a little kerfuffle on the second floor, one floor down from his office. Officer Boase is up there now. She was in the middle of negotiating peace."

Bridge raised her eyebrows. Boase, like her friend Torlay, liked it rough. She had grown up in a large, mixed-heritage family with an Irish father, who liked to swing his fists every weekend down at the local gym and an Indian mother who wasn't averse to beating her children in stern rebuke when the need arose and had once knocked out her husband with an unexpected uppercut when she discovered one December evening that he had gambled away the family's rent money on a 'sure thing'. The fact that the 'sure thing' had paid off and he had won three times what he'd laid down didn't matter to the matriarch. All she saw was fecklessness, and he was never allowed to forget it.

"You stay here, Parsons. Just keep an eye out for any reporters," Bridge instructed.

The media had been relatively quiet about this case; there were larger, juicier news items to report on. The national mood veered between hope and dismay, panic and elation at the touch of a keyboard and a swipe on a smartphone. And who could blame them?

Bridge strode up the stairs with authority, her shoes banging with intent, and announced her presence to the awaiting shouting crowd.

Claire Boase stood out like a sore thumb, in part because of the flame-red hair inherited from her father, but also because she looked ready to take on four angry professionals all by herself.

I bet she insisted that Parsons make himself scarce, that she could handle this minor disturbance by herself. She wouldn't have been wrong.

Despite being in awe of Officer Boase's ability to handle conflict, as the senior officer, Bridge knew she had to step in and take charge. It wouldn't do for the press to get hold of this, even if it would provide light relief from the panic and drama unfolding 140 million miles away.

As Bridge turned the tight corner of the second floor, she lifted her hand from the clean, white rail that had guided her to the sight before her. Clearing her throat with a touch of drama, she bellowed, a habit acquired from her youthful days on the terraces of various grounds, watching her father's unsuccessful attempts to transition from amateur football to the big leagues. In her mind, the vain attempt to catch a scout's attention by roaring her father's name was a gesture of solidarity and love.

"If everybody could stand still, stop pushing each other, and allow my officer to carry out her duties, that would be marvellous. If you don't, I shall have no qualms about charging every single one of you with affray and causing a public nuisance."

Never mind that they were all in a private building; those words were often enough to strike a measure of fear into even the most law-abiding of citizens. Thankfully, the four people surrounding her officer seemed reasonably sensible.

A strange silence descended over the group, broken only by Bridge.

"Thank you all. If you can just allow my officer to extricate herself from your company for a minute…"

The small crowd threatened to rebel once again, but Bridge was more than ready for them.

"Now, please, and once Officer Boase is back down the stairs, we shall all have a chat—one person at a time—on why you think it is acceptable to thrust your faces into that of my officer."

Only when the four people, three older men and a young woman, allowed Boase to pass did Bridge notice the painting. It was large and cumbersome, but with the senior detective quickly running up the remaining stairs while calling down to Parsons for assistance and shuffling everybody into a nearby room, the painting made it safely down to the communal car park. All the two officers had to do now was wait for a van to turn up and transport it to the police station for safekeeping.

A large panoramic window stood halfway open. Bridge noted that it almost spanned the entire width of the wall, offering the viewer with a sense of elevated ease as they looked out over the river. Half in shade from surrounding buildings and half caught in the reflections of a thousand other glass windows even higher than this one, the small community near Waterloo Station seemed separate from anywhere else Bridge had ever been before.

"Is every room in this building like this? So clean, stark, filled with large windows and whitewashed walls?"

Nobody commented aloud, but the small nods from each of the still-startled faces affirmed the uniformity of the building.

"Nothing different at all?"

The woman answered coldly, "Aside from personal details or some equipment, I have in my office downstairs a rather valuable specimen of a skeleton. It was a gift from a friend who was… the beneficiary of a will. Burke and Hare are rumoured to have handled the corpse to which it was formally attached."

Bridge wasn't sure whether to feel repelled or to admire the story. Even if the law had been broken, how do you enforce something that was hearsay? She decided to ignore it.

"So, you are probably aware that your… shall we say neighbour, has been attacked in his own home, left for dead by person as yet unknown. I wondered if any of you had seen anybody new entering the building of late, anyone strange hanging around?"

No answer.

The room was as silent as the morgue Bridge imagined the victim would eventually be in. Even if he survived the attack in the hospital, how could he hope to survive the initial assault which rendered him in a coma?

"I see."

This time, a short middle-aged man with a pencil moustache, who appeared to have a permanent table at the two-for-one buffet at one of the area's more fashionable restaurants, spoke up.

"No, I don't think you do!" He wheezed between each syllable, the fold underneath his chin acting as a valve in much the same way a trumpet worked, each breath caught in the act of desperation inside a jazz-routine-fused with lament.

"And you are?"

The woman spoke once more, appearing irritated by the other three's presence. On one level, Bridge understood that the constant interjection of men when a woman's voice should be enough irritated her as well, but there was something deeper than that. Bridge quickly thought back to what greeted her on the stairs, and now it made sense: the woman was the only one arguing for the picture to stay. The three men were adamant that it should go with her officer.

"His name is Belvedere. He's an accountant. His office is opposite mine on the ground floor. Behind me is Baker, he's a scriptwriter. He works in this building because it means he doesn't have to be at home with his awful, simpering wife. The man to my left is a physiotherapist, this is his room—his name is Fletcher. There's one room empty, has been for six months. My name is Dr. Flora Fawkes. What my neighbour means is that there are always strange people hanging around. None of us have secretaries. We make our own appointments. We might see each other in the hallway, on the stairs to use the toilet, or once every two weeks when we have a building meeting to discuss any issues, that sort of thing."

Bridge instantly recognised that Dr. Fawkes was the spokesperson for the building, at least was now. Bridge suspected that the victim had been the real power of this strange and eclectic tribe. There was no connection between them except for working under the same roof.

"Did any of you know him well, ever see him out of hours, perhaps have a drink with him? Did you like him?"

Once again, the doctor spoke for the group. Bridge's gaze drifted to the car park below, her attention wavering as she watched her two constables take turns holding the framed painting so the other could take a photograph of the curious-looking scene.

"As I said, we saw each other as neighbours, not colleagues, and while there might be a slight crossover of work—I, for example, might recommend a patient make an appointment to see Mr. Fletcher if I consider their needs to be in line with his skill—none of us really had anything to do with the man upstairs. I admit he was a good organiser. He was the one who called all the meetings and dealt with the landlord when there was a problem. He even arranged and collected the wages for the cleaner who came once a week. But she's been away for a month, called to look after her sister in Lincoln. Poor dear had a heart attack, apparently."

"I should like to have her name and a contact number that she can be reached on."

The doctor nodded in agreement to the request, but Bridge was oblivious to the act of compliance. Her focus was still on her officers. She shouted down to them both to stop mucking about and wait for the van.

"Don't lean too far out, Detective."

This time, it was a man's voice that had spoken. His concern was the complete opposite of the doctor's factual account.

"That's how Margaret…Mrs. Robson died."

"Tristan…" The name was spat out, a verbal warning that Bridge couldn't mistake.

"Tristan Fletcher, was it? What do you mean, that is how Mrs. Robson died?"

Flora Fawkes glowered at the young man. His openness of face tallied with him being the only one not dressed formally. The others were in expensive shoes and good-quality shirts; the scriptwriter, Baker, was wearing the ironic tweed jacket with leather patches on the elbows. The accountant, although a shabby man underneath his outerwear, was wearing a tailored three-piece suit, immaculately pressed. Yet this one member of the group broke ranks, still dressed appropriately for his profession, but when compared to the viper-like doctor, he was considerably more at ease in shorts and a loose cotton T-shirt.

Nonplussed, or gratefully ignorant of Flora Fawkes's daggers aimed his way, Tristan Fletcher explained the short and otherwise unremarkable life of Margaret Robson. If a person's existence can be summed up in fewer words than it takes to describe the process of pouring water from a tap, then that life was barely enough to fill a glass, driven perhaps by subsistence. The life of the ordinary man or woman who never attempted anything more than keeping a steady pulse was for all intents and purposes one of wasted opportunity, and the highlight should not be a sudden and dramatic passing. Death should not be the defining moment.

"She didn't fall. She was pushed!"

Flora Fawkes gave way to her consuming anger. Her eyes lit up as if sparked into life by a fuse and a flame, transforming from red to dead black in a millisecond. She picked up an ashtray from the otherwise orderly table, a clean decorative piece made of glass, never used for its initial purpose but admired for its solid craftsmanship, and threw it angrily towards Tristan Fletcher, who had moved from behind her and towards the detective.

When the brain and the eye work together, they can see remarkable things. They can map the path of an object as if it has already been thrown, so it was with little effort that Tristan Fletcher sidestepped the flying heavy-duty glass and watched it sail out of the open window.

Bridge was about to verbally warn the woman when, down below, a high-pitched scream rang out into the London air.

To Bridge, it was almost as if she'd had a premonition that had ticked away at the back of her mind as the ashtray skimmed through the air and then burst into reality as the scream left Claire Boase's mouth.

Both Bridge and Fletcher looked out of the window at the same time, heads peering out as though a cuckoo clock had struck twelve and the miniature wooden people inside had cheered at the thought of being reunited on the small platform afforded them as the chimes rang out. Behind them, Dr. Fawkes was hysterical. Belvedere made a statement later that evening that Fawkes had suddenly seemed to be possessed by a strangeness, an aura of cold, red anger. He had seen her lose her temper before, when she had threatened to assault a member of the public who had wandered into her room by mistake, but he had never witnessed this level of fury.

It was over with in a flash. Even before the ashtray smashed into the skull of Officer Parsons, Fawkes started to uncontrollably and wildly scream that she didn't mean it, that it was a mistake. A force had willed her to throw the nearest object to hand, just to get the Fletcher's attention.

On the ground, Parsons was undeniably dead, killed in an instant by the force of the ashtray. His mobile phone was in his hands; he had been taking a photograph of the painting with his partner Boase smiling broadly for her mum.

Chapter Twelve

THE INTERVIEW ROOM was far from Bridge's favourite place in the station. She had once witnessed a young-looking teenage girl take a knife to her wrists in a moment of panic when being accused of cyberbullying. The blood seemed never-ending; it didn't to spurt so much as to ooze silently out of her. It reminded Bridge of a Steve McQueen film she had watched with her father one dull and deserted autumn afternoon, the slow-moving creature pouring out of the bleak town, spreading itself over everything it touched, consuming.

Thankfully, the girl was saved from her own judgement. She understood the damage she had caused, the depth she had taken her victim to. It would be easy, reflected Bridge, to assume that the girl had turned her life around, become a model citizen. The fact that Bridge had not had to visit her home since that day, nor that the victim had said she wouldn't press charges, led her to believe the bully was keeping her head down, ashamed of her intimidation and harassment of a fellow pupil whose only crime had been to attention-seeking.

The interview room held bad vibes for Bridge ever since.

In front of her was the first of two people she had to interview under caution that evening. Drusilla Pero was the epitome of cool under pressure. Having been given the chance to clean herself up after being tasered, she sat in the sterile room as though she was queen of all she surveyed. It wouldn't have surprised Bridge to find out that Pero was contemplating her next setting for one of her classically inspired works.

Am I the hero or the villain in the painting? Bridge didn't want to know and rubbed her nose in the hope it would erase the scene into which she was mentally painting herself.

As if answering the unspoken question, Drusilla Pero gave Bridge her most affable smile and through teeth that resembled pearls, she spoke gently, an air of artistic illustration in her voice. "You are whatever you deem yourself to be, Detective. If you are the hero, then you will realise my crime was intended to bring down an evil. If you are the villain, then you will let the court decide on my guilt or innocence, and one evening, I will look out through the three bars of painted black iron framing the world, and I will watch it end."

Unnervingly, Pero's face did not alter as she spoke. Indeed, the whole case unnerved Bridge, but Pero, arms casually at her sides, her body language calm and fearless despite having attempted to take a man's life, her face scrubbed clean of make-up, not a hint of hiding behind a mask though she had been caught in the act, was as brazen as if she were already free.

"What's the difference between heroism and cowardice?"

Drusilla Pero grinned. Bridge wanted to reacquaint her with the Taser for that grin.

"He needs to die, surely you can see that. I saw one of his journals in your hands when I entered the room. You have got to know by now that he is a danger to those around him, to the world. He will bring untold destruction."

Bridge stayed silent, hoping that Drusilla Pero, formally Cilla Peros, would let loose a clue, and it was only as the one-sided conversation unfolded that the detective comprehended the confidence of the woman she was dealing with.

Normally, Bridge would be thrilled to have such a strong woman on the opposite side of the table. Someone of intelligence and pedigree to go into battle with, then go home, pour a beer, and replay the encounter in the mind. Bridge preferred it when women were the guilty party, especially in cases of murder. They were more calculating, so much more cunning than their male counterparts.

Adolescent girls who committed a crime made Bridge nervous with their false tears and sometimes false accusations, the need to be absolved for their lack of logic in the given moment, by pulling others into the web. She'd dealt with a few of those in her time, on the beat and as a detective. Then there were those who used their femininity to elicit a response from the police and to have their sentences cut short. Bridge could deal with those women easily.

All she wanted was a level playing field, a bit of back and forth, the evidence stacking up against her suspect, but the game being played to its full potential.

Allow me the sincerity of a female thief, the insight of a woman driven to murder, the calmness of a lady to whom all her lies ring true.

But not this woman; not Drusilla Pero.

"I believe you are responsible for the painting that hung outside of his office. Quite striking, the colours, the blend, the focus on the ambivalence of the struggle that had taken place."

"Where is it now?"

"It's quite safe. Until we close the case, it will remain in our custody."

"I painted it. He's never going to appreciate it again. I want it back!"

"Why?"

"Because I want to destroy it."

Bridge had already been taken aback once by the artist; refusing legal representation was not unheard of, but it could derail a case if the proper channels were not followed. By not having a solicitor present, all that Bridge said for the tape was fact, no one to caution her to keep away from certain phrases that may lead to her own downfall. But would the powers that be, those who decreed the foundations of law, see it as an act of coercion or the ramblings of a person looking for an insanity plea later?

The admission of wilfully threatening to destroy private property was enough to charge Pero even without the attempted murder. Still, Bridge felt troubled. Not only was this woman calculating, a worthy adversary upon whom Bridge would look back one day and consider putting in her memoirs, she was cold and consistently unemotional in her answers. There was an unkindness to her, one that didn't lurk under the surface but openly swam like a shark towards its prey.

For the first time in her life, Bridge felt as helpless as a newborn seal being pushed into the sea by a well-meaning parent, blind to the dangers of the water.

"You don't deny that you tried to murder this man today?" Bridge pushed across a black-and-white photograph of the man receiving urgent care in the hospital. It was as up to date as the detective could find, in a simple wooden frame, taken from the wall of the ground floor of the building in which he held his office.

A nod of the head.

"For the tape, please, Ms. Pero!"

A one-word affirmation of the charge against her, a truth in a sea of troubling, confessed reality.

I don't know if you are insane, or you believe what you just told me. No person in their right mind goes out to kill someone over a painting.

Bridge put pressure on her nose once more.

"Where were you on the night of the twenty-ninth?"

"The night he was attacked?"

"Yes!"

Bridge felt a migraine starting to appear.

"I was at a reception at a gallery on the other side of the river. Portia's in Whitechapel."

"Any witnesses who can corroborate your whereabouts that night?"

"Five hundred at least. I shook hands with them all. I signed several hundred books in full view of a gloriously attentive crowd, and even after the gallery closed, I was still encumbered by a dozen or more…sycophants who guided me to a terrific club in Docklands. Tamzin's, I believe it was called. There, I danced until five in the morning, and then those left standing were treated to a serenade and several warm cups of tea from a mobile café outside Sir John McDougall Gardens."

Bridge wanted to roll her eyes at the overflow and dumping of ready information. Surely, no one would be that precise for an alibi unless they meant it. That or they had some sort of OCD…or had it planned out in meticulous detail.

"So you're saying you weren't anywhere near Waterloo Station?"

There was no answer. None was needed.

"Final question for now, Ms. Pero. What is so special about the painting?"

Drusilla Pero looked long and hard at the detective. Her eyes flared brightly.

"You really can't see it, can you? The sheer depth of evil within. I felt controlled by another hand as I brought the image to life. I felt sympathy and empathy for the creature, and hatred for the man who had hunted her down. Like all men, he believes himself to be the hero, the slaughterer of a daughter of Gorgon, the ugly beast with weapon sheathed until he can spear the unique power in all women. The painting, the man, they are both the same. They are vessels within which hate is evident but concealed by a toxicity that is seductive…and patient."

During her explanation of the power of the painting, Drusilla Pero had slowly altered her sitting position. She had started out by leaning back in her chair, nonchalantly posed, almost as if any cares she had in the world were of little consequence, a speck of dust on the lip of a champagne glass easily removed by a deft flick of a finger.

Slowly, subtly that position shifted, almost unnoticeable to Bridge, and by the time she whispered the word 'patient', she was leaning across the table, her hands almost within touching distance of Bridge's neck, her face so close to the detective's own that she could have kissed her.

It was only the intervention of Detective Constable Richard Beaumont that stopped the artist from strangling or caressing the senior officer in the room. He sprang into action and pushed the accused back down, not with any force, but enough to subdue her back into the muse-like stance she had previously held.

Bridge nodded her appreciation towards the young man who had sat quietly observing the interview. Another of the new breed fresh out of school. He rarely said anything, but his views, when proclaimed, were always insightful. The young detective nodded back; he was, after all, only doing his duty.

"I want the names, as many as you can remember, of those in attendance at this gallery, Portia's. I want the name of the organiser. I want the names of those that you say stayed with you until the early hours."

Drusilla Pero rolled her eyes with exaggeration. Bridge could almost hear her sigh of exasperation, of deep-seated annoyance at having to comply with an order to exonerate her from one attempt of murder, despite already agreeing to the other.

"Portia Cullise will have the names of every woman who attended the evening, and no doubt will have a separate list of those men deemed worthy or interesting enough to be given the honour. She might even remember those who danced the night away at the club. I have no idea who was with me in the park, but if you send this boy down there in the morning, I'm sure the owner of the van will remember me if you show him my photograph. After all, I was the only worthwhile person staring at, according to him."

It hadn't escaped Bridge's notice that Pero had belittled her junior partner in the room, calling him 'boy', and that she spat out the word 'him' with such venom that if a man had said the same of a female, he would be thought of as a woman-hater, a misogynist. Bridge casually glanced at Beaumont; he continued to keep his own counsel, but she could tell by his stiff crossed arms that he had picked up on the woman's resentment.

"Fine. We will be sure to do that. Until then, I hope you enjoy the comfortable surroundings of one of our finest cells. I'm afraid there's no champagne for you to drink, but I do recommend the tea, which one of the many male officers will bring you during your stay. I'm formally booking you for attempted murder. I suggest that by the time we meet again, you find yourself a lawyer. You're going to need one."

With that, Bridge and Beaumont stood to leave. Bridge was already thinking ahead to the next interview when Drusilla spoke.

"He will die. He must die. Those on that craft, they are already doomed. But if he dies, we might all stand a chance of surviving what he has set in motion."

Bridge ignored the woman on the other side of the desk. She felt a wave of deceit and hatred wash over her. Beaumont left the room first; Bridge was barely out the door before she heard the artist in her custody add, "Although, I think it's too late, dolly eek."

Chapter Thirteen

FLORA FAWKES STOOD in stark contrast to Drusilla Pero. Drusilla exuded calmness, her demeanour resistant to police scrutiny. Flora, on the other hand, seemed on the verge of self-destruction as she was escorted from the cell into the interrogation room, where the enigmatic obstruction had previously sat.

Bridge knew she had no real case to bring against Fawkes; endangerment to public safety was perhaps the best outcome she could hope for, not the manslaughter she would have preferred to tie around the woman's neck.

She had sent Detective Constable Beaumont to conduct inquiries at the gallery across the river. It would do him good to get out of the building for a while, and it might give the gallery owner something to ponder if she was indeed harbouring anti-men sentiments, as Drusilla had intimated.

It was a learning curve for Beaumont. For Flora Fawkes, it was a hard-learned lesson.

Even before Bridge could ask her any questions, Fawkes was sobbing profusely, consumed by anguish and despair. This was no silly girl caught with her hand in the till, nor a manipulative teenager spilling crocodile tears and feigning remorse. This was a woman who, mere hours before, had been on the verge of a violent confrontation, and whose actions had led to a man's severe injury.

The woman who had thrown the ashtray with such ferocity seemed to vanish the moment she released it, her bravado replaced by fear.

IAN D. HALL

"Please, I'm begging you. I didn't mean to kill the policeman. I was just—"

"Angry, full of rage, trying to regain control of a situation that was slipping from your hands?" Bridge couldn't help herself; she had taken a dislike to the woman from the moment she laid eyes on her. It was the only trait Fawkes shared with Drusilla.

"No, no. Nothing like that. Please understand, I...I wouldn't...I couldn't hurt anyone. I'm a doctor, I take my oath incredibly seriously. It was just—"

"That you were being guided?" Bridge interrupted the inconsolable woman. It was a surprise to both the lawyer and the fellow female detective sitting in, that the question was asked without sarcasm, while Fawkes's face went blank, as though she had turned to stone. When she did speak, it was in a hypnotic tone, as if parroting someone else's words for the benefit of those present.

"She had to die. I see that now. She knew too much. She was a frightful old woman, always sticking her nose into my business, into all our dealings."

Bridge was perplexed. "She?"

"That old bag on the top floor. Sniffling around, eavesdropping at the door, spreading rumours, informing the council of any misdemeanour, any small infringement on the lease, opening our mail. That was the last straw, the day when I caught her going through my personal letters, notes from my husband, correspondence from my bank informing that I was out of credit, a letter of rebuke from the GMC. Oh, she loved that, standing beside my desk with the typed letter in her hand, waving it about as though it was a party favour."

"Dr. Fawkes...Flora...just who are you talking about?"

"And she didn't want cash! She wasn't normal. She wasn't going to blackmail me, not that I could have given her anything. No, she wanted me out of the building. The bitch wanted us all out."

The lawyer placed his hand on his client's arm in a vain attempt to get her to shut up and stop offering information on a crime the police didn't know had taken place.

"She's cold. Stone cold."

Bridge heard the lawyer speak, she heard the words, but she felt compelled to continue staring into the eyes of a woman slowly losing her mind. "She's flipped. This won't stand," she muttered out of the corner of her mouth to her colleague, who grunted her agreement.

"Okay, Flora. You can stop there. I think what we will do is get the medical officer to come down and take a look at you, perhaps give you something to rest for a while and then pick it from the beginning in the morning. Is that agreeable with you, Mr. Fencham?"

The duty lawyer nodded his approval. He went to stand and gently help his client.

"No!"

Flora Fawkes screamed the word as if denying a child from running out into the middle of the road as a bus passed by. The denial was long, guttural, spoken with force and anger. A different kind to the one on show in the office earlier, this was full of fury, demonic. Only the infernal laughter was missing.

"Margaret Robson. Somebody should have dealt with her years ago. She was once a member of the IRA. Did you know that? We found out by accident, of course. A man came looking for her. An American. He looked odd, as though he had seen hell and heaven and discovered they were one and the same, yet he was glad, brimming with excitement.

"I told him that she was most likely at the Globe. She spent her lunch breaks in the tea shop, swapping old stories with a couple of people. I saw her in there once before, when I went to buy a ticket for someone I was considering dating. It was the day after the cathedral came down in Avoncross. I closed my door, locking it behind me and followed the American at a discreet distance.

"Sure enough, she was there. He sat down beside her. I couldn't hear it all, their conversation. I was too far away, but I did hear him tell her that the building had come down just as he had planned. That she should have seen it, that in her day with those boys of hers, they would have celebrated long into the County Kerry night.

"It's funny, he was there as well."

Flora Fawkes had hardly stopped for breath. Both detectives and the lawyer were stunned into silence as what they suspected was the missing link, and it had fallen straight into their unsuspecting hands. If true, this was surely the man the nation had been looking for, the one who responsible for the destruction of Avoncross Cathedral and the deaths of over two thousand people, not to mention shutting down the city as it faced up to the challenges of rebuilding—a near-impossible job given the circumstances.

The lawyer forgot himself. He was just as eager to know what was going on as Bridge. He asked who was there with them.

"The man upstairs. He wasn't sat with them. He had been out all day, apparently, settling a dispute, but he confirmed what he heard when I cornered him the next day."

"The man upstairs?"

"Yes, him. The one whose head was bashed in. The owner of the painting of the Gorgon."

Bridge reflected on Fawkes's words for a moment. Just as she was about to ask a follow-up question, the lights flickered above their heads. It wasn't an unusual occurrence in the building. Its old corridors and small offices had been in place for more than 130 years; dust was a constant companion; newly installed electrics soon turned volatile. The blackouts were inconvenient, but many enjoyed the effect, as it made them feel at home, a throwback to a period when the law was not so transparent, when a beating in a room in the bowels of the building could lead to valued intelligence rather than a reprimand and dismissal.

Bridge was not of that opinion. She loved the history of the building: rumour was that Abberline himself was to be found there on occasion when he could be prised away from his beloved East End with its scares of the past, the villainy of corruption at the highest level seeping in from the nearby docks and factories, the meat markets where once upon a time both bovine and human meat might be eaten in equal measure.

Even Southwark Station was modern in comparison.

Bridge longed to work in one of the new offices, to be surrounded by light, by clarity, in serving of the populace of London on both sides of the river. That was her dream. But now in her early forties, she doubted if such a move would be possible.

The light flickered again.

Longer this time, more pronounced.

Bridge had continued to focus her scrutiny on the woman in front of her.

Flora Fawkes was still speaking in monotone, as though a murderous surgeon had attacked her with a sharp knife and damaged her vocal cords, destroying any emotional expression, but what her voice lacked in sentiment, her body made up for in violently convulsing.

The lights went out.

Groans of derision and voiced male anger filled the station. A couple of the female officers and detectives laughed nervously, a tea tray was dropped, a loud and indiscriminate bang echoed down the labyrinth-like corridors. Bridge could still see the woman in front of her, the sudden darkness not affecting her view. She had only been in such darkness once before—the morning she was caught in the terrorist attack on London in 2007. Her whole carriage was one of noise, at first complaints then cries of fear. The explosion from three stations further along the line had reverberated in their ears and buffeted the underground train, the tiled walls of the tunnel seeming to strain and bulge as the shockwave filled the corridors of power with astonishment and the public with enraged concern.

In that darkness, she had seen nothing and had been blindly groping her way along when an older man with authority in his voice announced he had a torch and that he was going to turn it on. Like moths to the flame, the people, the disconnected public, inched their way to the comfort of the light on offer, the sanctuary it provided.

This darkness, this inverting of order in the police station was extraordinary. The darkness in the Tube was frightening; nobody knew what was going on in the outside world. Was the city once more under attack? Was it a selected event? Nobody knew, and nobody in her carriage cared to guess or make light observation.

Yet even in the cowering darkness of the interview room—Bible black as her favourite poet once remarked truthfully—she could see her quarry. The image was engrained, seared into her mind, as if all the illumination in the world was trained on the doctor. Nothing else mattered except that vision. Impossible.

A scraping of a chair, a male voice asking repeatedly if all was okay. Still, she stared, transfixed. A door opened behind her, the unmistakable voice of her boss assuring all that the issue would be rectified almost immediately. Several blown fuses had been located and were being replaced.

The light came back on, yet the woman opposite still glowed brighter than the space around her.

Bridge's fellow detective was at the door calling for help. The duty solicitor was quaking in fear, his voice already hoarse from the panic that overwhelmed him.

"She's dead. She's dead. She's dead," he moaned repeatedly, his voice cracking under the strain of his grief. Bridge did not understand. How could she be dead?

She leaned across the table and touched the doctor's skin. It was, as the solicitor had said before the lights went out, stone cold. The fingers on her left hand were like ice, the wrist frozen. Bridge lifted her hand towards the doctor's face. Stone, rigid. The flesh frozen in fear, a half-crooked sneer as she had stopped speaking mid-flow, paused by a remote control that manipulated the living.

Bridge had failed in her duty. A suspect had died in her custody.

She felt a hand on her shoulder, a presence looming close to her ear, the slight lisp she had always found endearing speaking discreetly to her.

"Your man is back on the ward. You need to go. I'll clean up here, and we'll catch up later."

Bridge nodded her compliance.

"Be careful, Bridge. The doctors there are in a panic. There is something not right with our victim."

The detective took a final look at the dead woman in the chair. The glow was gone, if ever it was there, and had been replaced by a backdrop of brick and plaster. This was Fawkes's final moment, not consumed by fire, but to become as unfeeling as stone.

Chapter Fourteen

IT WAS ALMOST midnight before Bridge made it back to the hospital.

The streets had been fuller than normal. What seemed like thousands of people poured out of Waterloo Station's several exits, every service somehow packed to the rafters with late-night revellers. The pavements leading towards the old theatre were bruised with people dancing; cars came to a standstill from the river on the north side, down as far as Westminster Bridge Road. Even the alleyways, the old thoroughfares and newly built streets were lined with crowds, all acting as if it was the end of the world and they had every right to party.

It had been a spontaneous call-out by activists to reclaim the London night by all, but especially women. In fact, the organisers—unnamed, anonymous, internet-driven—had implored anyone who relished freedom to make London their own, to arrive en masse from eleven that night so that it would cause confusion and chaos, an impossible situation for the police to handle.

Bridge's station was right in the middle of this chaos. Officers were called in from all over London, yet the organisers, the invisible brains behind this civil disobedience, had prepared for this by having the greatest number of people on the streets of this small historical part of the city, cutting off almost every side street possible.

From the coffee shop on the corner of The Cut down to the corner of Southwark Underground and Blackfriars Road, to

Lambeth North to Kennington Road and down as far as Lambeth Bridge, it seemed to the detective that any road she tried to take to the hospital was full of chanting, demonstrative, fiercely proud people of all shapes, sizes, orientations celebrating the freedom that an internet site had promised them.

Every streetlamp was ablaze, shining with every watt of energy it had running through its wires. Every house, every flat, shop front, every factory, national landmark, museum, late-night café, empty and rotting pub—from Southwark's Christ Church to the Elephant and Castle roundabout to Vauxhall Underground—every light that could be on was on. Even The Oval's lights blazed merrily into the night. From space, it would have looked as though this one part of London was the centre of the universe—a giant billboard broadcasting *This is where you need to be.*

While this triangular-shaped wedge of inner London was enjoying the show, the chance to roam free and take in the night air with likeminded sisters and friends, those in surrounding areas began to see their electricity cut out. Brixton, Camberwell, Bermondsey, Peckham, Deptford—all lost power quickly. Then north of the river, Covent Garden, Farringdon, Clerkenwell, Whitechapel, and the city itself, were all plunged into darkness in rapid succession.

Bridge was unaware of this at the time. All she found was her way blocked at almost every corner. Every minute that passed, there seemed to be more people on the street, every second another stepped out of their house in a mass vibrant demonstration against misogyny and hatred.

Internally, Bridge applauded them. Even she had faced the effects of catcalls in her younger days when a policewoman's uniform was a mark of leering fantasy and not the symbol of authority that her male counterparts were afforded by the vast majority of the public. The first day she went to work as a detective constable in trousers was one of liberation. She still faced sexism

Ian D. Hall

head-on, but in that instant, a significant difference was made to her life in the force.

Internally, she applauded the crowd, but outwardly she objected to her passage in the pursuit of her duty being hampered. She started bulldozing through, almost knocking over a group of drag kings and butch queens. She apologised, making it clear it was not intentional, that she was in a rush to get to the hospital. A mouthful of abuse came back at her for her troubles. One person spat at her, catching her on the cheek. Another stuck up a middle finger and called her a traitor to her sex. The rest of the crowd just laughed, pointed fingers, and in parroted fashion yelled out, "Traitor, Traitor, Traitor!" as though they were hissing from the gallery at the spectacle of a hanging. Bridge didn't have the time to argue. It had taken her an hour to get to the far end of Lower Marsh, and there were still thousands of people dancing and screaming into the lit-up night ahead of her.

Security had been intensified at the hospital by the time she made the side entrance, recognised by a guard who had seen her earlier the previous day.

"What the hell is going on?" she asked as she brushed herself down, removing what looked like a muddied footprint from the side of her jacket. She didn't remember being kicked, but it wouldn't have surprised her to find out that she had been.

The man seemed both disgusted and fearful in equal measure. He noticed the quizzical look on the detective's face and explained himself.

"It's not the amount of people on the streets around here I object to. Even as a man of my age, I still worry about working nights and leaving the hospital tired and exhausted from the shenanigans of some people—the drug users, the drunks, the pimps and their toms who approach me as I walk home in the dark. It's what's happening in other parts of the city. Some arseholes, begging your pardon Miss, have used the chaos as an excuse to commit a terrorist attack in Tottenham. I'm surprised you didn't hear the explosion, but then again, with that lot out there, it's a wonder you could hear yourself think."

"A bomb?"

"Yes Miss. A big one by the sound of the report. Right by the ticket office at the end of the game tonight. Hundreds dead."

Bridge was struck dumb. In amongst all the revelry, all the overwhelming good spirits, and occasions of abuse, she had not expected someone to take advantage of the chaos by causing destruction, of mass murder on the other side of the river.

She thought quickly and composed herself. There would be hell to pay at the station. The fallout alone from the sudden influx of people hitting the streets of Waterloo would be a nightmare for public relations and paperwork. But this… atrocity, it was beyond her reasoning, and even as a survivor of a terrorist attack a few years earlier, she could not comprehend the scale of what would yet be revealed as homes across Britain turned on their televisions or laptops in search of light-hearted news only to find that they were once again living under the thumbs of maniacs.

The guard led her to the main entrance, made her sign in— "Can't be too careful," he whispered—and then escorted her to the new room in which her charge lay, surrounded by machines, the strange man at the centre of the web. He was alive but still in a coma.

A doctor caught sight of Bridge and the guard as they watched for a moment the apparatus breathing for him. It was almost hypnotic, mesmerising in its complexity, and it took a couple of hellos to get her attention.

The guard smiled and left her side, not wanting to get in any trouble with the doctor and mindful of the huge swell of people hanging around outside the hospital.

"Excuse me, are you Detective Inspector Bridge?"

"Yes. Yes, I am. Sorry. I was a bit taken aback by the number of machines in here. He looks so small in comparison." As she spoke, she removed her warrant card from her pocket and showed the doctor that she was indeed who she said she was.

"Thank you, Detective Bridge. It's been crazy in here for a couple of hours. I presume you had to walk here from the station and got caught in the crowds."

Bridge gave a weary, watery smile and agreed. He didn't need to know that she had never had a lesson, had never wanted to drive a car.

"The guard told me about the attack in Tottenham," Bridge said, changing the subject.

"Gosh, yes. The other part of the hospital has been put on emergency watch, but it seems with the huge crowds in the area and blackout in other parts of the city, all the wounded and dead are being taken to Watford, Hertford, and Stevenage," the doctor replied matter-of-factly.

The air grew stale around them, and there seemed nothing else to say on the subject. Neither had the energy to discuss it further; both would get their news updates from the same source during the rest of the night; both would give a nod of acknowledgement to the other passed as the horror unfolded.

"My boss got a message to say he was back from the operating theatre." Bridge pointed at the man as she explained why she was there. She may as well have been pointing at one of the machines surrounding him for all the good it did.

"Yes, that was from me. It's strange ,though. When I rang, it seemed you were in the middle of a local blackout there. I was going to say it could wait. I wish now I had said that. The terrible trouble you've had ,just walking a couple of miles."

Bridge shook her head; it wasn't an issue. Not now she was where she was meant to be.

"It is okay," she assured the doctor. "He's my patient as well, I guess."

The man was obviously relieved by her words.

"Well. It started in the operating theatre. We had to remove a blood clot that had formed at the surface of the brain. The person who attempted to kill him here had enough knowledge of how to create one that, if left untreated, it would have been more successful than the original attack he had."

"What happened?"

The doctor looked around and saw a couple of chairs. He motioned to Bridge to join him, and she did so willingly. The chairs offered a piece of normality in a world that had seemed to turn ridiculously off its axis in the last day or two.

Lowering his voice, the doctor leaned in as close as he dared without invading her personal space.

"It was peculiar. I would say weird, but after tonight's events, I don't wish to add laughable drama to your troubles. But I really think he caused all the lights to turn on in the area. His brain activity was off the scale. You see, the theatre is a well-lit room. Not as bright as you've seen out there, especially not over by The Oval by all accounts, but we can't perform surgery in the dark."

This last part seemed reasonable to Bridge. Yet the doctor's suggestion that the man in a coma on the bed, tied to machines keeping him alive pulse by pulse, had caused the surge in electric use was preposterous, naively insane. Still, she allowed him to continue.

"The machines we had him on initially, they went haywire. I've seen machines crash whilst in use—one blew up with such a bang, it set off the fire alarms and led to an evacuation. But several, all overloading at the same time? We were lucky the new system cut the supply and kept the damage to a minimum, that we have a facility in place to tackle a fire internally. But it was still hair-raising."

The doctor stopped for a second as a fellow doctor and nurse passed by. The sound of barked instructions and berated admonishment of the nurse made Bridge's teeth unconsciously grind.

IAN D. HALL

The doctor leaned in closer.

"When we hooked him up to another monitor, we noticed that the display was acting…well, odd. It was marking out all the usual signs, heart rate, sats and so on, but it was not regular. There was a pattern to it that didn't make sense."

Bridge was thinking. All the information seemed to come at once. She felt in her coat pocket for the journal she had been reading. The knock on his head as a small pre-teenage boy, the various hits he had taken, the attack in his home, again to the skull. The doctor spoke of patterns; there was another one revealing itself under her very nose.

"What type of pattern, Doctor?" Bridge asked with caution.

"Please, call me Tumas. Well, you're going to laugh. It was as if his brain was communicating in Morse Code. Stupid, I know. I doubted it myself as I watched it."

"How do you know it was Morse Code?"

"Before I came to London, I was in the Italian Navy."

"So you think that our man in there, beaten savagely, another attempt on his life, and though you might not know it, a blow to the head in his youth, is somehow capable of sending messages via Morse Code to an electric grid and shutting off power in North London, whilst at the same time overloading the local area with enough energy to create a dazzling show from here and beyond Waterloo Station?"

The doctor looked down. His eyes betrayed his inner thoughts, that he was going to be ridiculed for his belief. Bridge put a hand gently on his knee.

"Mate, I have heard weirder explanations than that in my life. But when you consider those people who have been going missing all over the country, the Government release of the clinic in Oxfordshire of children having their bodies turned to pulp in the 1980s, and the cathedral in Avoncross being blown up—don't get me started on the story of killer ants being hidden away in a secret laboratory—I think you might have something."

Tumas beamed. His smile was infectious.

"But surely," he said, "it's all bullshit, isn't it?"

Bridge didn't have a religious bone in her body, but she had read enough of the Bible to be fascinated by its ending—an end of days, the Revelation of St. John.

The three years she had spent at the University in Liverpool, the time she had spent following around a group of people on Hope Street volunteering for one cause or another in the Catholic Cathedral, and later giving up a large portion of her spare time in the imposing Gothic structure of the Anglican Cathedral... It wasn't a love of Jesus that had driven her to spend time in the buildings, attending prayers, quiet reflection and the occasional party where Spin the Bottle and the chance of a snog in the cupboard was replaced by appropriate action of changing the lives of others. It was because of The Gospel according to Henry.

Henry had enraptured her from the moment she met him. Her life had revolved around him, even when he was found guilty of child trafficking from Eastern Europe, even when he made it clear that her constant attention was making him anxious. Despite getting him through several end-of-term exams and one written paper in which she sailed close to the wind of being found out, he'd said she was 'too much'. In the years since, during her gradual if unedifying rise through the ranks where she had witnessed crimes that would have made the sternest stomach lurch...she had thought of him constantly, and now...

What else could she say to the man? The strangeness of the times, it was to her, an ending, a reckoning.

"Yes, it's bullshit," she agreed.

The doctor nodded in relief.

"It's funny, though," he said. "When I came on duty, and when I was assisting the operation, I couldn't help but think I knew him."

"Really?" Bridge asked a little too enthusiastically.

Ian D. Hall

"Yes. Then about an hour ago, I realised where I knew him from. He gave a lecture a few years ago on the grave mistakes of humanity's spread across the universe. He likened it to a disease, a virus reaching out and killing every host, every planet that they landed on."

Chapter Fifteen

THE DOCTOR STAYED with Bridge for a while longer, taking notes and asking questions about the case to which Bridge could not provide answers. On one occasion, he probed Bridge's marital status.

If Bridge had not been consumed by the information that the doctor had innocently dropped, then she might have been amused that whether she was married or not was a concern of the man who, it seemed, had taken a shine to her in the short time they had spent talking to each other.

In this day and age, was anyone truly bothered by such an outmoded institution and its effect on a person's ability to have some fun? Nevertheless, if she'd had her wits about her, she would have turned him down gently. She simply didn't have the time nor the inclination to be involved with anyone at the moment. Too much was going on in her life.

Sensing that Bridge was not interested in a date, or perhaps in his engaging conversation, the doctor made a tactical retreat. He smiled and told her that he would return later to check on her. Bridge accepted the offer with a gracious smile. *No need to give him a complex*, she thought.

For a while, Bridge simply stared at the man, her mind trying to work out what would make someone with such intelligence deny humanity's chance to walk amongst the stars. Why did this bother her? Why had it struck a nerve that she couldn't quite soothe or scratch?

The man's journal was still in her pocket, itching to be continued to be read. But the urge to search on her phone for the lecture the doctor had spoken of, to see for herself the damnation he had demonstrated during the evening at London's prestigious and historic Royal Observatory, was stronger.

It was ridiculously easy to find. A couple of bits of information, a few key words. The evening, which was part of a series of events commemorating the start of the construction of the great gift to London's enlightened and curious public, was more than 'a couple of years ago'. However, she understood that time, to a doctor, to a police officer, and to others, ran at different speeds. For a doctor and a nurse, a second in either direction could be life-threatening. For someone concerned only with filling their days with the mundane, Time became a more subtle animal, one that congealed, melded into one. So much so that she had learned that if a witness or suspect used the phrase 'the other day', it was quite possible they meant a decade back. In the same way that a school pupil might insist that the week drags on, and it is Thursday when they believe it to be Tuesday, so a doctor had every right to say 'a couple' when they meant almost eight.

What was not up for debate was the strength of purpose and disaffection for the observatory the man in the bed showed as he gave a perfectly lucid but unflattering account of the public's conception of the building. He even managed to bring Martial Bourdin's name into the lecture as he described the possible intentions of the anarchist. It was a car crash; the reading of the room was one of concern, and yet that was only to her. The lecture itself meant nothing. While she had spent time around Greenwich, taking in the history of the area and enjoying a picnic or two in the park when she was younger, with her father reciting tall tales of ships and sailors, the prestige of the event and the observatory itself were lost on her.

What was fascinating was the reaction of the crowd as they sat outside the building. She only had one camera to go on, a single viewpoint from which to gather any type of information. The camera was positioned side-on to the speaker, as if purposely focusing on the reaction to certain phrases, certain words. This was not a lecture of pomp but of circumstance. Even Bourdin's motive was of tenuous conjecture, but it served its purpose. Every time his name was mentioned, the crowd caught on camera was either appalled or enraptured. It was as if the man on the podium was testing the reaction, a devil offering a choice, and you had to climb down off the fence provided to take a side.

There was no physical reaction, no shouts of shame ringing out into the August summer warmth, no clapping or cheer of endorsement; it was all in the subtle movements on each face. The tics, the reflexes, the half-caught smiles, the downward glances, the raising of an eyebrow, the sense of fear, the joy of having certain ideals manifesting in the mind. These were the same micro-expressions she was trained to spot during an interview. These were the lies that each person was able to hide from their loved ones, their friends, and neighbours, but not from themselves.

Bridge watched the whole long lecture twice. Both times, she noticed more detail when the camera turned to focus on the crowd. Both times, the words sounded reasonable but off-topic. Yet some within the crowd were caught emotionally on the verge of ecstasy, while others were holding back from calling for him to be removed from the stage.

Then she saw her, or at least she thought she did. It was the right build, the same look of perpetual boredom running deep across her body language. A glass of champagne in her hand, tipped slightly away from her, as if she was perpetually chinking someone else's glass in good grace of celebration or of news received.

The hair was shorter, with a streak of red running through it from front to back as if to mark her out as interesting, but to Bridge, it was the arrogance of the woman that made her quietly punch the air. There was the connection; this is where the man in the bed beside her had first met Drusilla Pero.

There was another woman with Pero, who was more agitated than anyone else in the audience. Once again, there was no

IAN D. HALL

emotional outburst, just a giveaway signal that she was on the verge of creating a scene.

Creating a scene... wasn't that what Henry's wife told her when she confronted her outside the offices of *The Times* the day after the news broke of the charity founder's arrest? His wife had slapped her so hard that Bridge had the outline of the woman's hand on her cheek for over a week. It had stung, but not as much as being called jealous, not as much as the insinuation that Bridge must have had a hand in the whole operation. Thankfully, the action of a weak woman threatened by the truth—now that Bridge could see it herself—was not her business. The newspaper in question was taken to task by her solicitor, and she received a grovelling apology and a cheque, which covered the cost of a deposit on a flat. *Was it worth it?* she had often asked herself. Was it worth the silent treatment by all those she had once considered friends, the times now lost, the pariah status she was given by those who still to this day claimed that Henry had been set up...that he was innocent?

Yes, yes, a thousand times, yes. There was no reason to feel bad, to show weakness in the face of a major despicable crime. If she hadn't blown the whistle, if she had not found all the paperwork pertaining to the charity and seen for herself the ruin that Henry had brought upon those children, then he might have moved on from trafficking children to other, even greater nefarious offences.

Bridge paused the film and peered closely at the screen. Just beyond the woman next to Pero, barely visible and almost unrecognisable in what appeared to be a dirty-blonde wig, she was sure that the grainy, unflattering image was that of one of her fellow officers from the station.

Rubbish, she thought to herself. *Impossible! There is no way she would have been there.* She had a wife, two kids, no life outside of her family and work...did she? For all Bridge knew, her colleague could have been a huge astronomy nut, but then she'd asked for the television in the old canteen to be turned off during the series of interviews on the Mars mission...

Bridge stopped her train of thought and looked closer at the figure between Pero and the other detective. A man whom she definitely recognised; he was one of them, up there in space right now. Science Officer Jerome Brassington. He had been hailed a hero as he tried to save the life of Flight Engineer Thomskilyvan.

"What the hell?"

Bridge couldn't help herself. The words needed to come out and with force.

A nurse strode past quickly, tutting at Bridge.

Bite me, lady, Bridge thought brutally.

Brassington was one of only two British astronauts on board the craft hurtling across the blackness of space. He had been a late replacement for Kenyan Jack Kiplagat, who had a ruptured appendix a month before the mission began.

Bridge was about to call the station; she got as far as pressing the number before clicking it back off. If Brenda Beehaven *did* know either Brassington or Pero, then there was a conflict. She had two choices: either Beaumont or Torlay would have to do. The last she heard, Beaumont was on the other side of the river. Bridge had forgotten, had the young serious officer been caught up in any trouble?

She tried his number first. He answered immediately, and she blew a small exhale of relief.

Bridge listened as he informed her that he wouldn't get back to the station for quite some time. He had found the owner of the gallery, but it had taken a devil's age to get all the information from here. A spiky, untrusting woman was how Beaumont described her, a woman who visibly flinched when he walked in the door and asked to speak to her regarding a recent showing of Drusilla Pero's work.

It took hours, Beaumont said, almost as if she had done it on purpose. That, Bridge could believe.

　　　　　　　　　　　　　　　　　Ian D. Hall

"How are things on that side of the river?"

Beaumont's answer chilled her to the bone. She suddenly felt cold, the time of night perhaps or the sense of something being lost as the night took its toll.

He had been making his way back to his vehicle when every light in Whitechapel went dark. Every street became as black as pitch. The only lights unaffected were those on the cars and buses, but even they were ineffective as a means to get people moving safely as the roar of an explosion rent the air to the north and echoed as loudly as anything that the city had suffered during its dark days under siege from the raids by the *Luftwaffe*.

He had no authority to help, but help he had. Bridge was exceedingly proud of him as he explained what he had done in service on a night shrouded in death and destruction. He had initially pitched in and helped the local station house in Whitechapel. *Long memories in those parts*, mused the detective as a movement to her side caught her eye. She turned her head to stare at the man in the bed…

Nothing.

It wasn't long, though, before Beaumont and every available officer was instructed to guard certain buildings, to keep the public indoors where possible, and to assist those caught on bridges and the Underground. The last thing the prime minister wanted was panic on the streets of the capital. The scenes at White Hart Lane were mercifully kept off the national airwaves due to the inability of the major broadcasters to send any journalist to the area. All roads around the ground had been sealed within minutes. Nobody in or out of Tottenham unless you were driving an emergency vehicle. It was rumoured the army had been assisting, looking for another possible device, but as yet, it was limited to just a single attack.

Bridge thanked Beaumont and told him to get back whenever it was possible, but that as soon as he reported to her his findings, then he would be off duty for a couple of days. He was a good sort.

She was sure he would make a terrific detective one day…if he survived the storm across the Thames.

Beaumont thanked her and hung up. Immediate and to the point, that was the young officer to the letter.

London's burning, she started to sing in her head. Shocked by the flippancy and casualness of the moment, she admonished herself before calling to Torlay.

"Torlay, is that you? You sound muffled."

"It's me. I'm at Boase's mum's house. She rang me earlier to say Claire was feeling unwell. She's been asking for you and calling out Parsons' name. The shock of his sudden death, Ma'am…I think it's broken her. I've sat with her for a couple of hours, but she doesn't look right at all. I'm tempted to call in a doctor, but what with all that's going on…"

Torlay didn't have to finish the sentence. Bridge knew exactly what he was saying.

"Didn't they try to contact you from the station? I gather it was all hands on deck."

There was a small but discernible pause. Bridge laid a quick bet that he had turned off his other phone.

"Family emergency, Ma'am. Claire was in trouble."

Bridge didn't have it in her to rebuke him; his heart, as ever, was in the right place. He would certainly have a lot to explain, though, the next time he stepped foot over the thin blue line.

"Look, the reason I called is I need a little digging done, but I'm stuck at the hospital, and for reasons I cannot divulge at the moment, I also cannot rely on the right person answering the call. Do you have your laptop to hand? I only have my phone, and the battery is pretty low."

"Of course I have my laptop. It was the only way I could listen to the news tonight. You know what Claire's mum's like. Not a day shall pass when the news comes on in her house. The planet could be in mortal peril, and she would still rather watch an episode of *Bargain Hunt* or spit scorn at someone's attempt at cake frosting."

Bridge wanted to laugh. She really needed to, but the day had been long and there was too much at stake.

"I want you to see if you can find any connection between Brenda Beehaven and Jerome Brassington, and then see if there is anything that can tie them both to Drusilla Pero."

"Righto," Torlay answered with firmness in his voice. "By the way, Ma'am, I'm sorry you lost one today. That was harsh."

If Bridge was going to cry at any point, it would have been then. An officer killed in the line of duty, a bomb exploding in London, the effect that the case was having on her... it had all swum by her, but the woman in the interview room, her cold, dead eyes staring back at her—the memory was too fresh, too binding.

Weakness...

She breathed and composed herself. "Thank you, Torlay. That is kind of you."

He had meant it; he was sorry. No officer should have to see someone they've nicked die in front of them. It was a cruel joke played by an uncaring God.

"Look after Claire. Give her a hug when she is well, tell her I said hello."

With that, Bridge turned her phone off. It was all too much.

Her phone beeped once and went dark.

She sat back in the chair and closed her eyes. There was nothing she could do but wait. She would go home, have a shower, catch a couple of hours' sleep and start fresh in the morning. She would speak to both Torlay and Beaumont, keep an eye on Brenda, and then track down the police officer who looked after the boy that night many years ago.

Her phone beeped.

It had turned itself on again.

Damn stupid phone.

She fumbled at the illuminated keyboard, scrolled her way to the off position and put her hands on her knees.

The phone came on again.

As she held it in her hand, a quizzical frown forming, it vibrated, the usual signal that someone had sent a text.

With heavy eyes, she clicked on the text message icon.

Suddenly awake, her senses alert, she looked across to the man in the bed. His monitors all looked normal even if he didn't, encased behind a layer of surgical bandages, only his closed eyes revealing that underneath lay a human being.

She switched her attention back to the phone. The text message boldly displayed the words that made her cold body react as though she had been dumped in the Antarctic Sea with no clothes on.

I CAN FEEL YOU STANDING CLOSE BY, INGRID.

Chapter Sixteen

I CAN FEEL YOU STANDING CLOSE BY, INGRID.

THERE WAS A film that I once saw on television. I believe it was later given added...cool, I think they call it, by being the backdrop to one of those heavy metal band's songs. Now, I don't have time for the music, it's not jazz, after all, but I do find the blending of art in history to be a particular fascination.

I caught sight of the video when a patient used it as an example of his own neurosis. I recognised the spliced film, a much-undervalued performance by Jason Robards, I thought, and whilst the music did little for me, I felt the anguish and sentiment the group sang about. In my profession, it does help to be empathetic to new external stimuli.

This film resurfaces in my mind now as I know, despite me shouting to you, Ingrid, that you can't actually hear me. My eyes aren't open, yet I see you; my hands are impossible to raise, and the hairs on the back suggest that there is something in the air making them stand on end. That something is you, dear Detective.

They say that hearing is the last sense to go. I disagree. I would argue that it is the sense of self-awareness. I know I am not truly dead because I feel desire. I want to make you understand that what I did to those people was brought on by an ability to cause them harm, to think them, if you will, to death.

I am aware you are here, as sure as I know that somehow you have received my message, as clear perhaps as if you could hear me breathing in your ear. I don't know *how* you received it, but it's there, isn't it? And even now, you are staring at it as if it is a countdown ticking away to…what? An explosion? A big reveal?

Let me continue with my cautionary tale of Faith Croy'ance.

I wanted to marry her, Detective. There is my confession. Still waiting for the explosion?

Linus Rugren was a charlatan, a false man living high on the hog in a false world. I stared at him with a masked sense of dismay and disdain. This man had come all the way to England to tell me that Faith was a fraud. Yet he sat in my chair, cigar in hand, cheap and nasty, smelling of arrogance and wishful thinking, and informed me that Faith's mother had come forward and given a completely different account of the girl's childhood.

So far, the press had not got hold of the information; the studio had kept it under wraps, and the film was progressing as planned. The next stage of her career, financed and produced by Rugren, was to see her make a West End debut…out of the shadows of Hollywood, a natural home for the actor, backed by a man aware of the money she would bring to the three-month run.

The play was based on the life of Emil Hasda, a little-known Polish comic actor, who, it was said, is a relation of the man in front of me, and once received calls for six standing ovations for his act. This is remarkable enough; six standing ovations are to an actor like a shot of heroin to a desperate addict. The pleasure they both receive is a thrill, a rush, a relief.

Emil Hasda, on his final bow, took a gun from his waistcoat, aimed it at his head, and fired. All because the love he felt on stage could not wipe out the misery of having been rejected by the woman he loved.

Faith was to play the woman who had scorned our comic hero. The writer of the play, Ludwig Fulda, was to be played by one of those brothers who always seem to be on television only because they are married to theatre royalty, and Emil Hasda, well, that was to be a secret until the day before the opening night. I don't listen to rumours, but if it were true, then a particular cinematic heavyweight's career might have been changed overnight.

I had read an early copy of the script. It was decent, it had brutality, it had cheer, it would have been a smash, and Faith was going to shine like never before.

But then, according to Rugren, Doreen Tuttle re-emerged, and in her wake, there was enough damaging truth to see Faith never work again, hounded out of Hollywood, even dragged through the courts.

Of course, today it would be no big deal. You cannot be a star unless your baggage, your dirty laundry is on display to all and sundry—real sweat-driven, intestinal loosening of every colour running down onto the public below. The world has changed, now you must kill the angels to survive.

It seems, as Rugren was so willing to disclose, that Faith's past was not as clean and hard as she made out. Yes, she was abandoned; Doreen Tuttle was exceedingly clear on that. But it was done out of safety, out of concern for her own life.

If believed, Faith was always a monster. Deceptive, an unreliable witness to her own fictional autobiography. Doreen had shown the producer, his two lawyers, and his wife, a scar around her neck. The knife had not committed itself to the job, but the intent was there. Faith had caught her mother off guard, and she was lucky, she insisted more than once, to be alive. She had run away because if she hadn't, there was no telling what her child would have done next.

This, Detective, was not the end of Faith's battle with sanity and criminal acts. The family members who took her in, now all dead, had sent written apologies to the mother, now understanding her plight.

Doreen produced a letter from her father—Faith's grandfather—in which he wrote of wanting to have Faith institutionalised. Doreen's mother was living on her nerves, as every moment she feared another explosion of hatred and vitriol. It was signed by the man but without collaboration in any other testimony.

Doreen even insinuated that the child's father had left home because Faith had a possessive streak in her and had whispered to her father that she was going to kill her mother and replace her in his bed.

When it was put to Ms. Tuttle that her so-called husband never existed—after all, it was she who told government officials her daughter was the result of a one-night stand—she responded, "I made that up so I could get on the housing register. No one wants to help decent folk anymore.

"As the good lord is my witness," she said with remorse in her voice, placing her hand over her breast. "The man was decent. He moved out of our family home, but he never left me without. At least, not until that obscene child forced his hand and he had no choice but to put some distance between himself and us."

I was so stunned by these words of accusation that I sat in the chair I reserved for my patients, a chair of only moderate comfort, intentionally, so they feel compelled to talk. Ironically, it was a few minutes before I could open my mouth to ask a question.

"Do you believe her?" I asked.

Through a ring of foul odorous smoke, Rugren admitted that he didn't. "She's on the make. You see it all the time in the business. People want their time in the spotlight as much as an actor wants peace away from it. You've met the girl. Her aura radiates hope, overcoming adversity. She can barely do one film without spending a few weeks in a private clinic for her nerves. She's no murderous, incestuous being. She's a damaged individual upon whom fortune has gracefully fallen."

I mulled that over for a moment and then repeated my question.

"Do you believe her?"

A long draw of a cigar can be an excellent piece of theatre or an infuriating ego ride. It says, *Look at me! I can make you hang on my answer while I fill the air with a smokescreen.* It is deception. Mentally, I applauded and booed at the same time.

"There is a chance that she could be telling the truth. I've gotten a lot of money riding on the girl, not only on stage but with the film that's close to finishing production, and then there are three further films with her name attached to them. That's a lot of moola."

He'd allowed a part of his act to fall, a small casting aside of the mask he wore. The word came from a different age, and it was possible he'd used it to emphasise his meaning, but I looked closely at his eyes; he'd had work done. He was nearer seventy, even eighty, than he was the mid-forties he was trying to pass himself off as.

I let it go. His age didn't matter, but as a deceit, it was known to me now. So, he was willing to overlook his own lies but not take a chance on another's.

"That place you send her, that *facility*." He drawled out the word as if he were saying it for the first time, a child unsure of the pronunciation, seeking approval from their teacher. "What exactly do they do when she is in their *care*?" This time, the emphasis was of cynicism.

I admit, I didn't stay there. I found the management team effective, dutiful, their methods often groundbreaking. Faith spoke highly of them. But upon reflection, I was never in the room when they administered the help, the screenings, the sample takings, the monitoring. I only ever picked her up, travelled with her to the facility, hung around while she was settled in, and only once stopped in the area for a night—a pleasant old-style hotel on the edge of the nearest town, Perchester—to make sure she knew that if she needed me, I could be there in fifteen minutes.

I did not utter a word of my realisation. It would have been, if not career suicide, then a black mark against my professionalism. They had never instructed me to stay, neither the studio nor the man sitting in my chair. I had done my due diligence, and the facility was highly regarded within my peer group. Even that unfortunate accident, the fire, had been explained away. A new group took over, new doctors, new nurses, and they had come forward with information and paid deference to the government subcommittee about what happened there during the 1980s. And yet, I felt the stirring of panic.

"…back next week, could you maybe pay her an unexpected visit, see exactly what goes on there."

I had missed the start of his unusual request but soon caught up. I kept an outwardly noncommittal appearance, neither acceding nor denying him the satisfaction of spying on his asset.

"I will attempt to speak to the management there, but such things are not normally possible. They have their measures and protocols in place, but I might be able to get a warrant from a judge—if you feel it's necessary. Are you prepared to pursue that route?"

His face turned a strange mixture of green and red, an anger born of sickness, a rage threatening to spew pus and bile all over my wooden floor.

He composed himself quickly, as successful businesspeople are apt to do, and without missing a beat, replied, "Do what you can. If nothing comes of it, all well and good. If something should, well, you will be looked upon favourably."

He put his hands on his knees and went to stand up. I stopped him mid-motion, a tactic I use often when the patient attempts a quick getaway, believing they have made sufficient progress. It the perfect moment to throw a question in the shape of a hand grenade and has garnered some interesting results over the years.

"Where is the mother now? Where have you got her holed up? Somewhere nice, I'm guessing. Comfortable but not too pricey… and surrounded by ears that will report back to you if she gets drunk and lets her guard down."

Linus Rugren slowly sat back down. I didn't mind that it was in my chair; I just wanted him to know that I knew. I smiled, and it was genuine.

"Actually, she's in my home in Brighton. I'm heading straight there after we finish this edifying conversation."

"Freedom of the fiefdom."

"A two-week vacation—personal thanks for her part in her daughter's success. It is the least I could do for such an important client."

"The house is bugged."

The man in the chair said nothing, denied nothing.

"And Faith knows nothing about this arrangement?" I asked.

"No. And she will never, even if it turns out that the mother's story is true. The mother will be dealt with properly. Until then, she will want for nothing."

"And Faith?"

"Allowed to retire gracefully, a handsome payoff to aid her recovery. She will gradually be seen less and less in public until she is nothing more than a ten-dollar *Jeopardy* question—'Which twenty-first-century actress had the world at her feet and then faded into obscurity without a dime to her name?'"

He smiled at his own humour. I didn't think it was funny. I wanted to marry her. Yes, she was a client, but with enough effort, such things are surmountable. This was a man openly informing me that even if Faith's story had been correctly told all these years, she would eventually be cut loose and left with nothing more than the rumours of her past.

This time, I allowed Rugren to extradite himself from my chair, and I shook his sweaty, clammy hand goodbye. As he reached the door, he turned back to look at me.

"You know, you're good. You should have been on the stage yourself. Don't forget, she arrives back next Monday. You have two weeks from today to find out what you can and report back to me, and only me. I'll call you at noon on that day. Expect my call!"

He opened the door, stepped out of my office, and paused to look at the painting in the small narrow hallway that led to the outer door and the rest of the floor, building, and street below. I heard him mutter as he got to the second door, "Damn creepy painting."

So there it was. The mission I didn't want to undertake. I admit, over the course of the following week, I paid little regard to my other patients, pretending to take down notes during their sessions. I was in the doldrums. An unregulated melancholy had fallen upon my mind, and I felt sluggish yet listless, as the energy of Faith's return filled me with dread.

Would you like to know, Detective, that I am not a praying man? But I willed that I would receive a phone call, see on the news or hear on the radio that she had died on set on the last day. A bout of food poisoning, her private plane crashing into the desert, her long-haul flight ditching into the ocean or breaking apart as it tried to land. I despaired that this young woman was going to return with triumph in her heart, only to find herself suddenly cast off, a pariah and a leper. She would be better off living through one final moment of brilliance than to suffer for her sins.

Now, Detective! That's a little rude. I was in the middle of a great story, well, a true confession anyway, and you take a call. I wonder who that could be. We shall pick this up later. Maybe I will be awake by then, and then I get to see your face properly instead of it being shrouded by a darkness I cannot penetrate.

***

Bridge returned her phone to her pocket. The pace of the investigation was picking up, and her request to speak to a former serving officer had yielded a welcome but surprising result. She had an hour to get to Waterloo for the train down to Avoncross, where she would not only meet the policewoman who had sat with the boy the night his aunt died but also a woman who knew the lad at school.

She checked her watch and left the hospital room. Outside, the crowds had thinned enough that she was able to make the second train down to Avoncross. Those who partied on were fewer in number but still had the energy to get in Bridge's way during the walk to the famous old station. The electricity had returned to normal too, as though a valve had been released and the pressure had eased.

Chapter Seventeen

TRAINS STOPPED IN either direction a couple of miles from Avoncross. One old, neglected station that had been out of use since the days of Beeching's butchery enjoyed a renaissance. Tourists suddenly remembered the small town and made their way there to look at a living photograph of forgotten life—an easier life of summer evenings in the shroud of nature. It was a reminder of village cricket with tea taken liberally, of pubs that served ploughman's lunches and warm fruity beer in dimpled glasses, a slice of old England ruined by day-trippers in search of paradise.

In the other direction, on the route from London and Southampton, two temporary stations had been built, all show and no substance. They looked bleak on the horizon, almost within touching distance of each other, breeze-block grey and dull, with nothing to sit on while waiting. A Portakabin had been erected and put in place at the entrance, cordoned off from the main road where buses would drop the locals who were still reeling from the destruction in their midst and the occasional dead body that turned up.

Avoncross was becoming a ghost town. Plenty of people still lived there, played there and worked ,where possible, in the streetside shops that had been given the go-ahead to reopen and give the city folk a reason to believe, to hope. But it was all too much the same. The train station, though untouched, would not be operational for the sake of safety for another six months. The main shopping centre, housing mid-range boutiques, nationwide bookshops, the city's only remaining electrical stores, and record shops—established, much-loved names that had happily co-existed for decades under the spire—had all suffered terrible damage. As far as the Market Square, the city just died overnight and could not be resurrected.

It was fitting, Bridge thought with pity, that the hastily erected station she was approaching reflected the instant decay. She wondered what the man lying in a hospital bed would have thought about his birthplace being the subject of such world attention—the cultural and religious centre of the city being shown on television and the stories that came out of it. The nun who had been tied to the ground on the old settlement hill, the row of houses that had been left to rot where corpses had been abandoned, the silence that surrounded it all as the city folk kept their vigil of those who had been killed outright when the large gothic spire exploded and rained down ancient stonework around them.

"I have a horrible feeling he might have quite enjoyed it," she uttered under her breath.

Few people made the journey from London to Avoncross early in the morning. There was no need. Businessmen who had routinely travelled up and down to the capital had simply shifted their lives closer to the bright lights and the chance to forget the horrors that engulfed their bank accounts. Visitors from that side of the country chose to focus their attentions on less heart-breaking sights. And while Basingstoke didn't offer the same sense of history, it also hadn't had a recent tragedy where so many people had died and those who had not continued to live under the dawn of sorrow.

Is that how they will view Mars in the decades to come if that darned ship fails to land, or indeed leaves a scar in the darkness?

Bridge didn't know where that thought came from; it just seemed to randomly appear in her head. Thankfully, she didn't have time to dwell upon it, as the train came to a smooth halt. The station was deserted; the guard, tucked away in the back end of the train, activated the doors and allowed Bridge to disembark. It appeared that she and the man in the blue overcoat who had been waiting patiently on the platform at Waterloo, a half-folded newspaper clutched in his hands and his ears covered by headphones that were at least two sizes too big for him, had been the only two passengers during the entire journey. Why get up from a chair when the only thing to do is count out time?

Bridge looked around. The sheer emptiness of the area, a false construct to someone who had spent the vast majority of their lives in one of two large cities, and whose days out in Epping Forest had become a distant memory, gave her a slight chill. It was unnatural to see a tractor in a field only a hundred yards away, to hear nothing but the hiss of hydraulics and greedy birdsong.

She was glad that the two women had insisted on an early interview. Both had things to do, places to go and people they needed to help.

The elder of the two looked careworn as she held out her hand in greeting to her colleague. The younger was fresher, with a glint of authority in her eyes.

"Hello, Detective." The elder of the two women smiled naturally but with pain in her face as she shook Bridge's hand. "My name is Francis Meadows, retired officer of Avoncross Constabulary, and this is Alice Sidney. She…well, no doubt she will explain who she is. We thought you might like breakfast. There is a place that old coppers like me have been going to since the incident, and you'll get a decent cuppa there. I imagine you won't have had one in a while, not if what your commander-in-chief says is true."

The welcome thought of food pushed everything else aside. Bridge's last drink had been a cold can of cheap pop from the hospital shop, which a nurse had kindly liberated for her during the night, and food…she couldn't remember the last time she'd eaten a meal.

"It's been…an experience, the last few days. But especially the last twenty-four hours."

Neither woman asked for an explanation but nodded their heads sincerely in understanding.

"Come on, my car is over there in that lay-by. If we leave now, we'll beat the lunchtime rush of volunteers. That gives us plenty of time."

***

The journey took ten minutes, but even in such a short time, Bridge expected to see people out and about. The crush of people the night before on the streets near Waterloo had been an example of the craziness that London could experience, but here, in an area that could happily fit into her small world between the police station and the hospital, the pavements were empty. Away from the makeshift railway station that served one half of the eastern side of Avoncross, there was no one.

"A lot of this area housed commuters," offered the woman who had introduced herself as Meadows. "Many of them left when they realised how precarious the city's position had become. They will return when the area is fully cleansed, but that might take time. There is a huge hole in its centre where the cathedral collapsed. It was sinking by a centimetre a year, anyway. Imagine the depth of it now that it has sunk to, where the bowels of God's palace had been blown to seven hells and back."

The younger woman, who had been watching Bridge in the rear-view mirror, sizing her up candidly, added, "It suits the needs of the organisation looking after and instructing the volunteers and relief teams for the moment. They need somewhere to stay whilst the clean-up continues, and where better than in an area on the outskirts?"

The railway line they had followed for half a mile veered away, towards the bruised city. They turned off and joined a smaller road, which narrowed and wound snake-like to the north. Another set of fields, an old aerodrome. A small plane coming into land captured their attention for a moment before they turned left and went up a steep hill, arriving at a public house opposite the Neolithic hill and settlement around which the city once proudly stood.

As Bridge got out of the car, she noticed the skyline. She had never been to Avoncross before but had seen enough pictures in guidebooks and friends' endless holiday photos to know how much the historic Gothic cathedral had dominated the area. From every position on the rim of the bowl it sat in, it took prime position, since no building in the area could be over a certain regulated height lest it interfere with the view. The call to the faithful was ever in their sights, the view of heaven on Earth ever present—until somebody decided to blow it up, and if a witness statement could be believed, it was an American with a grudge.

Inside the pub, both Francis Meadows and Alice Sidney were greeted by name and with a smile. They settled at a table, and without a moment's hesitation, a young man approached their table.

"Three large breakfasts, Arthur, three pots of coffee," Meadows said. "I think our friend here is in need of substance more than she realises."

Arthur smiled and walked back to the kitchen.

As an afterthought, Meadows asked Bridge if she was vegetarian or had any issues with food intolerance. Bridge wasn't, and didn't, but she didn't know whether to be annoyed by the presumption or amused that even in the midst of destruction, there was still a semblance of carrying on with life, of being ignorant to the effects of disaster.

"Arthur was rescued from the rubble, one of only six people who had been attending an unveiling of a dedication to the cathedral that day to be found alive. His parents died, probably immediately, judging by their shattered bodies. He refused to leave the area when we evacuated, so they put him up here. He works like a hero, ten hours a day, cooking for the volunteers, waiting, cleaning, and then for six hours, he joins us, scouring old,

Ian D. Hall

abandoned buildings and empty homes for any sign of…well, you know the rumours."

The table fell silent. Bridge didn't know what to say. The news had covered the bombing and the disaster that followed with relentless glee, but nothing they said made sense. Many even thought that such an idea of creatures living underground that killed en masse was planted by the government so that they could tighten up security and place a cordon of secrecy around the city.

Arthur quickly returned with the coffee and then, a short while later, with three plates filled to the brim with food.

"Let's eat before we talk, Detective. You look as though you haven't eaten in a week."

Bridge nodded and tucked in, occasionally casting an eye over to the seat Alice Sidney occupied. If she hadn't been so damned tired, she would have asked why the woman kept giving her strange, awkward stares.

Eventually, Bridge put down her knife and fork and leaned back in her seat. It had been far too much, more than she had eaten at a single meal in years, long before she went to university. She rubbed her stomach, knowing she would inevitably pay for such apparent gluttony. Still, Alice stared at her; she had not taken her eyes off Bridge once during the silent meal.

Arthur collected the plates and asked if they wanted anything else. Meadows, once again taking charge, replied that all was well, but if he could make sure that they were not disturbed by anyone for an hour, she would appreciate it.

"I must be back on site in ninety minutes, and I'm there for twelve hours. When we're done, Alice will drive you back to the station. Like you, she works better in the nighttime, isn't that right, Alice?"

Alice didn't deny it, and for the next hour, Bridge asked both women questions relating to the attack on the man in the hospital bed. Meadows gave a frank account of the evening she'd spent at the boy's house after his aunt's death—how he'd acted, how upset he should have been, but how he seemed calm in the face of his latest tragedy.

Bridge stopped her in mid-flow.

"Latest tragedy? I have barely found anything on him apart from what I have read in his journals. He speaks of having lost his parents at a young age, but there's no indication of what caused him to become an orphan, and there's nothing online, not a single shred of information regarding their names."

Meadows sneaked a look at her younger companion. If Bridge hadn't been alert to it, she would have missed it—the look told her all she needed to know about the dynamic. It confirmed why Meadows had done virtually all the talking so far. She was the junior partner in this conversation; she was there to fill the foreground but had only so much to say. It was Sidney who was going to build on the foundations.

"Nobody knew his parents, well, not completely. You see, he was a child of the city, but he lived in his early years in a kind of bubble. I doubt he even remembers the time other than what he was told. His mum and dad were always around, on hand for all the big events, birthdays never missed, and he was happy... but it was a lie. His mum and dad weren't... well, they weren't his parents. They were guardians, custodians, wardens, there to make sure that he never found out who his real parents were."

Bridge felt her mouth open and forcibly closed it before her jaw dropped. This information was gold, but she couldn't express the shock of Meadows' words. She wasn't sure how this would affect the case, but it certainly raised more questions, and she was sure that the man had not known about his parents or it would have been in his journal.

There was no time for doubt, though.

"Do you know what happened to his biological parents?"

Meadows' mouth betrayed her imminent words. Her thoughts were on her lips before her brain even considered how to phrase the thorny issue.

"No. Nobody knows, not even the solicitor who came that day to inform him that he'd lost the house to the church. I only found out when I was given a series of boxes that were in the keeping of the cathedral warden. Before that, the boxes had been rescued from the solicitor's offices, which had suffered relatively little damage, but the partners evacuated along with everyone else while the city underwent a structural audit. I think they boxes were forgotten in the rush.

"I was there, when the solicitor told him about the house. I wanted to hold him, to soothe his troubles, but the way he looked at us both, well, more the old man, to be honest, it was like in that myth…what's her name? Medusa? Like he was trying to turn him to stone."

The analogy sent a bolt of cold dread through Bridge, but she quashed it and concentrated on Meadows. So much regret, so much sadness had been pent up within, only now released by telling the boy's story. A thought sparked in Bridge's mind. *You didn't meet your death because he cared for you, he could sense your distress.*

"What happened to the solicitor who met with him that day?"

If Meadows was surprised by the question, then Bridge didn't notice. She was carefully studying the younger of the duo.

"He died a few years later."

"So it was after the man who was tasked with taking him to the school in London was knocked down by a taxi?"

Meadows kept her composure but agreed with a simple nod of the head.

"How long after? Where and how did he die?"

Bridge emphasised the word *die* and felt the sheer depth of the burden within the retired policewoman.

"To answer that might take longer than I believed I had to spare. Let me make a phone call. I think we're going to have to order some more coffee. Alice, are you okay to catch Arthur and get him to bring over three more pots?"

Alice nodded in agreement, and both women rose. Meadows took her phone out of her pocket, dialled a number, and walked off towards the exit.

Alice followed her but not without pausing beside to Bridge, placing a hand on her shoulder. The words that passed her lips were spoken in a whisper.

"I think you know where this is going, Detective. I will tell you more when we're alone. But I warn you, what Meadows is about to say will make you wish you hadn't probed in this direction."

Bridge nodded silently. There was nothing more she could do now but listen.

Chapter Eighteen

I ROSE TO THE rank of sergeant, and then my career stalled, and eventually stopped completely. Several reasons were behind my decision to finally step away from the force; my children for one; my mother's bone cancer for another; and finally, my husband's death at the start of the glorious new century. I could not face another day of the routine sexism, the overlooked and underappreciated vibe I felt every time I walked into the station, which only got worse when the new one was being planned.

I don't complain now. It would have been nice…desirable to take another step up the ladder; I certainly deserved it. However, sitting here with you both now, I can say with hand on tired heart, I am glad I retired when I did. I could not have it all. I could not have done it without support. My kids were too young, and at the time, my husband was struggling with undiagnosed depression. He was a good husband and father, but he couldn't handle leaving the army, and he came back from Iraq a changed and silently suffering man.

I tell you this not as an excuse, Detective Bridge, but as a prelude to what happened next.

I was good at my job. I spent almost two decades at the wheel. I consoled victims of crime; I stood up for the vulnerable in our small city. I saved, proudly, three lives directly when I fought off and arrested a paedophile by the name of Creany, a despicable man who had gone from child porn to abduction of three minors during the summer of ninety-two, and I was part of the team that solved the Tremix murders a couple of years later. They were brutal, a family of six systematically targeted and slaughtered in their own home. The man who killed them was beaten to death inside jail in Manchester only last year. A relative of the family, a cousin, managed to get a visitor's pass and snapped his neck as if it were nothing more than chicken bone.

Then, just as I thought I was in line for a promotion, one that would set me on a new path, my husband tried to commit suicide for the first time. Suddenly the road I'd thought was leading to a motorway turned out to be a cul-de-sac, one I couldn't manoeuvre out of. I juggled it all with positivity. My brother-in-law took on the responsibility of keeping our bills up to date. He arranged with a solicitor to take care of everything financial so that I could keep working and looking after my husband and kids, and my older sister divided her time between our mum and dad and made sure that when I was at work, the children and my increasingly subdued husband were cared for.

Kevin, my brother-in-law, died when the cathedral was bombed, but by that time, I didn't see much of him. He had shrouded himself in a similar shame my husband's. Where Tommy couldn't face the innocent lives he had taken in a raid in a house where it was rumoured a girl was being held against her will, Kevin had been a victim of a scam set up by a solicitor who proceeded to lose all his money, and nearly losing what precious little we had.

Kevin wasn't the same after that. He didn't turn to drink like my husband, but he was desolate. He couldn't help his brother, and now he was facing ruin at the hands of an inscrutable bastard. He turned to God, and fair enough, it's not my bag, but do what you need to do to survive with a clear conscience.

That solicitor was the man who sat down and told a young boy that his aunt was the beneficiary of his parents' estate. A lie, a cruel trick played on a vulnerable lad.

Of course, there was no way to prove what had happened. The firm stuck by him until they could quietly dispose of him without shedding too much blood, and life's turning meant I left the force, my children grew up and left home, my husband's third attempt at

IAN D. HALL

suicide was successful, and my sister...she continued to look after our dad in his home until old age finally spared him the horror of facing his daughter every day knowing she had been diagnosed with the same horrible disease that took her mother.

In the end, I lived alone in a small house, having downsized to make my money stretch further. I'm glad I didn't live in the city itself, having moved to a village out of the valley, away from the destruction that was to come.

Anyway.

I have kept myself busy, Detective. Aside from this last...well, it seems like years, doesn't it since the cathedral came crashing down to Earth? I have been working on a part-time basis for my eldest daughter. She couldn't join the police force like her dear mum—forgive the smile, but I am proud of her regardless of what she does—and instead took the route into private detective work. I still had contacts in the station, friends, old partners who were willing to put information my way, I didn't necessarily need the money, but I was trying to give Kevin some freedom from his debts, especially after his wife left him for another woman. He was broken, and the church, for all its good, had its hooks in him to the point where I worried how far down the rabbit hole he was willing to go.

Five years ago, my daughter was landed with a case to trace the embarrassed solicitor. It was a very discreet request, dealt with by a third party, never by the client. She recognised the name of the person whose interest was barely concealed, and she sought my advice.

You see, Avoncross may be a city, but it is really a large village. Its darkest secrets are known to all, but they don't speak of them. It's all kept in the family—it's a little incestuous, to be frank. Want to rip open the wound? Be prepared for a lot of heartache and misery to come gushing out, to stain and contaminate everything that surrounds it. Like a sly pee in a public swimming pool, you may think you're only leaking a small amount of waste, but every part of that pool will have to scrubbed clean. That is what a village pretending to be a city does. It learns how to keep the piss in a tucked-away corner where the lifeguards cannot see it.

The firm the man worked for, they buried him well enough, but his living corpse turned up, as old as he was by this time, with a new plan, one that would make him a fortune and restore his name in the annals of the city, give him the power he needed to fight any accusation that might come his way. I suspect someone didn't like that, and whilst I have no proof, not conclusive, hard, fast proof, I do believe it was our mutual friend who saw red, who took the chance to bring him down and make him pay.

He didn't kill the old solicitor, not directly, but he did something that caused the old man to lose his senses. Money was transferred from the client's proxy and to my daughter. A very large sum of money. For every fact she could dig up, for every connection she made, she would get a flat rate, and you know what it amounted to in the end when the job was complete? It was the exact same figure that our friend's house was worth when he lost it all to the church and to the thieving hands of the solicitor. Not a penny more, not one penny less.

Coincidences will always brazenly stare you in the face. You know that as well as I, Detective. They are the falsehoods that slow down any investigation, but it seems mighty strange that as soon as that figure had been reached, my daughter was let go, told that the client had all they wanted and it was time to stop.

You wouldn't believe the ruckus the disgraced solicitor made on the internet. The sheer balls of the man. If he were running for prime minister, he couldn't have done it with much more fanfare. He caused a scene in Avoncross, to be sure. Everyone knew what he had done. It was a graft, a deceit, a festering wound; one small tug on the stitches could have split the city in two and allowed other secrets to come pouring out. Perhaps it would have been for the best. It would have been better then than now, what with everything my team has found in dark stairwells and the creaking attics of the survivors.

Coincidence? In this case, I truly don't think so.

The event, which was to coincide with his tell-all story of his crimes, was to be online, as so many of these things are today. An interviewer was to be out of shot, with our genial, supposedly repentant man being the absolute focus. In a similar vein to that created by John Freeman, the guest, our defrauder extraordinaire, was to be shot in the public glare, every possible inch examined, his life laid open for the camera and the hopeful thousands who would pay to hear him talk.

It was risky, so my daughter believed. We thought he would go to trial, be arrested, admitting fraud on such a grand scale, but he had a plan, you see, and he would reveal all during the broadcast. Did he want absolution? Did he want to go to jail, to face the wrath of people who lost their homes, their livelihoods? If my brother-in-law had given in to temptation and punched him to hell and back, I might have considered holding the old thief down and got in a punch or two myself.

My daughter did her job well. She found out where the film was being recorded, with an introduction by the now-legendary broadcaster Ainsley Corbett, who would also act as the host. I remembered Corbett as a rough and to-the-point man. I met him once; he gave an account of the disaster that befell our city from his last position, the fire he helped put out at the hospital outside of the city. It was riveting stuff. He was factual, interesting, but he kept some things to himself, his own secrets in a village full of mysteries.

If you're going to pee in the pool, do it amongst the other stains floating in water.

The place of the big reveal was a small studio in Southampton. Corbett was adamant that it would be near his home. He was feeling his age by then, a sharp mind, a healthy, inquisitive nature still rolling around in that educated journalist mind, but the fire had left him badly scarred—mentally brilliant but physically numb, which worked in his favour. He had nothing to lose and prepared to do what it took to take down his prey, for he also believed that the solicitor was guilty of more than he had admitted to and was ready to hang him out to dry.

The personnel consisted of a single camera operator, a make-up artist, a runner, a director, a producer, and a sound operator. Other than Corbett and the subject, no one else was to be found within a hundred yards of the cramped room. It was secure as anything. No one in or out for an hour before and an hour after—an air of mystery so tightly arranged that Corbett was sure it would be his final, most brilliant interview. And let's not forget he was the man who broke the news of the devastation in both the New Forest and in our sin city.

All went well, as far as we can ascertain. Corbett made his guest comfortable before plunging the knife into his inflated ego. The mood was good and genial; the broadcast was ready, a thousand guests had logged in via a specially created site. No one with any connection to Avoncross could access the online event—all vetted, all accounted for. Save one.

Nobody could see them. The producer only saw a shadow figure hiding in plain sight on his monitor. While the interview was taking place, the camera operator noticed that the solicitor was directly focused on a particular spot on a screen in front of him.

That screen displayed the specially invited and scrutinised online audience. No names, just a sea of lit-up faces, every emotion captured, every revelation framed in the eyes of the digital audience. It was the biggest ticket in town, a question-and-answer session with a thousand clear faces at the end, all for the camera—except there were a thousand and one on the screen. In the top-left corner, another face, shadowed, unseeable to the naked eye had crept in.

If you're going to pee in the pool, do it in a corner where no one can see you.

About halfway through the event, the director, so it is alleged, also noticed the feed. His communications device had been switched off, and he hadn't heard the producer talking to him. As it was in Corbett's control, the stipulation was that the producer was to be locked in the room so that there was no editorial interference. This was Corbett's show, perhaps his last major interview. It was no secret the strain of the fire had made him evaluate his life with more scrutiny than ever before, but he was still in charge for now, scarred arms and face aside. He was still the go-to man for great performance television news.

It is hearsay, a rumour from a source, but if you wish to believe such a thing, the old man finally saw the shadow in the corner of the screen. Corbett has stated confidentially that he watched the man's face and could see him fixating on something, his answers varying between frenzied and languid. Poor Corbett was losing him, from erudite and apologetic, from sensible to senseless…and all the while, the figure in the corner watched silently.

I have seen the tape. A friend of a friend got me a copy from Corbett's private vault. The episode didn't go to air; it cost Corbett a lot of money to hush it up at the time, but once you see it, you will understand why.

My words cannot do what happened next justice. You will have to watch it right to the end. Beyond the gore, you will have to look at the corner of the screen, look at where the old man was staring, and see if you can see a familiar, yet grotesque, distorted face staring back at you.

***

Bridge had not interrupted the former police officer once during her long speech. Not once had she asked her to reiterate or repeat her descriptions, to clarify or recap. Had she done so, then Meadows might have lost her nerve and her thread. The story had been a struggle to convey. Bridge sensed Meadows' distress at the memory of what she had seen on the video. Like a distilled horror film where the creature crawls out of the screen with its head turned upside down, the pain in Meadows' eyes reflected the conflict of knowing she could not undo what she had witnessed.

Bridge didn't push the woman. She seemed exhausted, drained of her will, sucked dry of her reason. It would have been too easy to push her onward, to get a full description of the event, but with a promise that she would send over the video to Bridge's email address, the detective was satisfied, for now, and allowed Alice Sidney to run her friend home for some much-needed rest.

There was nothing to do but wait for the younger of the two women to come back. The pub started to fill with people returning from their shifts in the valley below, and Bridge decided that the crowd was not for her. She needed some air after the one-sided conversation.

The crowd had an air of mournful melancholy attached to it, slow, quiet voices struggling to contain the emotion they felt as they gave thanks for the dwindling number of bodies they were finding beneath the soil, in damaged houses, in broken buildings. As Bridge passed by towards the door, a peel of laughter rang out. It was empty, hollow, a joke cracked against the will of life, something different to light the way in the vast chambers of the dead.

Bridge shuddered. The world was a crazy place.

Chapter Nineteen

B RIDGE HAD BEEN sitting on one of the small walls that surrounded the old beer garden of the pub for almost an hour before Alice Sidney returned. She was full of apologies and concerns for her friend. The detective had been thinking of calling for a taxi to take her back to the temporary station but doubted if she would find one in a city where day-to-day business had lost its meaning. Morbidly, she wondered if this was a prelude to what awaited London; again, she couldn't help but think of the end of days. The weird news reports that came in every day, the stories that a decade, even three years earlier, would have been one to chuckle over whilst having a game of cribbage with her dad, now made her skin crawl.

The place she had chosen to sit was in full sight of the valley below where Avoncross had been swallowed by the earth, and the site of the old prehistoric settlement. She felt pity and sorrow for all who had been caught up in the bombing, in the destruction of both the cathedral and the homes and shops that nestled in its once-dominating shadow.

The teenager, Arthur, had come over to her with a drink, a small bottle of beer, which she tried to wave away, but he had insisted, telling her she needed to take a moment away from her job if she was going to continue to look down on the world below with such sadness in her eyes. She graciously thanked him for his considerate action and fell back into quiet, sombre reflection.

The case notes in her brain kept churning away. The deaths, the bombing, the blackout, the loss of colleagues, all swirled into a gigantic soup of attempted murder. Then there were the victim's own journals and shelf full of notes. She hadn't even got on to the individual case files yet, the meticulously, slavishly written details of all his clients over the years.

Bridge had the sudden feeling of being overwhelmed. It wasn't a new feeling, more of a companion in the darkness that she occasionally felt. She was a dutiful daughter, a dedicated police officer; she gave all to her job, the replacement of her youthful faith which had been burned out by the discovery of the object of her affections being as corrupt as any villain she had put behind bars.

She noted her breathing had become slightly intense, labouring under the weight of her thoughts. She started to name album titles in her collection out loud, an aide to calm herself down when the world started to spin.

She had reached Marillion's later period when she spotted Alice Sidney's car coming back up the hill and turning off the road into the car park adjacent to the pub.

The apologies were accepted and understood; Alice had taken her colleague home and settled her in bed. Meadows had been shaking all the way back to the house, and Alice wanted to make sure she was as comfortable as possible before leaving her alone.

"She has bad days, we all do, those of us left behind to deal with the aftermath. Then when you add in this…I'd be surprised to see her for a few days. I've let her daughter know, and I suppose the other child might drive down to look after her, but I doubt it."

Bridge nodded. All that she had been overwhelmed by seemed suddenly insignificant. The city below would never truly recover; its people were hanging by a thread. What did she have to worry about? Once this case was cracked, she would go back to her home, put on some music, and within a couple of days, she would see the world anew. People like Meadows, they would become echoes of their former selves, slowly drowning in time and in their own memory, symptomatic of what they had lost.

IAN D. HALL

Bridge stood up and took the decisive step of requesting a favour of Alice.

"I want to see the house where he grew up, or at least the outside. I want to be able to visualise how his aunt lost her life, and while you're driving me around, you can tell me everything you know."

Alice Sidney was about to decline the request, motioning that it wouldn't do any good. Bridge held up her hand. She didn't want to hear 'no' and would assert dominance any way she could.

"I can make it an order if you wish. Even in amongst all this chaos, I can still find a judge who will you direct to help me. Besides, you know more than you're saying. Like Francis, you have secrets, but hers are killing her. You—you seem to be revelling in them."

Bridge's words sounded harsher than she'd intended them to be. However, she didn't apologise; she just stared intently at the young woman for a moment before Alice relented and headed off in the direction of her car.

Bridge followed, listening carefully for any slyly muttered words of dissent. None were forthcoming. Indeed, Alice Sidney didn't say another word until she'd parked the car at the far end of the road where the victim lived as a boy.

The yellow tape across the road looked worn, a tattered gateway to the carnival of the macabre, its two ends wrapped around bent lamp posts that had yet to be taken down and replaced. The road also looked bent out of shape, as though someone had worked out that it was possible to use a street setting as an accordion and pumped away until the ripples were filled with air, almost but not quite flat. The houses, all bungalows, looked fine from the outside, but Bridge would've laid money down right now if she were to walk into any one of those houses, she would see buckles, small ridges in the walls from the shock waves of the cathedral's collapse, even this far out of the city.

Bridge got out of the car and walked towards the yellow tape. She felt the presence of fragmented order in the slightest touch of the plastic.

"Nobody lives in this road anymore," Alice explained. "Although a safe distance from the site, it was considered too dangerous to let anyone stay. Just look at the roofs on the other side. See how they bow inwards?"

Bridge nodded. She saw what Alice was describing, the upheaval of thousands of lives, the death of many more. *End of days*, she reminded herself once again as she ducked under the frayed police tape. Alice followed.

"Look. I'm sorry for what I said earlier. It has been…difficult, the last few days. Seeing all this with my own eyes, it puts it into perspective, and you guys, the city, you have had it hard."

Bridge offered her hand in a note of conciliatory apology.

Alice took the peace offering, a measure of relief flashing across her eyes, a glint of pleasure even. Bridge couldn't be sure.

They walked carefully down the road. Abandoned cars had been left to gather dust; some had mounted the pavement, and on two occasions, both women found they had to walk along the road in the swirl of dead leaves and rank rainwater that had backed up from the sewers because the cars were completely blocking the path.

The road was just shy of a quarter of a mile long, but what would have been a ten-minute stroll in normal times took them almost double that. Bridge thought back to the previous night (was it only that short a time ago?), when walking a mile and a half took hours; at least this time, there were no drag kings and queens blocking her way or thankful women reclaiming the darkness.

"It's just here, on the right."

Bridge walked another couple of steps and was greeted by a home that had seen much better days. The windows had not just been smashed; they had been blown out with a force resembling a rocket attack. The frames, what remained of them, were broken

IAN D. HALL

bits of kindling jutting out into the open air, swaying in the breeze. The roof had buckled inwards and had started to collapse as if compelled by a force of unearthly power, the gravity of a black hole sucking everything towards its inevitable doom.

The space in front of the destroyed house was covered in circular potholes. Bridge didn't dare step beyond the gate; the prospect of the ground opening up as she strode towards the door, which was half hanging off its hinges, filled her with anxiety, a dread that was preposterous but suddenly very real.

In all this destruction, all this ruin and carnage, someone had taken the opportunity to deface the property with graffiti. This was not an unusual sight for Bridge; she had gone into some of the worst estates of inner London. She had been part of raids, even led them, in areas where the overwhelming feeling was one of neglect, of human relinquishment to chaos. Cars had been placed strategically to hamper police presence and then set on fire; tower blocks had become rat runs, tunnels created between flats to aid the criminal in their escape. Petrol bombs had once rained around her as a riot spiralled out of control, and she had seen her fair share of graffiti that proclaimed death to the 'pigs', that Donna was a grass, that sex was available for a price—ugly words, ugly sentiments, but none held the impact of the graffiti that greeted her and Alice as they took in the rant painted on the dirty walls.

Across the middle from side to side ran the legend, GOD IS DEAD, the capital letters not just declaring the viewpoint, but an insistence, and it certainly felt that in this small, forgotten, tangled heap of a form home, God had lost the will and taken her own life to spite humanity.

Surrounding the declaration were short passages from the Book of Revelations. Then there was the cold and unfavourable, the allusions to the church being a whore, that thieves and clergy alike steal from the poor.

Bridge lowered her head in sadness. In amongst all the desolation, someone had found the time to deface a home with words of anger and rebellion. She felt an urgent tug on her arm and looked up. On the wall, words began to appear as if the spray can was being held by an invisible hand.

EVERYONE WILL DIE BY HER HAND

Bridge took a step forward, reaching for the gate.

Alice stayed where she was, her hand, which had tugged on the sleeve of Bridge's coat, suspended in mid-air. Neither woman felt the electricity in the air spark and arc around them. Both were caught in the image of the words being scrawled on the wall, guided by an unseen hand.

The detective was about to push the gate open and step inside, an invisible sound urging her onwards when Alice spoke. It was soft and muffled as though spoken through a hundred layers of cloth, a murmur to the ears, and barely understandable. Alice forced herself to grip the shoulder of the woman she had not long met, and with might, she pulled her back as the sentence completed.

EVERYONE WILL DIE BY HER HAND, BRIDGE.

IAN D. HALL

Chapter Twenty

BRIDGE AND ALICE sat on the temporary station platform outside of the city, staring out across the countryside, barely able to contain the fear that had run through them like a high-voltage electric shock. One train had already come and gone; Bridge found she didn't have the energy quite yet to return to the crowded and squeezed-full capital.

What they had both witnessed had driven a stake into their guts. Alice had screamed so loudly that it broke the spell of the words and pulled Bridge away from the desolate and damned property.

Both women were unaware that as they sat down on the cold metal platform, they were holding hands. It was a natural act, a sign of comfort in a moment that had terrified them both.

They'd been lucky. As they reached the car, having sprinted as well as they could through backed-up sewage and past the wrecks of other cars, they happened to look back down the road. The sound of a building collapsing is not one that many people have heard, but Bridge had once witnessed the demolition of a factory not far from the Thames, which was kind of exciting. Ear-splitting, yes, but the crowd that had gathered was caught up in the opportunity the empty space would symbolise. Away with the rust, down with the markers of chemical waste and pollution; the factory's demise was a chance to change the area's old-fashioned and outdated outlook, to relinquish the grip it had on the mind of the people who had seen it slowly become tarnished and diseased.

This sound, though, was terrifying. It was one born of agony, the cacophony of resident ghosts and memories being torn apart and pushed together, their spectral forms squeezed, pressed, and forced to share the ever-diminishing space.

Neither woman wanted to hang around and see the damage. The experience had already burned into their psyche without having it engraved on their eyes forever. The sound was, to Bridge's mind, akin to victims of war's wails for the dead, the cries of women and children amplified by bricks, mortar, cracked and broken tile. This was the scream not of a poltergeist or banshee distressing a family, but of the world ending in fire.

Bridge didn't dare close her eyes. It was all too much; the case was a phantom, mired in the obscenity of the spirit. If she hadn't long since abandoned her faith to logic, she might have been scurrying to her jewellery box in search of a long-lost silver crucifix to fondle and fidget between her fingers.

It was Alice who broke the silence. "Are you aware of The Daughters of Gorgon?"

Bridge wanted to scream internally. She felt as though she were losing her mind. She gritted her teeth and shook her head.

"I'm not surprised. Very few people are aware of them. And yet you have met at least two women who are a part of their number, and I suspect that you have a colleague who is a member."

Bridge turned her head and looked Alice Sidney in the eyes. "Gorgon, as in the Greek legend, as in the artwork that was outside of his office?"

"One and the same!"

Bridge once again found herself sizing up the woman who had been reluctant to explain why she had joined the former police officer at the pub. *It wasn't for comfort, friendship, or support, was it? Not a bit of it.*

"Look, who are you? Really. What is your connection to the man? Please don't spin me a line. This whole case is starting to leave me…restless."

Alice removed her hand from Bridge's grip. The detective suddenly felt cut adrift, the tether she had to reality had been loosened. It was a feeling she didn't particularly enjoy.

Alice eased herself up onto her haunches, her slight frame giving her the appearance of a praying mantis hovering over her next meal.

"I work for a special case unit called The Division, and I knew the man in that hospital bed in London from before we were teenagers…though I doubt he would remember me."

This time, Bridge afforded the talker no time to explain. She couldn't help herself. *First Greek myths, now special case units, what am I being fed?*

"What's The Division?"

Alice laughed, a genuine expression of apathy. She didn't care what Bridge thought, not in this case. She sighed heavily.

"That really isn't important. Suffice to say, it's a government-backed initiative that deals with certain individuals who show a greater degree of ability to inflict harm and damage on society. Think counterterrorism, but concerning itself with those who lead by example, who can inspire others to believe they are capable of deep hatred, not with bombs or bullets, but in more malleable, unseen ways."

Bridge didn't follow the meaning. Wasn't that the definition of a terrorist? Killing behind closed doors, inspiring others with rhetoric intended to kill hundreds, maybe thousands if the wind was pointing the right way?

A smile of sympathy appeared on Alice's thin lips.

"I see your pain in trying to understand my meaning. I get it—too big a scope to understand. Let me put it this way, influence does not just come from politics. To be able to kill someone by simply looking at them, to affect the way they think by a simple unknown command—"

"You mean like hypnotism."

The smile never left Alice's lips.

"Sort of, but we all know that hypnotism only works on the truly weak-minded, the susceptible, the impressionable, those grieving over a loss, for example. They have an aura, a certain way about them that a seasoned hypnotist can tap into, to encourage them to act the fool for pure entertainment. No, I'm talking about something that is much deeper in the mind, much more alarming when studied. You have heard of Stockholm Syndrome? Of course you have. You may even have witnessed it in your job. I see it in those with absolute conviction, a faith perhaps. They've been put under so much pressure, endured such terrible moments, that they have turned to an impression in their minds of a being that can offer them comfort, that they truly seek to do their master's will.

"If you look at it in that sort of sense, The Division becomes clearer. We look for those who are so assured of their purpose that they can simply will someone to death by convincing themselves they have a higher power within them!"

Alice was still perched on her haunches. Bridge admired that. The ability to process thought while in an uncomfortable sitting position showed mental strength.

"So you're saying that our man, he's one of those people, able to manipulate a person just by purely thinking it. I mean, in his journals, he talks of having caused several accidents and some deaths, but I thought they were the ramblings of a delusional mind, the aftereffect of the knock he took to his head when he was younger."

"Ah, yes, the two lads who had been messing around with a boomerang on the field as he walked to school. That did happen. It happened right before the test in the computer science class. I know all of that, Detective. I was in his class when he was constantly failing the test, always finding a sea mine on his first go. I was sitting right behind him. I saw it happening in the reflection of the glass above my head. Poor lad, he was getting so frustrated.

I was relieved that he was pulled out of class early...but then I found out the reason, and I felt terrible for him."

Bridge suddenly recognised the girl from the brief description he had given in his journals, and Alice kept smiling. Her grin was almost hypnotic.

"You asked a good question, but no, he is not capable of such control. He talks a good game, though. He has the ability to look at a person's life and offer help. Is he worth looking at as some sort of beast, a man who can urge people to die spontaneously? Not a bit of it. No." The smile grew larger, more intense.

"Then why the interest in him?" asked Bridge in bewilderment.

"It's not the man that concerns me. It's the woman you have in custody, suspected of his attempted murder, the artist. She's a Daughter of Gorgon, a founding member. She's someone my organisation would very much like to hold in a cell and bring to justice."

"The Artist? You mean Drusilla Pero? But she has a rock-solid alibi as far as we can ascertain."

"Does she, or is that how she hides in the shadows? She's a clever woman, a manipulator of incredible depth. Your man in the hospital, he is a person caught in his own delusion. He's unwell. I'm sure you've already been told that the knock he took as a child unbalanced him. Well, as he lies in the hospital now, surrounded by machines that are keeping him alive, he is just a man for whom brain damage is part of his DNA. His background is one of sadness that he didn't even know. Not even Francis knows this, it would upset her too much, and her daughter doesn't need to know either, but he is the product of an illicit affair between a mentally ill man and his sister. He is a child of incest."

The sound of a distant train slowing down caught the air around them. It broke the spell. Without even seeing it, Alice was on her feet and offering her hand to the detective to get up off the cold metal floor.

"Look into The Daughters of Gorgon. That's where the truth of all this lies. I will be in touch, you have my word on it."

"All that he has written—it is a lie?"

"Not at all! He is an honest man. This is how he truly sees himself. He just cannot see the delusion!"

With that, Alice Sidney turned and walked briskly back to her car.

Bridge realised her mouth was hanging slightly open. She quickly shut it, even though there was nobody around; she didn't want to appear to be gormless. *All ridiculous, all insane.*

A thought struck her as the train's brakes squealed at close quarters and the conductor opened the door for the one passenger to depart.

"Alice, what about the message on the wall? What about my text from him? If he cannot do the things you say, then why did it happen? How do you know about all this anyway?"

Bridge couldn't be sure whether Alice hadn't heard the first part of the question due to the electric hum of the overhead cables or if she just ignored her, but as she reached her car, she turned to face the detective once more.

"I know because I was one such child they investigated. That day, I showed an aptitude that filled them with fear for what I could become."

Alice Sidney hadn't shouted the words, hadn't expressed the explanation with a bellow over the sound of the train. The words just appeared in Bridge's mind, clear, concise, deliberate, as if she had placed them there by simple thought.

Chapter Twenty-One

IT SEEMED LATER than it was by the time the train rolled into Waterloo Station and not just because Bridge had spent the entire journey feeling utterly bewildered and exhausted from the events in London and Avoncross and the unceasing pace of the last few days. As the train approached the city, she, and others in the several carriages that had joined the train at Basingstoke, noticed that the area was shrouded in darkness. Aside from the odd square of dull yellow in a building here and there and the sweep of torch beams along the pavements, not a light could be seen from Battersea Power Station in any direction.

Thankfully, the hospital's emergency generators were keeping pace with the demand of patients and the lifesaving performances of the doctors and nurses inside, but it stood as the sole beacon, a lighthouse shining a warning for weary travellers to keep away.

Even inside Waterloo Station, the usual bright lights were subdued to a level barely above the illumination gifted those of a bygone age by the candles they carried gingerly to their beds.

Bridge, as with the rest of the passengers, took her time departing the train. The announcement suggested this was just another problem for a creaking system to deal with, without people being hurt, and accordingly implored passengers to not run, to pay attention to the staff, and leave the station promptly so that the next train could be guided in safely.

Bridge looked across the rest of the platforms; there were no passengers waiting to depart, to get out of the madness. Leaving the surprisingly orderly queue, she stepped to one side and caught the attention of one of the staff, a young lad who barely filled his uniform.

"It was the strangest thing," he said, "and that's taking yesterday into account and all. The electric to the track's still running, but everything else just…well, not shut off, but it went dim all of a sudden about half an hour ago. Makes the station feel kinda like those old photographs you see, the black-and-white ones from the war, all ghost-like. Full of hidden shadows."

The lad, no more than twenty, probably still a teenager, was smiling and no doubt saw it as an adventure. Bridge thanked him and re-joined the queue. *Half an hour, just the other side of Woking, as though a welcome mat was being prepared for me.*

She didn't mean to think that sentence; the words came from nowhere, a stab of unconscious drama, which made her utter under breath, "Stop it."

The person in front of her half turned while continuing to walk along the platform—was no mean feat, especially in the gloom of an ill-lit station—and pulled a face that signalled displeasure and concern of being close to someone who berating themselves aloud in public. Bridge ignored him.

On the other side of the gates, Bridge was caught between going home for some much-needed sleep or walking to the police station and locking herself in one of the cells for the night. She didn't want to go home; it would be cold, it would be lonely, assuming she could even get there, which seemed unlikely, given the hastily pasted notices and unhelpful tannoy announcements reminding people that the Underground in the local area was out due to electrical failure.

No, it was too far to walk home, and she would have had to pass the police station anyway. Besides, it wouldn't be the first time she'd spent the night in an empty cell. Failing that, she still had a chair that was comfortable and out of the way.

"All passengers please leave by the exits marked. Please be reminded that lifts from the upper concourse to the lower street entrances are

IAN D. HALL

unavailable this evening. Please do not run. Please leave in a quiet and orderly fashion."

The words, though delivered by a stressed-out, low-paid rail employee, sounded metallic, brutal—an order given by a weary commandant of a prisoner-of-war camp, devoid of the sympathy the management and shareholders might have hoped for.

The red carpet doesn't extend out past Bermondsey then.

Nothing was open. It was only early evening, and the concourse would normally be full of those heading out for after-work drinks at one of the many bars, catching a film in a nearby cinema or a play at the Old Vic.

Bridge praised her luck when she saw that Nico's mobile burger van was open, operating off a small generator. He had survived court orders, temporary shutdowns, a food-contamination scare (which was finally traced to another trader attempting to discredit Nico), so it was no surprise that even now, when the lights in Waterloo had fallen dark, he kept going. The smell of chips and vinegar, of burgers and hotdogs, filled her senses with extraordinary delight.

"Nico, my man. One sausage and burger roll, lettuce, no tomato, mayonnaise, chips on the side, and a tea, please."

"Coming right at you, Ingrid. Unreal, isn't it? Last night, the lights wouldn't shut down. Tonight, they won't turn on. Only London, am I right?"

Bridge smiled as he called her by her first name. So few people did that. Only her dad seemed to remember that she had a life outside of the force, although these days it barely felt like it.

"Only London, Nico," she agreed with a song in her heart as she realised how hungry she felt. The breakfast served to her by the young lad Arthur had kept her ticking over, but now she needed to chow down on fat and conversation with someone who wasn't afraid to call her Ingrid.

There was a small line of people waiting to collect their orders of various offerings from the limited but tantalising menu that Nico had detailed in the neatest handwriting Bridge had ever seen on a blackboard.

Bridge marvelled at the dexterity of the man's cooking. Nothing ever burnt, nothing caught on the griddle; even if the gas ran out in the middle of preparing an order, he managed to keep the food cooking while swiftly changing it over to a full reserve that he kept underneath the counter.

"I took a fortune last night, Ingrid, so many people about. No police down under the arches—they couldn't get past the drag kings and queens. I sold out completely. I had to get my daughter to come from home with another supply of buns and bacon. It was a good night."

"Good job you don't live that far away, Nico. Or on the other side of the river. She wouldn't have made it across."

Nico flipped an egg with the mastery of a juggler and laughed. Pouring tea with one hand, he presented it to Bridge and passed the egg-and-bacon roll to the hungry man to her left with the other.

Bridge leaned against the metal plate counter and smiled. Nico was a good man. Despite knowing a few dodgy people who could have asked favours of him, he had lived comfortably on the right side of the law all his life. Like his father before him, who escaped Cyprus before the Civil War and the partition, he knew that there were some lines you didn't cross if you wanted to make a fortune from selling late-night, open-air food.

"Did you hear about that poor bloke who was found with his throat cut, Ingrid?"

The woman next in line made a face of disgust as Nico spoke of the mutilated body. He half-grinned at her and passed her a soft drink from the fridge.

"On the house, darling. Sorry about that."

Nico never gave anything away for free, except maybe his time and the odd bit of information. Bridge didn't voice the question she was itching to ask until the queue died down to a mere trickle.

Nico passed her the food, and she tore into it like a savage animal being fed for the first time in days whilst he regaled her with the story of the man found the night before in the park over on the Isle of Dogs. Bridge wasn't squeamish, but regardless, her hunger kept her eating, even as Nico got to the part about the head being found several feet away from the body.

"The weirdest thing, Ingrid, is that it was being held aloft by a statue—one of those that look like they're pointing to some far-off land. I mean, I know the Isle Of Dogs is out of bounds for some, but it's still London, you know what I mean?"

Nico believed that almost everywhere was London. He could have been describing a murder in Huddersfield, a rave he once attended in Southampton or Brighton, or a day out guiding a barge down the Manchester Ship Canal, and it would have been London to him. His life was Waterloo; he breathed it, had never left it; his family were all within walking distance. London was just everywhere else he wasn't.

"Wait, Nico, are you talking about McDougall Gardens?"

Nico nodded enthusiastically, then remembered why they were discussing the area in the first place and grew solemn.

"Yeah. He was one of us. A cook with his own van. Decent bloke, though I bet he didn't cook chips like me or have my sparkling conversation." Nico chanced a grin. Bridge returned it with a half-smile.

McDougall Gardens. It was virtually opposite where she lived. She hadn't thought of that when Drusilla Pero said that was where she'd ended up after the gallery reception. It couldn't be a coincidence.

"I didn't know there was a statue in that park."

"There isn't?"

"No…" Bridge was about to ask another question when a large group approached the van, another set of people who had been caught out by the lack of electricity and had followed the scent of the delights of Nico's van through the darkness.

The orders flew at Nico, and Bridge admired the ease with which he dealt with them all. Over the loud appreciation of hunger being sated, she quickly asked Nico if the dead man worked early in the morning.

Nico laughed, simultaneously pouring tea or coffee into several polystyrene cups. "Ingrid, always asking questions. Some of us never stop, even when we're at home asleep. There's always someone in the van to serve. Do you think we can live on a nighttime trade alone?"

Bridge understood where he was coming from and wished she could just rely on one or the other, nick criminals at night or during the day. But crime, like people's stomachs, never rested, and like capitalism, always needed to be fed.

A familiar buzz in Bridge's inside pocket alerted her to a call. She turned away from the slowly rebuilding crowd shouting their demands to a genial and money-drunk Nico and looked at the display before answering the call.

"Torlay, how's it going?"

"Boss, are you back from your day out yet?"

Torlay wasn't a man to unduly panic. He wasn't that kind of officer, but something in his voice gave Bridge a moment of acid reflux. She excused herself from Nico's presence, the last of her meal finding its way into the plastic bin, and answered her colleague with an affirmation.

"You need to get back to the station, Boss. Something weird has happened and the place is erupting!" He might have said more, but his voice was lost to what sounded like a riot was going on around him.

What in heaven's name could have happened for pandemonium to break out in a police station? It was so loud, so raucous, that even Nico could hear it over the sound of the bacon spitting on the hot plate and the constant thump of the hot water in its boiler.

"You okay, Ingrid? Do you need a round of rolls for the squad?" He laughed heartily for the crowd but gave a glint of concern towards Bridge, his way of showing he was there if she needed him.

Bridge nodded to him, making light for the paying public while leaving him under no illusion that she thought there might be trouble.

The relationship between the pair had always been good. She had taken on a surrogate-mother role to Nico's family when his wife became seriously ill, the same disease that had taken Bridge's own mother, although Florentia was still going, after many rounds of chemotherapy. Bridge and Nico were friends and had never taken it any further; neither side was tempted, but Nico would have stood in the way of a thousand axe-wielding maniacs to keep Bridge alive.

She waved him a fond farewell, not once taking her phone away from her ear. When she was far enough from the burger-van crowd, she resumed the conversation with her trusted officer.

"Talk to me, Torlay. What's going on?"

"I can tell you that we have had to release the artist. The other thing…I don't think you'll believe it unless you see it."

Bridge swore under her breath, and then out loud. The echo of the words bounced off the walls of the narrow alleyway through which she had taken a shortcut, away from the ever-emptying railway station.

"How the hell has that woman been released? We had her bang to rights on attempted murder in the hospital."

"You need to take that up with the super."

A loud crash hurtled down the airwaves.

"What was that? Torlay, is everything all right?"

The man sounded shaken when he answered.

"Boss, just get here quickly, will you?" Another loud crash accompanied his words, and then the phone went silent.

Despite the lack of sleep, the travelling to Wiltshire and back, the scare she had endured, and the overall bizarre way the day had unfolded, Bridge found a residue of energy that she wouldn't have guessed was possible and ran as fast as she could towards the police station.

Her mind was so preoccupied with every facet of the case that she didn't notice a figure watching her. In the darkness, the bright eyes burned with hatred and condemnation, jackal-like vision tracking her progress along the road and up the old, impractical stairs, which she took two at a time.

The watcher didn't move away as the detective disappeared behind the oak doors that had seen better days; they merely shifted their focus up one flight of stairs and three windows over to where the commotion was taking place. They couldn't see behind walls, but they were able to visualise the anarchy taking place, the chaos and lawlessness as male police officers, with the exception of Torlay and Beaumont, smacked seven bells of hell out of each other, beating each other to a pulp, leaving blood-streaked faces, broken noses, and myriad other injuries that would take several hospital visits and months of therapy to put back together.

A window smashed, large pieces of glass slicing down to the pavement below and narrowly missing a couple returning from visiting a terrified elderly relative. With the window now a gaping hole, the noise could be heard easily. Shouts of derision, threats, and near revolution in a place of order. It was all too perfect for the watcher, and they smiled, their eyes blazing with satisfaction.

As a banshee-like scream pierced the night, and the couple who had barely escaped being impaled by shards of glass ran for their lives, pounding feet and pulses providing a beat for that scream born from bedlam.

That was enough for now. The watcher could walk away knowing they had caused a fracture in the male-dominated order of the thin blue line. Even Bridge, as pivotal to the end game as she was, could not put things back together that quickly.

The night was turning cold. Perhaps some tea down by the arches, or a coffee, and a roll. After all, they were only human, compelled to do what humans do best when they have brought commotion to the world; they celebrate.

Chapter Twenty-Two

BRIDGE HADN'T SLEPT for days.

Not proper sleep, not the sleep that a woman of her age should have.

As she surveyed the scene before her, the effect of the whirlwind, the human tornado unleashed, she envisioned rest was now beyond her; all there was, was carnage.

She was seated in her chair; three badly injured policemen were being tended to by ambulance crews and as she gulped down an energy drink, the sticky, bitter taste of which her want to throw up, but she swallowed hard; she needed to keep going. Officers Beaumont and Torlay stood close by, thankfully unscathed, speaking to Superintendent Barbara Lenton, their graphic description of the violence, the near slaughter that took place in the building over the course of ten furious minutes being replayed and retold by the two men who somehow had remained unaffected by the sudden surge of animalistic desecration.

And there, by the side of the wall, was the cause of the problem...if Beaumont and Torlay were to be believed: Drusilla Pero's painting of The Gorgon in the moment of her most famous contribution to the world of art.

Bridge felt the sickly liquid crawl down towards her stomach and closed her eyes, preparing to aim the deluge of disgust at the painting.

It didn't work, the resultant belch earning her a revolted, silent rebuke from her superior. Beaumont turned away, looking as if he might vomit himself, while Torlay grinned at her with a mixture of pride and admiration.

All around her was a mess. There was no way to cover up the wanton destruction; the noise alone had drawn a sizeable crowd to the darkened station, and a few photographs and amateur videos had already been uploaded to social media for the nation to enjoy.

Video...Bridge suddenly remembered the file that had been promised to her by Francis Meadows.

With her back to the three unaffected officers and the painting just in her line of sight, she pressed the power switch on her computer. Thanks to the back-up generator having been restored and so far behaving itself, the login screen appeared. She quickly logged in and navigated into her email account, scrolling through the impossible amount of turgid spam—cheap Viagra, insomnia relief—past a message from someone claiming to know the man in the hospital and an invitation to spend an evening at the cinema with a colleague in Croydon, until, finally, she found the message she was looking for.

The video began with a warning for graphic content; she ticked the agreement absolving the creator from prosecution and leaned forward to watch what had obviously caused Francis Meadows to refuse to say more than she had.

She didn't hear the three officers behind her stop talking to watch as well.

The credit titles rolled, and the interviewer appeared on screen. His was the face of a man who had suffered tremendous adversity but who wore the burns on his cheek and neck as though they were a badge of honour. Bridge felt sorry for him. According to his bio, he had caused a sensation more than once in his journalist career, but the way he'd acted in the fire that threatened to engulf the entire hospital at Avoncross had seen his stock rise nationally. Bridge had not heard of him until that day; news often drifted past her, just another confession delivered by another soul in search of redemption.

As he introduced his guest, she picked up on the contempt in the voice, hidden beneath waves of platitudes, inaudible to most, but to Bridge's ears, the insincerity and hatred ran deep.

"No denying he's got a game face," Torlay uttered from behind her.

"Who is he, Bridge?" the superintendent asked.

"Ainsley Corbett. He's interviewing the lawyer who ripped off our man in the hospital when his aunt died. A stitch-up by someone in the church in Avoncross and a guardian of the law."

The unaired interview ground on, the solicitor playing on his age and sense of guilt as he went toe-to-toe with Corbett. The answers were all plausible, all contrite.

A small flicker from the screen, a blink-and-you-miss-it moment, but all four officers saw it.

A few more minutes passed.

"What's he looking at?" Torlay asked. "See how he keeps looking past the camera?"

"That's what Francis Meadows was talking about when we spoke this morning in Avoncross…or what's left of it anyway."

"That bad down there, is it, Ingrid?" the superintendent asked with a soft voice, suddenly mindful of what her best detective had probably seen that day.

"It's a mess, Ma'am. A frightening mess. The city will recover eventually, but I suspect its residents, those who lived through it, will ever be the same." An image of Francis Meadows flashed before Bridge, eyes that had begun to sink in on themselves, hollowed cheeks, an expression of defeat. "Too much emotion for the city to hold."

"See?" Torlay interrupted. "He's doing it again, fixating on something in the corner. He looks…scared."

"That's what Meadows said too, but it's the bit after this that we need to concentrate on."

They all fell silent. The quiet unnerved Bridge. The station seemed to close in around her, lifting her, folding her in half until her paper form could not be doubled or creased anymore. She wanted to scream, to allow the chaos that had inflicted the station to channel itself through her, to envelop her; anything was better than the sudden, two-dimensional silence.

The only sound came from the video, and that had lost its strength, as if there were some malfunction in the studio that left only the solicitor's words, stumbled over and then caught in his throat as his eyes widened and bulged, threatening to poke his steel-rimmed glasses off his nose and tumble to the floor below.

And then he was dead, the top of his head sliced majestically from the rest of his body. It happened so quickly, none of those present could work out what they had witnessed, just how somebody's life can be snuffed out in a single second.

Not a sound passed between the four of them for what seemed an eternity. The video kept playing, Corbett, the experienced journalist, was shouting to the director to turn off the footage, to stop recording. The make-up artist could be heard screaming, the camera operator abandoned his position and stood over the body, his mouth gaping as he stared in at the same point the solicitor had before he met his end.

The camera operator bent down and hesitantly picked something up. For an appalling moment, Bridge thought it was the top of the solicitor's head, to show all that the mound still contained part of the brain, which, like a spoon holding a pudding that had lost its consistency, it would start to slop over the side.

It was a brief relief for all four officers when they saw that in the camera operator's hands was not a pudding bowl of brain, but a light in its metal sheath. It must have come loose and swung down, the thin edge of the casing slicing right through the solicitor's head like a knife through a peeled boiled egg.

Bridge didn't blame Beaumont for walking away; his face had turned a sallow shade of green. He walked down the corridor, past the last of the policemen who was being seen by the paramedic, and into the men's toilets.

Right there with you, my friend, Bridge thought sympathetically.

She dragged the play bar back, the digital images blurring the effect of the partial decapitation. When she reached the start, she paused the film and looked at the two remaining ghouls in uniform and asked if they wanted to watch it again. To her surprise, they both nodded.

Their faces were solemn, respectful, understanding of the event they had just witnessed, one which very few people had the unfortunate privilege to see or even know about. Yet beneath the thin-blue-line veneer, she sensed something else take hold in them, a gruesome want, to which she was now a party, as she clicked play on the screen.

They watched a second time in silence, and then a third, and it was only when Beaumont returned that Superintendent Lenton pointed out a nanosecond of the footage that they had all missed.

"There, go back about two seconds and then freeze the picture."

Bridge rewound the film a few frames.

"Do you see it? Just to the side of the solicitor, there's a reflection of a spark. That must be where the light broke loose. But look closer." She leaned over Bridge's shoulder and placed her index finger on the screen just millimetres below the image.

The camera had caught a brief reflection of the small audience. Six rows could be seen, but only two of them clearly.

"Jesus, it's him," Torlay uttered. "How did he manage to get an invite?"

Bridge shook her head. "The audience was vetted. He must have rigged it somehow."

"And then watched in delight as the solicitor was beheaded. That's sick." Torlay was almost beating his chest in delight. He'd always embraced his 'alpha-male' status in the team, but there was more to it this time, and as he high-fived Beaumont, Bridge picked up on the underlying aggression. Turning away from the screen, her attention was drawn once more to the painting standing against the wall.

"You all never said. How did that get up here? It was meant to be in evidence storage."

Nobody answered her. They hadn't heard. Bridge went to stand up, to move her legs, but it was as if the painting was draining her will to think or act.

Hadn't she asked Torlay to gather some evidence for her? Why was the super here at night? That beat, the hiss of snakes, the text message on her phone, the graffiti on the walls of a home that fell violently to the ground within minutes of her reading it. A vicious end to a man's life captured on film...another louder hiss, a rattle of keratin filling every space in the room.

It grew louder, angrier, a den of snakes spraying venom over the unsuspecting.

The air grew thin.

Each breath felt as though it was clawing at her throat, refusing to enter her lungs, to sustain her life.

Still, she could not tear her gaze from that picture.

She wanted to gasp, to call out to her colleagues, her friends... could they not see her losing consciousness in front of them?

The head of Medusa morphed, flickering between Pero and the dead woman who had slowly grown cold in her interrogation room, faces she didn't recognise, faces that meant nothing to her, faces...faces...faces, all different, all skipping along as though they were drawn pictures in a child's flip book.

She fell to the floor.

She didn't know she had done so until she opened her eyes and saw the painting from a different angle. Her head pounded, the sound of snakes increased, and it was only as Perseus became the man in the hospital then the face she saw in the mirror every day that she realised she had been poisoned or drugged, her system flooded with a hallucinogenic.

She felt an arm take hold of her.

She was in the picture, the canvas displaying every pore, every pigment shade, the mole that sat above her left lower jaw, her

IAN D. HALL

eyebrows that were thick over deep-set eyes, her hair bristling, caught in a breeze coming through the open doors of the temple in which Medusa was now screaming, her face contorted, her features writhing in pain and fury, her hair of snakes alive and spiteful, dead yet cunning.

It was Bridge who was holding aloft the severed head of Medusa. It was Bridge whom the figure in ancient dress was staring at, accusing with her eyes, damning with those thin moving lips, speaking in an unknown, unspeakable language that she seemed to understand in her delirious state.

"Hold her down, she's going into shock."

Bridge heard the words but didn't know they were being spoken about her.

She reached out and tried grasp the head of Medusa, to yank it back, pull it away from her prone body on the floor of the police station.

Where's Brenda Beehaven?

That had been her only concern when she first ran into the station and saw all but two of the male population fighting en masse. Assault and battery, common assault, attempted murder… where in all of that was Beehaven? Why wasn't she in the room? Why wasn't she in the station now?

She's my equal. Where the hell is she?

Bridge held on to that thought as she watched Medusa's head attempt to turn and face the painted version of herself. It was a moment of surrealism, a fight between the two women on canvas that continued as Bridge's will drained from her.

"It was in her drink. Her can of drink, look. There's a pinhole in the top of the can. She's been drugged like the others."

So that was it; she had been drugged, but instead of going into a murderous rage as her fellow male officers had, something different had happened to her, something far more devious, more frightening.

She's killing me.

With all her might, Bridge smashed the head of the Gorgon down onto the chequered marble floor.

The painting showed the struggle, the conflict that Bridge's mind and soul was facing as her heart started to give out.

The Perseus/Bridge character swung a hefty arm, and the head caved in and smashed into a thousand fragments, the nose shattering first, followed by the forehead and the cheekbones and finally the snakes, all crumbling to dust as the head of the Gorgon was obliterated in a fit of violent outrage.

Bridge felt the needle go into her body; she felt the drug tear through her system, but it was too late. The only pleasure she would take to her grave was the knowledge that she had defeated the mass of serpents attached to the head of one who could turn men to stone.

Even drugged, hallucinating, and convinced she was on the verge of death, Brenda's name kept unfolding in her vision. Bridge fought off the sympathetic darkness valiantly, and as she passed out, she understood that the viper in the nest was her colleague. She had been right, but that knowledge was no use to her now.

Chapter Twenty-Three

THE DRUGS HAD been delivered by design. The only reason Beaumont and Torlay had not been affected was because neither man had taken the drink that had been offered them. Torlay was convinced carbonated drinks gave him gastric distress, but Brenda Beehaven was insistent.

"I really thought she was going to have me on a disciplinary charge, the way she was going on. She started out with a smile, and then by the time I told her to get lost, she was almost scarlet with rage."

"I just told her I didn't like fizzy drinks," Beaumont said. "She left me alone, although I did hear her mutter something derogatory as she walked away."

Torlay asked what Beaumont heard, and then laughed when told. Both men grinned at each other like schoolboys hearing of a teacher's misfortune and realising they had got away with not doing their homework.

They stopped abruptly when they remembered where they were and the seriousness of the moment.

"Do you think she'll pull through?" Beaumont asked.

Torlay focused his attention on Bridge in her hospital bed, where she fought internally to come back to the land of the living and the sane.

"I think so. I hate the phrase 'tough cookie', it sounds patronising, but she's faced worse than being drugged, even if it was a large, concentrated form. Far more than was given to Biggs, Donaldson, Ferris, and Daley. She survived a bullet once."

Beaumont gazed down at his boss with renewed respect.

"I guess there's no doubting Beehaven was behind it," he said.

"None at all," Torlay agreed. "Polly Nicks downstairs confirmed that it was her who took the painting out of evidence. That she has gone missing is a fact, and the hallucinogenic was only in the lads' drinks and not in the superintendent's, Nicks', or Griffiths'."

"Good job Claire was still at home ill. She'd have snaffled a can."

Torlay nodded vaguely. The energy drink might not have blown Claire Boase's mind, but the painting would have. The fact that she'd been raving about it causing Parsons' death when Torlay left her with her mum had upset the seasoned police officer, so much so that returning to the station to find his colleagues trying to kill each other felt like getting off lightly. Watching grown men fight each other under the influence of narcotics was preferable to listening to Boase clutching at straws and if-onlys as she tried to reconcile her partner's death.

Both men fell silent.

In the silence, Bridge heard everything.

Her vision was of darkness, but her hearing was acute and rampant.

The secretive nature of the black void consoled her, welcomed her, gave her a chance to rest and be at one with her mind.

If this is death, then it's not as scary as I thought, she mused. It was like sleep, minus the dreams that often plagued her. In here, this empty black chamber, she could not see the Gorgon, could not see the snakes as they writhed and thrashed insanely on the canvas that held them prisoner.

"Bridge?"

The voice was almost ephemeral, so light in its delivery that thought she had imagined it.

If this is death, then is it really so bad?

She was happy here…wherever here was. Her cares, her past, all seemed so unimportant now. Those memories, she could still feel their presence, their consequence, but their rank, their

Ian D. Hall

substance no longer mattered. It had happened, once, and she saw each one in the darkness, but they were fleeting glimpses of what was being taken away, the sense of duty, the fear; she was carefree and disinterested in covering the distance between that which she had been and what she was now.

There, just to her left, a touching distance away, the evanescence of her earliest memory. A small child looking up at her mother and then seeing the stars in the heavens surrounding her. Her mother smiling, loving her, no thought of what was to come, how she would soon leave the precious bond as she became more her father's daughter.

The image was not a dream; it was focused, a brilliant burst of light in the raindrops of sorrow, and she allowed it to fade, happy in the knowledge that her mother had loved her, even if only for a time.

There, just to her right, the memory of the first boy she kissed. The taste of his breath as it collided with hers, all pineapple juice and ice cream, a party for a mutual friend on their tenth birthday, the seizing of the moment as she fell in love for the first time... and then felt her heart break when he told her that she had a funny smell and he didn't like it.

What once would have upset her, a recurring waking nightmare when dating was, if not a priority, then at least an opportunity, that unconsciously drove her to wear more deodorant than was probably advisable, that made her scrub her teeth until the gums bled... now was just nodded at in understanding, forgotten with a smile.

If this is death, then I am fine with it.

The first time she heard a record by Judy Garland, the anguish of her father when she dyed her hair bright blue at fourteen, the detention she received for answering back when a teacher described her performance on the trumpet as woeful, the immense pride she saw her in her father's eyes on the day she passed out of Hendon, the sadness of the suffering she had seen in the darkness that followed the explosion further down the tunnel as London was once more revisited by terror groups; all flashes, all soon wiped away.

She was getting closer now. She was ready…

"Bridge!"

This time, Ingrid heard the voice coming from deep inside the void. She did the only thing that made sense; she answered.

"God?"

Silence.

The darkness suddenly felt disturbed by her single-worded response.

"Really?"

This time, the silence was maintained by Bridge. It seemed to stretch for an eternity, enough time for other memories to form, coalesce, and then slowly fade.

"Do you want to try again? Surely, you know who I am. I thought we had become quite close!"

The voice was natural, not supernatural and not as low as some, but certainly a man's voice.

"Are you Him?"

The darkness revealed a reddish tinge, a border that deepened in its hue until it hit the pitch-black Bridge had become accustomed to.

"Him?" The question posed by the voice was full of promise, almost seductively pulling the detective into believing she was conversing with that which she once feared.

"The devil. I suppose you must be. It makes sense. I thought I was heading to heaven, but I suppose hell is just another place in which you get to meet those you loved."

The striking red border altered, shifted colour, became violet.

"To meet the devil, you have to be dead, Bridge. There is no God. For that fact, there is no devil, no horned king, arch fiend, Baalam or Baphomet. They're just names hanging out together in their own nothingness, and Satan is a myth. Lucifer could be acceptable, but that's pure fantasy. If you want evil, look into the hearts of men and women alike, give credence to the greed of a person who worships but one thing. Avarice. Check out those with the fur on the inside, the ones who wish harm on others, who seek revenge for those who had harmed another out of pure spite and malice. To that end, I guess I am a devil, but I prefer to think of myself as Death."

"Death?"

"All-powerful, eternal, plucking the living from the cruelty of their existence, and giving them…hope."

Bridge saw nothing, no vision to take her mind off the exposed thought that perhaps the prophets were right after all: God and the devil were one and the same but had been extinguished by humanity's insatiable need to bring about its own destruction. They didn't need deities and demons to influence them.

"I never said anything about there not being demons."

The voice seemed to laugh at the notion.

"Is Death, you know, real?"

The silence spoke once more whilst Death collected its thoughts.

Bridge lost her way. She had been walking straight, towards some sort of resolution, but the voice had waylaid her, made her question a fundamental belief, and now she wasn't sure which way she was supposed to go.

"You are as close to solving this as you believe you are. It's just a shame that there is a larger scheme at play, that the heavens alone should not touch the Earth, and humanity should not seek their place amongst the stars."

"How does that answer the question?"

"Which one? The one you seek, or the one you already know?"

"Can people be willed to death?"

Death ruminated over the problem she was having with the concept. Was she seeking an affirmation of life after it had been extinguished? Or was it deeper, crueller? Did she actually believe that someone could be held responsible for a passing stranger falling down from a sudden stroke just because they looked at them the wrong way? Could a child wish their mother dead just because they had a stupid falling out over nonsense such as toys, food, bedtime? *In the same way that people look for portents in disasters after the fact, so we feel the need to place blame for someone's death in a random accident on the likelihood that it must mean something more, something other.*

"No."

"No?"

"Except, someone can influence another to take a life without realising. That is the crux of the matter, isn't it? Your colleague, you know she is part of The Daughters of Gorgon, even without the evidence. Why? Because you feel it. You know she somehow killed your witness. A toxicology report will attest that there is a minuscule puncture mark on her neck, delivered by syringe, poisoning her...but what about the woman in the building? How did she die? Word is she was ranting in her office and the door was open. Her words carrying down the corridor to our patient, who promptly shouted that if she was suffering that badly, perhaps she should consider suicide..."

Bridge knew that she was hearing the voices again, dull, indistinct, but there all the same.

"You're not dead, Bridge. In fact, you have never been more alive. You're having a bad trip!"

The detective looked into the void and was disheartened to find it wasn't staring back.

"Bridge, I am Death, but not the death you seek. You are on the side of the angels. But while I still have your attention, before the effects of overdose you were subjected to by a coward and a follower of that cult wear off, let me tell you further of Faith Croy'ance."

"It's you, isn't it? You're in my head. Making me think I'm conversing with Death."

"I never said any such thing, dear Detective. Now buckle up. Before you come round, you're in for one last trip. It might even send you insane. I do hope not. You're worth more to me alive and cognisant than you are residing in a mental home for the rest of your life."

The words of the man in a bed two hospital floors above Bridge echoed around her fragile mind. She saw the man's face appear out of the darkness, and she screamed.

Chapter Twenty-Four

FAITH CROY'ANCE LIED.

Once I began to look for it, I could see she had manipulated me and others with an ease that is shaming.

She was dreadfully abused by her mother. Of that I am content to admit under oath. Indeed, there was more mistreatment doled out to the young girl than I was comfortable knowing. Some of the danger the mother posed was such that was she now not dead herself, having suffered a genuine accident by electrocution as she dived into Rugren's swimming pool and some old, exposed wiring fell into the water at the same moment as the inebriated women bellyflopped her way to hell, I would have happily had her prosecuted for the sheer, nameless evil she had put her child through.

Faith, though, was not as innocent as she made herself out to be.

I met her, as arranged at the airport.

She sailed through customs with ease, apparently having taken a few moments out to pose for the camera of a smitten captain and his number two and had the official who pulled her over to confirm the contents of her bag almost falling over herself to aid an unrequited unknown female lust so that the extra cigarettes she had forgotten were in her carry-on bag, and the unique pearl-handled gun she had purchased were given clearance to pass.

There is no other way to describe the way she walked out of the airport and was met by the gathered press. Serenely elegant are the perfect words to capture the way she glided towards them.

This was the first time she genuinely looked pleased to be swamped by magazine paparazzi and the tabloid hacks. She was especially gracious to the two journalists from the higher-quality end of the much-maligned British press. She was a star. Everything about her screamed demure and tantalising, garnering undaunting love from the crowds. She answered questions with frankness and playfulness, and was full of conviction for the film she had shot, thanking the producers and her co-stars alike with enthusiasm and assuredness.

She even dragged me into the frenzy of photographers' flashes and a cacophony of queries, introducing me to the world as the man who helped her career and mental health. Who believed in her in the darkest moments.

I am grateful that aside from some of the more salacious and obnoxious newspapers, the photo of us together never made it to print, my soul preserved by the fortune of being less than photogenic.

I removed myself from the omnipresence of flashing lenses and false decorative smiles and walked to the car. I opened the passenger door, and as was always my cue to her, nodded in expectancy of her compliance to wrap up the photo call and allow me to drive her to the facility.

She smiled in appreciation of the gesture and then, as she was going to thank you to everybody for welcoming her home, an unsightly man raised his voice and dropped the biggest bombshell of her life.

"Ms. Croy'ance. What do you make of the rumour that a woman claiming to be your mother is in England?"

Faith looked the man dead in the eyes, the smile never leaving her face. The only way you could tell she had been ruffled was by the tightening of her lips, the moment where annoyance mixed with uncertainty.

The assembled photographers and journalists didn't catch it. They weren't looking for it, but I was, and it stung as sharply as if she had slapped me with her bare hand.

The grace remained, at least on the outside. But inside, I could tell she was ready to blow. The volcano had been stirred by the unexpected question, one she thought she was never going to have to answer.

"I'm sure that if my mother was in the country, the authorities would by now have had her arrested and charged with child abandonment. There's no time limit on such a horrible act of wanton disregard for a child's safety."

"The rumour is she is holed up in secret. That she has come to bury the past and reconcile with you."

A buzz of interest, like mosquitoes sensing sweaty bodies unpeeling by an outdoor pool. It was time to step in. But I didn't need to; a change had come over her while she had been away, a sense of determined resolve. She gave the reporter a flattering, if completely insincere smile.

"I'm sure that is not the case. A reconciliation? I'd sooner play opposite a gorilla in a remake of that old Ronnie Reagan movie, darling. If you see her, check out the resemblance. Perhaps that is why she is here—to be in films herself."

The crowd laughed.

She laughed.

The journalist smiled and wrote down the quote quickly.

All around were in on the joke.

Only it wasn't funny. Only on the inside was Faith not laughing. As a woman scorned, her mother would have nothing to lose by blabbing all that she now knew. No studio executive would be able to control the narrative.

Faith walked determinedly to the car, closed the door, and opened the window to say thank you and goodbye to the still-amused crowd. I hurried to the driver's side; no doubt my face

IAN D. HALL

betrayed the urgency I felt was required to get her away from the damage she had set in motion.

The journey would not normally take long. The route, one which avoided the motorway, was always a pleasure, a chance to share a pot of tea in one of the many pretty villages dotted through the Oxfordshire countryside between the airport and the facility.

Not so this journey. Even with relatively little traffic to hinder our progress, we seemed to get embroiled in an endless loop of argument and accusation. For my part, I never once brought up the subject I had been instructed to investigate. I wanted to, I desired to have it out with her as quickly as possible, to prove that the mother was a con merchant, a callous lying bitch who threatened my own love for Faith. Instead, I focused on the way she had effectively invited the press to take her to task in the morning editions.

Faith asked me if I knew her mother was in England.

I wasn't going to lie, but I could obscure as much of the truth as others saw it. *Of course, I knew, but I only found out when it was too late to inform you.*

"What's she doing back here?"

Again, I concealed the whole truth.

"I don't know. Maybe it's what the press guy said, that she's returned to face the music. Maybe she's seeking forgiveness."

That seemed to enrage her, and she smacked the dashboard with fierce damnation. She started to swear under her breath, the words riven as though she were possessed by verbal tics, language that would have made a sailor blush.

I won't go into all the expletives, Detective. I know you are still under the influence of the drug in your system. Let's just say there were more F- and B-words than you might imagine, and all of them were directed at me. She kept hitting the dashboard as she delivered her cruellest line to me.

"You're supposed to protect me from this. You're supposed to stop all the bad things from happening to me. This is all your fault, all your fault, you damned useless husk of a man. Oh, you're ready to smile and take credit for putting me on a path to assured superstardom. You're ready for the cameras to capture your arm around my waist as though we are two inseparable lovers. You are a weak, childish man. What were you hoping all this time? That you would get to fuck me?"

I didn't know how to respond. I had wanted to marry her, but I had never once admitted my feelings to her. I certainly would never have been coarse enough to use that word, not even in the heat of passion. I had been wronged, and yet I couldn't bring myself to rebuke her or to feel anything but shame. In this instance, and for now, I remained silent, avoiding eye contact and conversation with her.

The journey felt like hours. I could have driven to Edinburgh, had a slow leisurely dinner in an upmarket restaurant, enjoyed a fine cigar and driven home in the time it took me to calm down enough to notice that I had almost overshot my turn-off for the small town and the facility that nestled in its midst. It might have been better for me eventually if I had just dropped her at the front gate, told her I never wanted anything to do with her again, and then carried onwards to the Athens of the North.

She had hurt me, but for the first time in my life, I didn't want to exact revenge in the way only I could.

You see, Detective, no matter what you believe, Death is very real, and I am that harbinger of silence hereafter.

We arrived. Thankfully, she had stopped assaulting the dashboard. I was relieved that she didn't have a knife to hand; I dread to think what she would have made of the upholstery, or even my face.

I slowed down, the gravel grinding under the weight of the car, and stopped almost right outside the stone steps that led upwards to the impressive building. It was, for someone of my profession, a wonderful place to admire; a vast improvement on the one that stood on the site decades before, so I was told.

I was angry but humiliated and meekly bade her good fortune and that as ever her mental health be restored before her next adventure. I waved at the nurse as she walked down the steps to greet us and waited for Faith to depart.

"I'm sorry."

To the untrained ear, they were words of reconciliation, heartfelt. I knew better…or I thought I did.

She put her head to her hands and howled. This woman who, only an hour before, had been beating the hell out of an inanimate plastic object was now howling horrendously and with passion. She clutched my arm, buried her head in my suit and begged me to forgive her. She blamed jet lag, the change in temperature, the distance, the need for rest, and the way she had been sidelined by the press. She blamed everything but herself. I couldn't help but be moved. After all, whatever I was feeling that day, I did know I loved her.

The nurse opened the door, and Faith wailed once more.

The nurse cast a sympathetic look my way and said, "Come now, Faith. It's always the same. I know how much the doctor means to you, but you have come here for rest, for peace. Let the doctor go."

"I shan't," she squealed. "Don't you realise this man is more than just a doctor. He is the man I love. Ask him! He won't deny it. Please, Nurse, ask Professor Seward if the doctor can visit me tomorrow. We have so much to talk about, so much we need to discuss."

I started to decline.

In truth, I was startled by her sudden declaration. My head, as is apt, seemed to explode. Was it true? At that moment, it didn't matter. Nothing mattered. I was ready to absolve her of all, to take my conclusions back, biased as they would be, and declare her a saint.

I stammered. If this was a love story, it might have been endearing, the soft focus on my face, capturing the essence of drama. Thankfully, my life has been one of horror and abandonment, one of death. The only love I've felt, when I look back now, is one of chaos and retribution.

The scene would have been over in a flash had the nurse stuck to her guns and job description. To turn my back on Faith at that moment would have been foolish, disagreeable, an affront to what I had felt for the woman, and a small, calculated response lit up my mind like a match being struck in a dark void. If I were to stay a couple of days, if I made the most of the time available, I might have the perfect excuse to delve deeper into her psyche, to unravel what I could not in the privacy of my own practice with all the distractions therein.

The nurse seemed unsure. Who could blame her? If she had said no straight away, I would have got in the car, waved Faith goodbye and given a verdict of damnation, swearing to all that I would never seek to be in the same room as the actress again. That pause, much longer, aggressively deeper, than my own initial hesitation, gave me the impetus to regain control of the situation…especially after the display of anger from Faith on the journey from the airport to the Oxfordshire facility.

I had to play it with intent and be seen as though it would be a favour.

"Nurse…?"

"Elizabeth Blackmore, you don't know me all that well, but I have read all your papers, and your book. That was one of the reasons I joined the team here."

"Elizabeth…" Always lead with a first name if offered by the speaker. "I understand the predicament my patient has put you in. It was unfair of her to ask such a question knowing full well it would put you on the spot. I tell you what, get the professor to give me a direct call. I will stay at the hotel in Perchester tonight, the nice one near the old manor house, and if he believes I can be of use tomorrow or the next day, then I shall gladly make myself available to him. I think that after the declaration observed by us both, I shall need to step back from treatment anyway, so it might be a chance to hand over all my notes on Ms. Croy'ance, face-to-face."

It seemed my suggestion, delivered with a smile that was dripping with concern, was taken on board with a touch of sympathy—and was one she might pass off as her own idea. If it went well, I thought, I would allow her to believe that for the rest of her life.

"I will speak to the professor. I know he has long admired you. He would relish, I'm sure, a chance to actually sit down and talk to you properly."

Looking at Faith, I nodded my head, hoping she would take it as a sign of my compliance. I knew she wouldn't argue; she wouldn't create a scene in public. That was only ever reserved for the film set or in private.

She nodded, a little too enthusiastically.

"That's settled then. I look forward to a call, one way or another. Thank you, Elizabeth, I know she is in excellent hands."

Before another word could be said, I hopped back into the car, executed a gentle three-point turn, and drove back towards the main road to Perchester.

I checked myself into the hotel. In the past, it had been one of the finest places to stay in the area, and I'd had the pleasure of visiting a couple of times.

Inside, I found a genial welcome, and beside the unlit fireplace, surrounded by décor from another age, of fashions that had come and gone, and mysteriously returned, I spied a man I had spoken to for a few hours on my last visit, a former local journalist turned historian and writer. Whilst a room was made ready for me, we conversed a while.

He was an impressive figure, having seen unfathomable things in his life, and I often wondered if he would have made a good case study. Perhaps he still would, if ever I become whole again.

We conversed and whiled away a couple of hours. He treated me to a story of a badly disfigured man who survived a witch's cult, and I nodded in approval at his fascinating way of delivering a cold, juicy tale. I wish more than anything, Detective, that I have learned from him and given you reason to learn more.

Later that evening, the call came. I was alone in the bar, nursing my second glass of water, when the barman informed me of the professor's call. We spoke only briefly, but there was a sense of joy in his voice, which I reflected back, for many different reasons, and we agreed upon a time when I would be able to finish my sessions with Faith.

It was to prove enlightening.

Chapter Twenty-Five

B RIDGE RESURFACED INTO the light with a gasp, a large, emphatic drawing of breath. Her ribs hurt as she struggled to control her emotions, coming back to life with haunting memories of someone else's pain and existence firmly etched in her mind.

Torlay's face swam into view, a haze, a puzzle box where one small square seemed to be elusively always in the wrong place, making the picture one of obstinate refusal to make sense.

There's only one thing worse than being stuck in your own dark thoughts, your own questionable sanity as you analyse every decision you've made, and that's being held captive in someone else's explanations as they feed off your emotions, guiding you through the detail of their own perverse nature.

It took time for Bridge to gain full use of her faculties, to see the world as more than just a swirl of odd arrangements.

"What the hell?"

Torlay smiled, a sight she was not used to, especially one that wasn't a sarcastic grin or a weather-beaten grimace. His uniform looked as though it had been slept in: the creases in his shirt matched those in his face, the lines almost running together, merging as though they were intersections of railway on an island map.

"You gave us a horrible fright." Despite the smile, his words were filled with great concern, his outward demeanour pressing down on emotions he didn't want to reveal.

"I need to get up. I need to go to Perchester," Bridge insisted, trying to move, but the multiplex of wires connecting her to the machines barred her way to freedom. "Get these things off me, Torlay."

"What are you doing?"

"I need to talk to someone who can shed light on the state of mind that our victim was in when he was attacked. He's not as innocent as he seems."

"Well, we knew that, but what about this cultish group, The Daughters of Gorgon? They're the key to him being strapped to a bed unconscious."

Bridge was in the middle of pulling off tubes and wires, sticky-backed pads that were monitoring levels in her body, when she realised what Torlay had said and froze.

"He wasn't tied down or anything before."

"No, he wasn't. It's the oddest thing, or perhaps not with everything that has gone on just recently. Doctor Wasteacre was adjusting a monitor when the patient started thrashing about and ranting. A nurse videoed the commotion. He's absolutely gone, his brain activity's a jumble, the doctor says, and he's almost certainly still in a coma. It was when he started talking about the Mars mission, parroting the TV coverage word for word—that's when Wasteacre restrained him. And he said your name."

"Have you seen this video?" Bridge ripped off the last of the tubes, and the machines around her grunted and beeped in annoyance. "Where are my clothes?"

"In the cabinet to your left," Torlay answered reluctantly.

"Well, don't just stand there gawping like a fool. Help me get dressed!"

He did as he was asked. Bridge often hid her body behind baggy clothes as a damnation of those who sexualised the uniforms of policewomen, but she was not one to care about delicate matters of nudity when there were more urgent matters to deal with. However, Torlay have only ever seen three women naked: his mother, his ex-wife, and a prostitute who laughed him out of her room in Berlin when he was eighteen years old. It was no less excruciating aiding his superior into her trousers and shirt, and he was thankful that he caused neither of them embarrassment as he finally pulled on her socks and then her boots, even if he did feel slightly used.

Bridge could not have cared less. There was a job to do, and she was struggling to keep balanced. Never had she felt less sexual, less as though she was being ogled, and in a way, she found her colleague's unease reassuring.

"How long have I been out for, Torlay?"

Torlay finished tying up the lace of Bridge's boot and carefully stood up. What he was about to relay to her might cause her to relapse; he had heard of such cases.

"Almost two and a half days, Boss. Beaumont stayed here the first night with me, but he got called back in, lack of staff. I...I decided to stay, and I've been here ever since. It's a good job the only thing they can do is discipline me."

Again, that smile that hid the pain of his life appeared. He used it as a weapon of disarmament. This time, though, Bridge found it better utilised as a lifebuoy thrown out to sea to capture the body of one who was in danger of being dragged under forever.

She had been in the process of standing up, unsteady but driven to complete the task at hand, even if that was only walking out of the hospital and acting as though it was normal for someone who had been attached to wires and tubes only minutes before. But as she fought her disbelief at Torlay's revelation, she could not help but lower herself back onto the bed.

"Two and a half days... How? I mean...impossible."

"You were lucky. You had such a volatile reaction to the drug that was injected into your drink. You could have ended up like the woman in the cell. The superintendent has issued a warrant for Beehaven's arrest, but it's likely she has gone to ground by now."

Bridge absent-mindedly touched the cloth sheets, the roughness of the texture reminding her that she was awake, that she was not in a madman's dream.

"Anything else I should know?"

"The Daughters of Gorgon have issued a statement claiming responsibility for the bombing of the box office at Tottenham. The death count now stands at over five hundred. They've also admitted that their actions are a response to the patriarchal system that protects men such as our friend in a coma."

The machines that had been gathering data on Bridge's vitals sent out a high-pitched squeal, which alerted a nurse and brought Doctor Wasteacre to the room. As soon as they entered, Bridge defied her mind, which felt in freefall, and went with her gut. She held out a palm and roared her disapproval of being kept in the hospital any longer.

The nurse was upon her, almost rugby tackling her down onto the bed in an attempt to get the detective back under control so that she could be sedated. She would have succeeded, too, had Torlay not manoeuvred his body into such a position that the nurse was pushed aside and staggered backwards, landing on her backside on the cold, tiled floor.

"Detective Bridge… Ingrid… what do you think you are doing? You've been seriously unwell. You need to rest, you need to recuperate." The doctor appealed to what he believed was Bridge's strength, that of order, but Bridge was having none of it. She was determined to walk out of that room. A sense of doubt that had begun to shroud her had been cast off; whilst all the answers were not there, might never be completely known to her, she was going to see the case through.

"I'm sorry, Doctor, but there are a lot of bad people out there determined to see slaughter on the streets of London. I need to leave."

"Please, Ingrid. I'm only thinking of your health. You had a violent reaction to the drug you ingested. You might think you're okay now, but what if in a couple of hours you have another reaction? Who's to say just how your mind will respond? You've already been out of it for a couple of days. What happens if next time it is longer than that? A week maybe…a month… What if you never recover at all and spend your existence in a vegetative state?"

The doctor meant well. Bridge understood his concerns. Yet she persisted onwards. She felt as though she had been manipulated from the start, that her actions had been manoeuvred by others with desires, with ambitions and objectives that she could not fathom. That malignant influence needed to be cut out like the tumour it was, its remains burned to ash.

"I'm leaving, Doctor Wasteacre. You cannot stop me."

Wasteacre saw the flash of madness in her eyes, the resolve, and threw his hands up in appeasement.

"Ingrid, I couldn't stop you if I tried. You've proved that with the way you handled Nurse Caryer there. Before you go, though, I do need to take you to the room of the man at the centre of your troubles."

Bridge responded as the doctor hoped she would, a small degree of interest popping the bubble of indignation. The mention of the man she had centred her life around for a week gave her a moment to reflect on why she had been in the hospital in the first place.

"Okay, but if that woman comes near me again, if she so much as looks at me funny, I will do more than break her nose."

The nurse staggered to her feet and shot Bridge a look of pure hatred.

"You have my word, Ingrid. No one will harm you. No one will touch you. And when I have shown you what you need to see, I will gladly give you any aid you ask for as I walk you to the front door and wish you and your officer good fortune."

Bridge flicked her eyes towards Torlay, who responded with a subtle nod of the head.

The woman whom Bridge had defended herself against was led out of the room by a stunned junior nurse. Wasteacre was as good as his word, and Bridge soon learned that the fuss and clamour that was buzzing like cheap flies pestering over a leftover piece of rotten meat in a back alley, was for the man and not for her.

Several doctors were rushing around, bellowing orders to all and to no one at all. The doctor, Bridge and Torlay walked in single file, avoiding the panic-strewn white coats and uniforms of those trained to care.

The doctor she had met a few days before, Tumas, was at the centre of it all, a medical pitcher throwing a curveball in the hope it would be caught by another member of the team. He spotted Bridge and gave a smile so watered down that it struck her that he might be under the illusion that his opinion mattered.

"Detective, I'm surprised to see you up and about. When last I checked on you, I was worried that you might be in bed for quite some time."

"Well, you were wrong," she retorted with more than a hint of viciousness in her voice.

Wasteacre raised his eyebrows at his younger colleague in an attempt to get him to back off. It was fortunate the man who had shared a drink and conversation with the detective in the dead of night understood the older doctor's meaning and went back to writing down vitals on his clipboard.

The television in the room was on once more but muted, a silent interloper in the maelstrom of noise and pent-up frustrations. On the screen, the latest from the Mars mission was being discussed by a panel of experts and individuals. Bridge paid them no attention, but something caught Torlay's eye, and he stopped to watch.

"This is the problem," Wasteacre said with an edge of fear catching itself against his teeth. He pointed directly to the bed and the man strapped tightly to it.

His eyes were wide open.

His pupils were fixed and dilated. They stared directly, coldly, no sign of life in them whatsoever, at the ceiling. Bridge watched him silently for over a minute, the hustle and constant reports emanating from every healthcare professional not even denting the detective's unyielding concentration. This man had penetrated her mind with images of rampant, unceasing anger, with malignancy, hostility, and a malevolence that had crossed into the waking realm with her when she escaped her dream-filled solitude.

"Is he awake? Can he hear me?"

Her words hung in the air, a nuclear cloud of unkindness waiting to rain down on the heads of those to whom life was sacred.

Finally, Wasteacre answered. "He's still in a coma. But every time we close his eyes for him, they spring back open. His brain activity is going through the roof. We muted the TV because he was verbalising the reports, word for word, simultaneous with the broadcast. Then, about ten minutes ago, he started saying something new. They sound like coordinates, but none of us have any clue. They're not map references or survey marks. They don't point to any British or European military establishments—"

"What are they exactly? " Bridge asked. "An example, please!"

The use of the word 'please' caught Tumas's ear. *As if she is having to force herself to remember how she would have once asked a question with interest and not hostility.*

Wasteacre looked at the notes that he had scribbled down, the mix of single letters followed by single- or double-digit numbers.

"The last set started as N12, then L15, followed by a small gap, then G13, F19, F20, F21…another gap and then finally M23, M22, L22, L21, and then nothing. We even thought about postcodes, perhaps a signal to us that some atrocity was being planned in those areas, but that didn't make sense. There were some consecutive numbers, but then a set that seemed to be random, haphazard."

Torlay had been half-listening to the conversation as he watched the television, but said, "It's from a game. I played it years ago. It was almost impossible to get the right numbers down before the box blew up. I was hopeless at it. We all were. A man came to the school, and it was loaded up to the computers in the lab. He offered us money—a fiver, I think—if we found all one hundred bombs on the screen without blowing them up. The best I managed was about thirty. Such a maddening game."

Bridge turned and faced the back of Torlay's head.

"A game. I had a conversation with someone about that recently. It was part of a government initiative, some sort of scheme to identify those with a kind of potential." Bridge knocked the side of her head with her fist as if restarting an engine with a lump hammer. "It was down in Avoncross...where the boy learned of his aunt's death."

Torlay didn't answer.

A couple of the doctors were tapping at their phones, trying to find a game that fitted the description.

"Torlay, are you listening? I'm talking to you."

Torlay pointed at the screen. "Isn't that the woman from the gallery. I'm sure it is. Beaumont printed a picture of her from a screenshot from CCTV in Whitechapel."

Bridge focused her attention on the screen.

"Someone turn the television up, please," Torlay requested, and as the sound crept upwards via remote control, Portia Cullise's exotic accent filled the hospital room. This was followed swiftly by the man in the bed, eyes wide open, staring blankly but with purpose at the ceiling, copying the gallery owner's words exactly, right down to the rhythm and pace, as they left her mouth.

Chapter Twenty-Six

STANDING IN PROFESSOR Seward's office, Ingrid Bridge peered closely at the photographs adorning the walls. An ungainly sword in a glass case rested on a mantelpiece above the cold, unlit fireplace, but Bridge paid it no attention; such weapons of barbarity held no significance for her. Instead, she focused entirely on the photographs, which seemed to chronicle the facility's history.

They told the story from the grass meadows that once served as a barrier between Wendlefield and Perchester, a natural boundary separating the small village from the slightly larger town, through the building's inception as a drug rehabilitation centre in the early 1980s, to the fire that covered up various wrongdoings, and finally, its grand rebuilding and rebranding as a catch-all facility, catering to drug dependency, alcoholism, mental health services, and even child services.

Bridge had done her due diligence; she had read about the facility's history in the car as Torlay drove her along. She had meticulously searched for any connection between the man in the hospital bed and the facility and concluded that there was no sign of vested interest. Whatever had happened to Faith Croy'ance seemed to have no link to any member of staff, directors, or the long-standing overseer, Professor Seward.

Despite her thorough investigation, one small newspaper cutting from three days after Croy'ance's death caught Bridge's attention: the professor's name appeared as having attended the play in which the actor died.

The series of black-and-white photographs on the wall served as a reminder of renewal and change. Those of the outside of the building portrayed a landscape sculpted by time. However, as she turned her attention to the large picture window, the scene outside seemed almost timeless, except for the gravel pathway that would have been the same a hundred years before. Fields stretched for three miles, separating the modern world inside the government-backed facility from the rural Oxfordshire town beyond.

Torlay had driven through Perchester to give Bridge a glimpse of what lay beyond the facility's reach. The main road, now a designated pedestrian zone, showcased a parade of shops gradually evolving over time. Gone were the old institutions and family-run enterprises, giving way to glossy, contemporary establishments. Though old buildings still stood in the market square, they no longer held the fascination of local historians.

This town had forgotten its own past, both structurally and physically. Despite seeing more than its fair share of horror, its people seemed ignorant of it, and those who remembered only spoke of it in hushed tones, as if trying to keep it hidden.

As Bridge looked out of the window, watching Torlay lean against his car and relax in the still cold air, she wondered if the fate of Perchester was being repeated in Avoncross and in her part of London. Would the pavements she had once strode with pride, where she'd conducted searches for missing children and participated in community outreach programmes, eventually succumb to collective amnesia? Would they, like Perchester, forget or ignore anything sinister or out of the ordinary?

The door behind her opened, interrupting her thoughts. She had seen photographs of the professor in his prime, exuding pride in full glorious colour as he posed for the camera on the day the facility celebrated its tenth anniversary. He had been a handsome man, with a full head of hair, glasses that lent him an academic air, and a suit that shimmered in the photographer's lens, capturing

Ian D. Hall

a moment of resplendent respectability that urged people to trust in his methods.

The figure before her was admittedly twenty years older than the photograph, yet life seemed to have played the cruellest trick on him.

Gone were the locks of bushy, rampant hair, the sleek figure, the broad shoulders and fresh-faced appeal that would have sent shivers of lust down anyone's spine. In their place stood a hunched-over, virtually bald man with a shallow, haunted complexion as though his face had been encased in plaster of Paris and left to harden. Bridge recalled reading in a Sunday supplement about a Middle-Eastern cult where human skulls were covered in plaster and used as a horrifying spectacle to frighten people to death. That was how the professor looked, giving Bridge reason to worry about his future health.

When he spoke, it was with authority. That, at least, was a relief.

"I see you are disturbed by my appearance," he said, with a smile that defied the deep wrinkles in his forehead, hinting at a lingering lust for life even as his body began to crumble. "Please do not worry. Time has been unkind, but I am still here, more than capable of doing my job. I flatter myself that few could manage this place as well as I have over the decades and remain sane."

"I apologise. I didn't mean to stare. I was just admiring the picture of you on the day you took over the newly built facility. It sort of caught me off guard. You don't expect to be confronted with the past and present all at once."

"I suspect I might be saying the same thing to you if what you want to talk to me about is Faith Croy'ance."

Bridge bowed her head apologetically at the wizened-skinned man, who brushed it off with ease and another smile, although once Bridge and he were finished discussing the actress, she doubted he would smile again for quite some time.

"Seward, an auspicious name for a man with your responsibility," she remarked as she sat in the chair that the professor had pointed to with his walking stick.

"Ah, the great Irish soak's creation. I would like to tell you that it was appropriated from my great-great-grandfather, a nod to two intellectual men and the friendship forged."

"And the truth is?"

"Very astute of you. In actual fact, like many names, it is a corruption. My grandfather was a humble steward for the White Line Shipping Company, but he had rather a thick accent and found difficulty pronouncing certain letters. When World War One started, he was transferred from commercial and passenger shipping to the merchant sea. The perfect combination of his thick accent, a slight impediment of the tongue, and a hard-of-hearing captain meant that he was recorded as his profession rather than by name. He went from steward to Seward in one stroke of a pen."

Once again, the professor smiled. Bridge wasn't sure if he was pulling her leg. She decided it was best to nod and smile back at the man. He became serious. Bridge had asked the question to disarm him, to make him feel comfortable while being informally questioned by an officer of the law. Why did she feel that he had the upper hand, despite his obvious frailty? He had turned the tables, and now she felt subordinate to him.

"How can I help you, Detective Inspector Bridge? The death of Faith Croy'ance was quite some time ago. I'm sure that all you need to know about that horrid night has been archived by now and is a matter of public record. There was even an open coroner's court, which gave the public reassurance that it was a terrible mistake... an accident, an awful, awful accident."

Bridge leaned forward, determined to reassert the power she felt she had misplaced. "I have read the reports, the news coverage, the gory end to the life of a woman seemingly at the height of her profession. I have gone over every inch of that night in the theatre, and yet you only come up once, a throwaway line, and no mention of your relationship with her within these walls. I find that odd, don't you?"

Bridge relished the question. The two days or so stuck in a hospital bed had given her impetus to see the case closed. She would rather believe that it was the rest and not the intrusion into her mind by the man she strongly suspected of playing a part in at least one death and being true to his word, that he was an embodiment of the Grim Reaper.

The old man didn't take the bait. He remained stoic in his chair, aloof to the pressure Bridge was hoping to place upon his dropping, saggy shoulders.

"I was there, yes. A matter of public record. Is it my fault that the press largely ignored me? That only one of those tediously terrible tabloid papers found a way to place my name in the column inches provided?"

"You weren't even called to give evidence to the coroner."

"That is correct."

"Why was that? A man of your prominence, a man who knew the dead woman, if not intimately, at least in his position as… what exactly, a therapist? That cannot be so, unless you did take on the role after our mutual friend abandoned her as he makes clear in his journal."

Bridge noticed Seward's eyes blink rapidly. The chance she had taken had paid off.

"Journal?" Seward repeated.

"Yes. He kept a series of journals over the years. I have read almost all of them. He names you a couple of times, well, quite a few actually, especially around the time of Faith being brought here for what was to be her last time. He goes into detail about that last visit, the one you sanctioned against your own ethics team's advice. Yet somehow, none of it was mentioned, not a single minute of it was recorded for the benefit of a report into her death."

"I assure you, Detective, that anything I would have had to say would not have had any bearing on the poor girl's death."

Bridge heard the condescending words mixed freely with deflection in the man's voice. He was lying, and she aimed to press him on it.

"Why don't you let me be the judge of that? From the top, I want to know why you allowed him to come back the next day, why you broke the facility's rules, your own rules of conduct for the patients under your care."

"It won't make any difference."

"Why you were at the opening night of the play, the night when Faith's mother was also present, and how she came to kill, indirectly, her only daughter? Don't forget, I have the journals that back up my theory, his skirted-around confessions. I can easily present them to the Department of Public Prosecutions. They will not be swayed by the demand and insistence of 'not in the public interest.'"

Seward's eyes dropped sullenly to the floor, then lifted again. His pupils had shifted from sparkling wit to symbolic rage. The autumn sunshine peeking through the window and refracting of a red glass trophy of some kind made his eyes gleam like fire. At least, that was what Bridge hoped she was seeing as she rested back in her chair and straightened the cuffs of her blouse, which had started to poke beyond her jacket sleeves.

She hadn't wanted to distress the old man, nor had she ventured into his domain with the explicit intention of bringing him to his knees. But if there was anything she had learned to be intolerant of in the last week, it was someone keeping secrets from her.

"If you insist, Detective," Seward conceded, his defeat easily won. It made Bridge light up from the inside out. She even accepted the offer of a pot of tea from the professor, for as he put it, "What is the point of the truth without the satisfaction of a hot drink to aid its digestion?"

If Bridge had not relaxed, if she hadn't been caught up in the pleasure of believing she had the upper hand, she might have noticed a name that would have meant something to her, a name that might have stirred a memory.

As it was, she missed a vital part of the story of Faith Croy'ance's death because she had touched arrogance. As the tea was brought into the professor's office, she barely noticed the darkness surrounding her. If there was an evil in the room, she would have believed it to be Seward, not the creature who stared at her with dark-set eyes and stitching at the back of his head above his left ear. It was a telltale sign of a brain operation, and Bridge gazed upon it long enough to make her wish she hadn't.

For now, she was content. She urged the professor to tell his tale, a tale for which she had fabricated the means to ensnare him.

Outside, Torlay stretched his arms to relieve the onset of cramp. He glanced at his watch, noted the time, and decided to stretch his legs. It wasn't a long drive back home, but he still felt constricted from having sat in a tight-fitting chair in the hospital for a couple of days.

He felt his phone vibrate and retrieved it from his pocket. The message had been sent from Beaumont. The words saddened him, tears forming in his eyes. His friend and fellow officer, Claire Boase, had been found unresponsive in her bed. She had overdosed at some point during the night and subsequently died.

Torlay lifted his head and looked beyond the fields. He couldn't see the nearby town, not even the spire of the church that for generations had been a symbol of hope in times of adversity— when children started to die without reason, when some went missing, when some went mad.

An overwhelming surge of despair washed over him. He felt as though he was partially to blame. He had left her to attend a call at the station when he knew she was having trouble, and then spent the next couple of days by Bridge's side. An image of a loyal but unwanted lapdog came to mind, wasted time on one person when his loyalty and care should have been on another.

Rage swept over him, and he smacked the bonnet of his car with all his might while the phone was still in his hand. The screen withstood the first hit, but not the second, and it cracked into fragments—a spider's web of plastic and electronics across the heartbroken words of Beaumont's message, now lost to time.

His legs went weak, buckling underneath him, and he sank to the gravel path.

Claire Boase was dead, another victim of that damned painting. It had affected everyone, the Medusa infecting people, turning them to stone, eating away at their souls. He could do nothing now but weep.

Chapter Twenty-Seven

YOU KNOW HOW she died. Of course you do. I can see you are an intelligent person, a detective of the highest calibre, but you do not yet know why.

If she hadn't died at the hands of our mutual friend, I suspect I may have killed her myself for the way she mistreated my facility by using us as a vehicle for her own success. And she did use us.

At first, she was broken; I cannot deny that. The first time I met her, she was a child—a child who had suffered neglect and parental abuse, compounded by a lack of self-esteem, and horrific burn scars that could have only come from lit cigarettes being pressed against her skin. Her back, the soles of her feet, the backs of her knees, and her bottom bore the marks of unspeakable cruelty. It made me and the nurses that attended to her sick with guilt by association. As responsible, mature, and developed people, we could barely look at her without wondering how others could be so abusive.

That first summer when she was in our care, suggested with enthusiasm by the doctor at the heart of all this, we made significant progress in allowing her emotions to be released, to be confronted—addressing all the small details, all the large disturbances. I pride myself on how we cultivated her from a bedraggled weed to the picture of security that she presented on screen and to the public.

There was so much more to do, but we were confident that the progress made in such a short time would manifest itself, altering her outlook in such a way that she would fulfil what the studio and the doctor believed was her destiny.

Destiny, such a closed book outlook. A word that suggests, no...*insists* upon inevitability.

When we said goodbye on her last day, we had such high hopes.

She was whisked off in a private car and taken directly to the studio where she spent three months making her second film, relishing the key supporting role, perhaps understudying the leading lady.

I expected her return; I thought she was an interesting woman, one for whom the facility could be seen as a benefit to her mental health. I won't lie, I hoped it could further our cause in certain circles, that at some point we could introduce Ms. Croy'ance as the face of positive mental image.

I did not expect her to arrive back in such a state—a huge mental breakdown that, between us, we managed to keep out of the press, and even from the doctor. A make-up artist found her on the floor of her caravan having taken an overdose; not one that would have killed her outright but would have certainly made her very ill for some time. Her liver would have suffered terribly, but she would have lived.

After a week of isolation, after refusing to open up and participate in her therapy, and I admit to feeling frustrated, she finally attended a solo session with one of the heads of the department, and she made allegations against one of the stars of the film, claiming that she had been the victim of systematic racism and bullying. It set her back in terms of her recovery. She retreated into her shell without a hint of regret. It was another two months before she would even talk to me, by which time the studio had taken her complaint seriously enough to conduct an internal investigation and discreetly drop one of the major actors from the roster.

It was at that point that the doctor and I concluded, far too late, that Ms. Croy'ance had the taste for another type of fame—that of attention.

IAN D. HALL

Eventually, I found myself informing the doctor of the whereabouts of his patient. I anticipated some professional recriminations and was surprised that he understood the position of the studio; all he cared about was her welfare.

The warning signs that surround this case, to my shame, eluded me until it was too late. I never suspected that the doctor had romantic feelings for the girl, and while she was of age to give the man the benefit of the doubt, the fact that he was a good number of years older than her should have alerted me to the possible question of control.

I just never thought that the coercion came from her.

Over the course of several years, she returned, sometimes in triumph, just needing that extra validation of her craft. She was a delight in those moments, projecting herself as a strong-willed woman who the past would no longer send spiralling into fits of depression. Then there were other periods during which she was overwhelmed by anything and everything.

It was in those times that I despaired. Nothing I could do, nothing I could prescribe would give her a sense of peace. It was in those moments that she would become more urgent, more pained to talk of injustices, of attempted rapes, the numerous times she had been subjected to every 'ism' under the sun… and we ate it up, we believed her. Why? Because she was convincing, because she would produce the evidence, because it suited our needs as much as it did hers.

In the end, I started to find inconsistencies in her statements, the 'candid' talks she held with various interviewers. Whether she thought that no one would investigate further, or perhaps she had started to believe every tale she weaved, she started to falter. When I realised how deeply embedded her elaborate lies had become in the lives of others, I resolved to unmask her.

My problem was that while I was in charge of the facility, I was not her primary therapist; the doctor was, and he was in love. I was sure of that, convinced that the feelings he had for her were not those of a professional therapist but instead those of malignancy, a stereotypical descent for the caring class to fall for their patient. I have seen it numerous times in my long years. I have a sister who succumbed to the Nightingale effect, and thankfully, she landed on her feet. She left the profession and devoted herself to him, and he reciprocated with kindness and honesty. A good man.

The doctor is not a good man.

Something changed. It happened quickly. It was as if Faith had finally pushed him too far and the scales had fallen from his eyes, dropped as one would smash a previously thought of as precious and expensive Chinese vase when it has been revealed as a cheap, nasty replica put together in a sweatshop in a factory near Bradford.

That day he dropped her off here and made a request to meet me, I was almost overjoyed. We had spoken, but never spent time together, and despite my misgivings about his earnest appreciation for the girl, I was a huge supporter of his work. I found his papers fascinating. This was a man to whom the human condition was no stranger, and I was desperate to lock horns with him and discuss his insight.

I allowed him to think that it would have been an imposition, a question of timing, when in truth I was chomping at the bit to have him sit in the chair you are currently in, to have tea, maybe something stronger to cement a friendship, or at least a friendly, cordial arrangement.

I knew he would be staying at the hotel. It is the only one in town that caters to the more discerning type. There are others, but they offer standard fare. The doctor is not a man to suffer the indignities of not having a bar or a decently cooked meal over which to feel the pressures of the day dissipate into the air.

I rang him and he displayed an air of humble thanks. He put me at my ease, said all the right things to make me smile, my own subterfuge pulling him into my sphere of influence.

I regret that phone call now. I see with clarity just how impressive he is, how good a liar he is. He and Faith are well suited.

Are you a fan of theatre?

I can take it or leave it myself. It's not that I don't enjoy it, I just find the meaning at times to be strangulated, hidden, and I like to uncover emotions completely and not be left with a gratuitous ambiguity riding on my senses.

Theatre…that is what it was. Ambiguous theatre. They both shared equal billing as star and director in their own play, but neither one would admit that the other was just as important; as far as each was concerned, in my opinion, they were the understudy in their unspoken game.

I greeted him the following day, we shared initial pleasantries, we spoke cordially in here, we exchanged a few stories of our profession, nothing really that would ever interest the police, I assure you, and for a time, I thought I may have found a like-minded individual to whom I could relate. You find so few in this game, and the friends you have, at my age, are all memories of what they once were.

We spent an hour together.

I wish I could explain how valuable that hour was, but I am bound by patient confidentiality, unless you wish to make this formal. If you are able to navigate the government red tape I have at my disposal, then please arrange a time when we can meet, but until then, Detective, you will just have to trust me. Some conversations are off limits.

He then requested, and I acceded, to meet with Ms. Croy'ance alone. As I have said, it may be my facility, but he is her primary contact. I hoped that over the dinner we arranged for later that day, he might be forthcoming with any information raised, but if he wasn't, then it was my loss.

A nurse brought Faith to us; the look on her face was one of pleasant surprise and instant gratification of having, as she fiercely insisted the day before, the man she loved stood before her.

I removed myself from their presence, affording them the comfort of this room to talk. It is as near soundproof as it is possible to get, but there are always ways in which an errant conversation can be captured. A window left open, a communications device such as this intercom between here and the several others throughout the complex. I was not privy to the conversation. However, word got back to me that in the time they spent together, it was nothing more than a blazing row, a heated and terrible commotion, and had the doctor not stormed out, I suspect we would have had to call the police.

What was certainly heard as he reached his car were the words, *"I refuse to treat you anymore. Your mother is going to enjoy her moment in the limelight."*

In hindsight, that sentence meant more than those who heard were aware of. But they were not to know that, as their main concern at that point was Ms. Croy'ance's welfare, and she was beside herself in emotional pain, screaming out that he had abandoned her, that he was the devil.

Over the course of the next few days, she wrote letter after letter to the doctor; she phoned him several times a day. Each time, she was met with either an answering machine or with the ominous metallic click of a telephone being placed off its hook. Which is more maddening, that which cannot answer, or that which refuses to speak?

She drove herself insane with it all. She refused to settle, and I could not allow her to leave in the state she was in. In the end, I managed to get her to sleep. The drugs we used were…perhaps inadvisable, but you must understand, I was quite sure that had I not acted in the way that I believed was right and just, she would have died a lot sooner than she did.

I too made several calls to the doctor. I was disappointed that we never had the dinner together I'd hoped for. A pot of tea over menial small talk does not qualify as knowing a person well, but a dinner in Perchester's top-rated restaurant—now that would have been marvellous, simply exquisite.

Several calls to no avail.

Not a single reply, no prospect of imploring upon him the situation that Ms. Croy'ance now faced. I was almost at the end of my tether. Our patient had grown quiet, sullen, detached from the experience, and I wondered if she might commit suicide in the dark hours. I made sure that there was always a nurse close by, and I had the door removed from her room; something I had never insisted be done before, or since.

I had no idea what he was doing. Was he punishing her for some transgression that I could only suspect? Was it a chastisement, a form of suppression? Was he even castigating himself by avoiding her? I don't know, but just as I was on the verge of calling the studio and speaking directly to the producer, he called me.

It was late in the evening on the fourth day. The rate at which Ms. Croy'ance had declined was incredible. I would expect the time it would take for such depression to reach the point it did to be at least a week, and I began to realise that she had been truly masking her desperation with a fantasy joyful spirit. She must have been exhausted. She was carrying the weight of the world on her shoulders, and those lies, that mountain of smears and slanders, must surely have added to her burden.

He was not able to make the journey up again, but he wished to convey, with Ms. Croy'ance in the room beside me listening via the speakerphone, that he harboured no ill will, that he would keep the secrets shared, and she should make haste to ensure she was in fine condition when the rehearsals for the play started the following week; he would be there on opening night to support her.

From sheer despondency to elation, an instant high delivered by that most gracious of drugs…forgiveness. She flowered as if drenched in water on a hot summer's day. She apologised with grace and beamed as if she had been kissed for the first time by a crush. Was it a scam? Was she really that bad in the first place? I have asked myself that question many times, and not just with her, with other patients.

I lost a good friend once, my deputy, who allowed a woman to be used by a criminal mastermind posing as a doctor; he took her life. I was sure that this wasn't going to be a repeat, but somewhere niggling away at the back of my mind, I felt a sense of unease, as if there was something occurring that was going to embroil me in someone's dirty work. It was a feeling I quickly dismissed, as I also got caught up in Ms. Croy'ance's uproarious joy, and another's despair.

It seems that whilst I had been but a passing stranger to the doctor, he had affected others in a way I could barely believe possible. I have heard men and women describe him as the devil himself. That much may be true. However, I have also heard him being described as a model citizen who gives his all to the lives of those in need. Make of him what you please, Detective. But don't underestimate him. One look, one cross word, and you will go from investigating his attempted murder to being a muddied corpse like his schoolteacher.

Now, if you will excuse me, Detective, I see that my secretary is buzzing me. I will return momentarily.

***

As soon as the professor left the room, Bridge leaned back in the chair and breathed heavily in and out as if she was catching her breath. She was overwhelmed by the professor's words; she felt as though she had sat through a lecture on diminished responsibility and coercive control, and it was heavy going. Useful, enlightening, but heavy.

The professor returned quickly.

"I'm afraid I must go, Detective. An urgent case. One of our more established residents has become a little agitated by your presence. Nothing sinister, he just feels very uncomfortable when members of your profession are close by. He blames you for his being here, always protesting that you never cared for him when he was attacked. My secretary will show you out."

He departed hurriedly, leaving the approaching secretary to smile at Bridge with concern as she showed her gently to the outside world where Torlay was sitting with his head in his hands, hiding his face as though he had been weeping.

"Oh, before I forget, Detective," the secretary said loudly. "I found this on the floor earlier. I think it belongs to the man you were talking to the professor about."

The secretary handed her a medium-sized, hardback journal. It had burn marks along its edges, as if someone had taken a match to it, allowed it to flicker for a while, then thought better of it. The pages inside had not suffered much in the way of damage, a singe of smoker's fingers brown, patted out by the same hand.

Bridge knew that scene-of-crime officers had passed everything they had on to her, several small journals filled with names and dates, with drawings, some brief notes, and sometimes full confessions, but this was larger, heavier. It was the weight of someone's truth as opposed to their lives.

She thanked the secretary for the journal and apologised for disturbing one of the patients with her presence.

"I don't know… Oh my, no! It wasn't you. The professor probably just said that because it would be too embarrassing for him to say it was over a bunch of flowers."

Bridge looked at her quizzically.

The woman took the bait. She expanded on her reasoning.

"Well, I've been here for three years now, and once a week, every week, a large bunch of beautiful flowers is delivered here for one of the patients. They really are gorgeous. I often say to my Derek that it's a shame he doesn't put in as much effort, but men, eh?"

"Flowers for a resident—is that usual?" Bridge asked.

"Not at all. Some receive them around their birthday. I say it's a peace offering, a watered-down attempt at an apology for not visiting them on the one day a year when they should...a terrible thing to do to someone."

Bridge nodded quickly, hoping the secretary would get to the point.

"I rang the woman who had the job before me a couple of years back, lovely lady, she spoke with such diction. She said that the patient had been receiving flowers for more than twenty years, and even before that, so her predecessor before her said."

"Is there a name or a message on the bouquet?"

"Never. It's pre-paid for as well, so the boy who delivers them says. A long-standing account."

"Where do these flowers come from?"

"There's a shop in the town, bit pokey, but very clean. It's owned by a couple, Donna and Terry Glosh. They might be able to tell you more."

With that, the secretary smiled broadly and abruptly said goodbye in a voice that made the detective wince.

Chapter Twenty-Eight

Torlay was in no fit state to drive, but Bridge rarely sat behind the wheel of a car. She found it disagreeable. In truth, she knew she would always go too fast and could cause an accident. She just found it easier to go by train, by any public transport possible, or when the offer was there, hitch a ride and allow someone else to have the worry of a fine and a three-point penalty. It was the reason she had never learned to drive, despite the pressure and demand of the job.

It wasn't that far to Perchester, a route made simpler by the addition of the dual carriageway that took travellers directly to Oxford and onto the motorway to Banbury and Birmingham.

In the short journey, Bridge thought about the journal that was in her possession. She hadn't had a chance to speak to Torlay about her stroke of luck; her focus at the time had been on consoling her colleague, helping him up and into the car, and allowing him to shed more tears before swapping seats with him and asking him to take her into the town.

She only felt concern once. Torlay drove reluctantly into the town and seemed to promptly lose his bearings. He managed to ignore the simplest of road signs and somehow ended up going the wrong way down a one-way street. Bridge let it go; there was no need to add to the man's grief. She wasn't as close to the fallen police officer as Torlay, but she also felt the damage in her heart; so many had died, so many had lost their lives, and for what?

Torlay managed to turn around without too much trouble, just wounded pride to add to the regret he was feeling in his soul.

Pulling into a space in the multistorey car park, he turned off the engine and sank back in the chair with the effort of those ancient Greeks who had watched Sisyphus roll the boulder up and down the hill and couldn't help but feel the pain in their muscles in sympathy.

Bridge debated quickly in her mind whether she should suggest that the gruff but well-meaning man stay in the car and allow him the privacy to release his emotions in comfort. However, she determined that he might do something stupid, reckless, or even leave her behind in a fit of anguish and temper. Her father had done the same once, taking her for a pint in a local pub on the night his mother had died. He sat down with his only daughter, two pints on the table, and shook his head. Before Bridge could do or say anything, her father had stood up, tears streaming down his face, and walked out of the pub, leaving her to stare at the walls and receive sympathetic looks from the locals and the barman, who thought that she had been stood up by a man who suddenly remembered he had a wife at home.

Would she feel the same sense of confusion and the looks of those shoppers returning to their cars if they saw a man drive off, leaving her stranded?

"Come on. I'm going to buy you a coffee, and then we're going to the florists. You can pick up some flowers for Claire's mum."

Without a word, Torlay removed the keys from the ignition, opened the car door and stepped out into the cold.

Bridge followed him into the cavern-like space. With the car locked and the keys in his pocket, Bridge relaxed slightly; at least she could be certain she wouldn't be catching a train back to London and then be stuck on the Tube all the way to Waterloo.

They found a small independent coffee shop close by on what Bridge would have guessed was once a major thoroughfare of the town but was now, like many of the smaller towns of the country, completely pedestrianised in the hope of attracting shoppers away from the large out-of-town retail parks slowly strangling the life out of historic marketplaces.

The drink was welcome, and the slice of pie Bridge splashed out for was enough to get Torlay talking. For an hour, Bridge put all she had learned on the back burner, and while she was itching to read the new journal, she felt it was kinder, more productive, to give her time to a friend, to a person who was in mental pain.

Torlay painted a picture of the young woman that was endearing and informative. Bridge had been pleased with Boase's advancement, her keenness of spirit, her willingness to improve on all areas of policing. She was a woman who harboured a punk-like streak, which only made Bridge like her more, though she'd known Claire's mother better; they were of similar ages, just a few years separating them, and it would be to Claire's mother that she would think of when delivering the expected eulogy on behalf of the station.

It was a statement rather than a general reminiscence that reminded Bridge of the matter at hand. She had been sucked into the gentle pace of life that the town offered, the taste of coffee on her tongue as she was lulled by nearby countryside…until Torlay yanked her out of the unknown dreams of peace and quiet.

"I don't think he saw me watching him."

"Who?"

"The man, a shabby-looking guy. He was hanging around by the window when you were talking to the professor."

"What was he doing?"

"He was just standing there. I would have said something, but I didn't think it was my place at the time, and then I got the text message off Beaumont and it all sort of ceased to matter."

"Can you describe him?"

Bridge could see the smear of wiped-away tears on his still-red cheeks. It gave the police officer a glow that radiated with emotion and thought. Her pity was replaced with sympathy.

"As I said, shabby-looking, but not out of place when I consider the building and its history, what it stands for. He was tallish, maybe five foot ten, no more than six feet, thin, painfully so, not just his stomach, but his arms also, they looked like branches that had withered, and he wore a cap, I thought to keep out the cold, but he removed it for a moment when he scratched his head, and there was a scar…"

"Just above the ear, one that looked as though it had been caused by a knife?"

Torlay's eyes narrowed, an air of suspicion crossing his face. It pleased Bridge to see his mind working in the right way, not completely crashing into the arms of melancholy. There would be time to mourn, to appease, and apologise later, but now she needed the man to think of the crime at hand, not of what might have been.

"He served the professor and I just before I heard what may have been a truncated version, or at least one-sided adaption of the death of Faith Croy'ance."

"The actor?"

"One and the same!"

"I read the brief note that you sent over to us, but I wasn't sure how much of it was speculation and how much was other people influencing your judgement."

"You mean the man's journals?"

"Those we could find. There were a few missing, if the order is to be believed."

Bridge smiled, her teeth showing that slightly yellow tinge that affects all who drink too much caffeine over time and who refuse to give in to the temptation of whitening their teeth out of vanity. She allowed a little growl of delight to escape her mouth as she pulled out of her jacket pocket the journal that had been given to her by the professor's secretary. There was a sparkle of interest in Torlay's eyes.

"I haven't read it yet, but I will as soon as we have talked to the proprietors of the flower shop, Donna and Terry Glosh."

"What do you think is in it?"

Bridge took her time to answer. She wanted her officer on spurs, to feel the case biting into his soul as it was hers. He was hurting, but this might give him the edge to see it through with her; then she would allow him to have the breakdown that was bubbling away in his heart. She drained her drink, took a ten-pound note from her purse and placed it under the saucer of the now-empty mug.

"No idea, but for once, I think we're on the front foot."

Torlay didn't argue, but he did return her smile.

Yes indeed, we have a chance here, Bridge thought brightly.

***

The florist was situated in the town's market square. The secretary had described it as pokey. Bridge's first impression was that it resembled the size of a jail cell; every available space on the wall and floor was filled to the limit with flowers of every colour, shape, size, and description. The smell irritated Torlay, and he was relieved to find that he could not stand in the cramped shop at the same time as the inspector and the Terry Glosh. He elected to stand outside and finish the cake that he had hurriedly wrapped in a tissue as they left the coffee house.

The florist reminded Bridge of a man who had once existed in the minds of Edwardian novelists, the pencil-thin moustache barely covering the top of his equally thin lips, the waistcoat elaborately designed and augmented with a single red rose stitched delicately on each side of the buttons. Those buttons, if one got close enough to see them, had been handmade and contained at their centre a poppy. The man's trousers were pressed impeccably, an old-fashioned use of starch keeping them pristine. Even the man's hair was dripping with quaintness as it shined slickly and glinted in the desperate rays of sun peeking through the narrow window and framed his demeanour as a throwback to the era of the cad.

Ingrid Bridge held out her hand and the man took it, nominally, weakly; Bridge felt an urge to wipe her hand on the back of her trousers and rub away the feeling of disgust she experienced, a reflex which she immediately admonished herself for.

She listened to the man explain that his wife was out on deliveries and would not be back for some hours; the young boy they employed had phoned in sick an hour ago, saying that he had been ill on the way back from the facility and needed to go home.

"Does he often get sick?"

"Not normally, but he always tends to do so if he must deliver flowers up there. Normally. the wife goes, but on the odd occasion I have sent Trevor, he always ends up feeling the worse for wear."

"Perhaps it's the building, maybe it gives off a vibe."

Terry Glosh stared at Bridge in wonder.

"You know, I hadn't thought of that. Stupid old me. He had… well, he never met her, but his aunt was hospitalised there decades ago, taken there after being found freezing to death in a field that ran alongside the river to the south of the woods that separate Perchester and the county border of Buckinghamshire. Well, I never, Inspector, you have solved a puzzle for me. I shall not send him there again. Now, how may I return the favour?"

Bridge had barely listened to a word the man had said with a voice that dripped silk. She had been wrestling with a personal matter of how she had become less tolerant since the man in the hospital bed had infiltrated her unconscious psyche. She recognised it as PTSD, but she also only now understood she had been violated, corrupted.

"Detective, is everything all right? Do you feel ill? You went deathly white for a moment. You lost all the colour in your face."

The man touched her arm, out of concern, and she felt herself shiver.

"Yes, thank you, I am still feeling the effects of an accident I had a couple of days ago. Nothing serious, just phased out for a moment," she lied.

Terry Glosh bent his head to one side and drew his eyebrows together, expressing empathy.

"What can I do for you, Detective Bridge?"

Bridge pulled herself together; in her mind, she slapped herself around the face, leaving an imprint that only she would see.

"I'm investigating an attempted murder, and as silly as it sounds, I have information that pertains to the flowers that are sent to someone at the facility—in fact, to the person who your lad Trevor delivered earlier on today."

"Oh my, how exciting. Of course, I know the person you mean. His name is Alexander. We have been sending flowers to him for years. Even when we used to run our business out of our garden shed, we had the privilege of handling the client's express wishes with care and attention to detail."

Bridge nodded, hoping it came across as sincerity.

"I need to know who orders the flowers. It's vitally important to my investigation."

For the first time, Terry Glosh looked distressed, physically sickened to be asked a question that would betray a customer's confidence.

"I know better than to try to block you. I say that it goes against the client and our agreement, you come back and say a warrant will enforce me to tell you. I moan and threaten to make it difficult, you arrest me or my wife, and I am left feeling bitter about the experience. If you promise that it will not get back to my other customers, I will give you the name on trust."

Bridge sized up the man without giving quarter to the sense of hate she felt for him. She wanted to sneer, to grab him by the lapels of the flower-laden shirt and buttons that lay beneath the open waistcoat embroidered with roses.

"I give you my word, Mr. Glosh."

The florist looked relieved, and she wondered cruelly if the wife would have put up more of a fight before caving to the inevitable.

Terry Glosh looked over the inspector's shoulder to make sure the policeman was out of sight and that no customer was about to come rushing through the door.

Bridge was stunned when the florist spoke the name of the consistent purchaser of flowers for the hospitalised man. She should have realised; it was there all along. In the first journal she read, she had seen with her own eyes the confession of having had flowers sent to a sick man; he was practically proud of himself for having done so. This Alexander chap had suffered an attack, a mental attack of violence, if you believed the written confession.

Bridge composed herself quickly. "I suspect that you might find your order from him might soon expire, or at least be delayed a while. He was viciously attacked himself a few days ago and is, as we speak, in a coma. I'm told that if he recovers, he might be as damaged as the man he has been buying for."

Rather than appearing disturbed by the possibility of a cut in profit and revenue, Terry Glosh took it on the chin. Too well, Bridge thought.

"Whilst I'm sorry to hear that he is…unwell, it would mean nothing in terms of the business. The contract we had with him is fully paid up, including price changes, for another decade. For the last twenty years, it has been paid in advance and secured by the bank. If he dies, I lose a customer, but I don't lose the money."

This time, a sense of begrudging respect seeped through Bridge's heart, and she smiled at the florist with actual candour.

She shook the florist's hand and wished him well, thanking him for the information. As she reached the door and pressed down on the handle, she remembered to ask what Alexander's last name was.

"It is Peros. Alexander Peros."

Chapter Twenty-Nine

"**H**IS DAUGHTER?"
"His daughter!"
"His bloody daughter?"
Torlay's jaw half-dropped; he couldn't find the words to express his complete and utter disbelief.

The pair stood in the town's marketplace and attempted to fathom just how the case had been so caught up in the idea of identity, in believing that it was all paranormal. The daughters of Gorgon were obviously a cover for Drusilla Pero's retribution.

Torlay looked around him and spied a restaurant, a favourite from his youth when he would hang around on a Saturday morning with others who rode their mopeds around town and generally caused havoc. He wondered if they still served the burgers he liked, the link sausage, and the chips, and realised that the cake Bridge had bought him had not quietened the gnaw in his stomach, nor dampened the grief he still felt under the surface. He needed to eat.

He turned his attention back to Bridge, pointed at the quaint-looking memory of fast-food heaven, of girls in tight leather skirts and leather jackets that were out of place on a moped, and asked her if she wanted anything.

Bridge shook her head but urged him to go and eat, telling him he had twenty minutes and then they had to make haste to get back to London.

Torlay smiled in appreciation. They both knew he was hurting, but if he got through it by eating his emotions for a while, then what did it matter?

She watched her chief officer stride purposefully towards the bottom end of the triangle-shaped market square, and then turn around as he walked backwards for a few steps, his arms open wide, and a scowl of bemusement creeping across his face.

"His bloody daughter!"

Then just as quickly, he faced where he was going, crossed over the road, and disappeared into the grey-fronted building that housed the feelings he craved.

Bridge wanted to laugh. She had never more felt the desperate need to let go of the swelling anger and rage crawling around her mind and soul. She hoped one day it would come, that she would spend an evening with a friend and find a way to laugh so hard that she would be gasping for breath.

All she could do for now was respond with a broad smile that tried to dampen the… It wasn't anger, though, was it? She could have smacked her head in exasperation as she came to terms with the emotion writhing in her, poking its stubby curious nose into all she had experienced, tainting the belief she had and giving it anxiety. She thought it was anger, but it turned out it was its more alienating sister, that of fear.

"Face everything and Rise."

Bridge spoke the words out loud, as if the expression of positive vocal belief would be the validation that she needed to quieten down the worms of despair that wriggled and spawned in her.

She took out her phone and called Superintendent Lenton. Even though, from this distance, Torlay, if he was watching, would not be able to make out her words, she turned away and faced the other end of the misnamed Market Square.

She spoke quickly and only the facts as she knew them; there was no time for conjecture. She needed Drusilla Pero found immediately. Yes, she was aware the artist had a cast-iron alibi, but she was at the centre of it all. The connection to her was inexhaustibly clear.

Ian D. Hall

She listened intently as her boss filled her in on the events in the case London end. It seemed that her fellow Inspector, Brenda Beehaven, had been picked up in Bristol's Temple Meads station. An anonymous tip-off from a member of the public had aided in the capture of the corrupt detective. If Bridge wanted to have a crack at her, no one on the station would stop her. She would be brought back to London the next day. Bridge grinned without mercy at the prospect.

The town seemed quiet, or was that the city girl speaking? The town was prosperous enough; it had the air of country gentility wafting through its wide streets. But she felt out of place. More than anything, she wanted to go home. Despite the terror, the strikes, the lack of space, and the constant sound of pain that the city seemed to scream out each day as car horns and human dissatisfaction made thinking almost impossible, towns like Perchester were, as far as she could see, cold and impersonal. They offered little commitment, and the community seemed aloof and uptight.

Again, she recognised the thoughts as fear, the dread of being invisible in a town where the highlight of life was falling out of the local pub after several games of close-call cribbage. She wanted life to surround her; of that, she was certain.

Bridge remembered the journal. She gave her thanks to the superintendent, confirmed that both she and Torlay would return as soon as they could and put her phone back in her inside pocket. Then with a deft hand, she pulled out the missing piece of the journal. She had fifteen minutes in which to make a start on the man's writing. She found a nearby bench, ignoring the hard bulldog looks of a couple of old women who moaned under their breath about some people having nothing better to do than sit and read.

The first couple of pages seemed to be a jumble, a mishmash of thought that made no sense whatsoever. Small diagrams faded out and led nowhere, words that, if spoken, would have been mumbled, incoherent, rambling and disconnected.

Bridge recognised some of the names from previous books; some jumped out at her like a snake uncoiling to attack an unsuspecting passer-by. Some were ignorant of their part in the increasing delusions of a madman.

There was a small piece that gave weight to the death of the man who had been overheard by the doctor in the Globe of planning and executing the destruction of Avoncross Cathedral. As with the alluded death of Faith Croy'ance, it seemed the man at the centre, the spider in this carefully spun web, had taken at least one other life forcibly, physically, with no sense of it being driven by an otherworldly hand.

If Bridge was reading the journal right, psychologically this was the testament of a man losing his grip on reality.

There were ten pages dedicated solely to numbers, similar to the ones that Torlay had said were from an experiment that some schools had undertaken during his time as a pupil. Bridge had no recollection of such experiments; she thanked her father's insistence on sending her to a school that would have had her marked out as posh and subject to derision from some members of her family who thought such practices were against the faith of the working class to which she proudly belonged.

Bridge stopped reading for a moment. It all seemed convenient. Why had this one journal been saved? She examined the cover. Those singe marks, on first look, showed the signs of having felt the searing heat of a deliberate fire in which its comrades would perish, but on closer inspection, they looked more like the result of having been placed quickly against a low flame, a quick burst of light, just enough to give the aura of belief…of faith.

Faith and fear.

The edges of the paper showed the same burn marks, but they were desert brown and hadn't spread in the way one expected paper to burn; they were almost circular, a quarter of the bright-yellow sun in the corner of a child's crayon depiction of a summer's day.

Faith and fear.

Bridge skimmed a few pages along, the flicking sound catching her ears in a playful manner.

Halfway through the book, she came upon a chapter that was simply headed in the doctor's handwriting.

Today

The heading puzzled Bridge. Throughout each recovered journal, the separation of thoughts and opinions was marked by a new date. Some of the man's written musings were disjointed, flitting between past and present, perhaps triggered by connections he witnessed or gleaned in confidence from his patients.

How would those affected by their own troubles and trials feel if they discovered they were part of an attempted murder investigation? How could they confide in another human being without fearing they might become fodder for a story, a tale of the divine split of the human mind?

Today?

Why not the date? Bridge glanced up, observing Torlay standing in the doorway of the chain-fed restaurant, stretching his arms, seemingly content despite the weight of circumstance and loss. She refocused on the question at hand: why write just 'Today'? Each journal entry typically bore a date in the format of dd/mm/yy—never deviating.

Today?

Did the writer anticipate something significant happening? Was this a final communication to the world? Today? Today? Today?

She spiralled in her thoughts, seeking meaning. The answer might lie within, but the question itself captivated her, consuming her attention.

Her concentration was so intense that Torlay's touch on her shoulder nearly startled her out of her skin. It didn't matter that his gesture was gentle; it caught her off guard, prompting a spontaneous expletive that echoed in the stillness of the day.

The glare Torlay received was one he later described to Beaumont as bordering on hate. It was a fleeting moment, but in that millisecond, he saw something haunting in her eyes, a glimpse of existential pain, of entropy and the end of all things; a confrontation with mortality.

Then it was gone, a mere flicker in the vastness of time.

"You scared me to death!"

Unnerved, Torlay attempted to regain his composure. "Yes, I see that."

"Are you ready to leave?"

Torlay, still shaken, feared he might scream and run if she had said 'depart' rather than 'leave'.

"Have you got your phone on?"

Bridge's mild panic surfaced as she searched her coat pockets. It wasn't in its usual place. She muttered under her breath, puzzled by the sudden change in habit.

"No. I must have turned it off when I said goodbye to the super."

"Okay. Look. I've just read the news whilst finishing my dinner. That spacecraft—all communication has been lost."

Bridge felt a small stab of pain in her temple.

"That's bad news, but what has that to do with us?"

"Before they lost contact, a string of numbers, rapidly spoken by a male voice, could be heard in the background. I listened and then replayed the news item, recording it on my phone as I did so."

Bridge felt the headache spread. She didn't like where this was going. Before she could reply, Torlay had already pressed play.

Bridge held her nerve as she listened intently to the string of numbers being relayed to the world only a few minutes before. This was a message from space, a communication from a place where humanity had taken its first tentative steps beyond its initial reach, but the significance of it came from a place much closer to home. In this eerily quiet Market Square of a small town just a few miles away from the learned seat of education of the Oxford Colleges, a town which stood in its own isolation with pride, she knew she was listening to the numbers that the man in the hospital had been reciting whilst in a coma.

Chapter Thirty

THE JOURNEY BACK to London was filled with terror, ears firmly tuned to the latest news and updates. Word had got out, likely from one of the doctors in the hospital, that the numbers heard two minutes before all communication was lost with the Mars expedition had been spoken by a man deeply lost in his own unconsciousness. Bridge had hoped that people would dismiss it as a hoax, that the internet would shout conspiracy loudly and with a sneer, persuading the public that such a thing was not possible. But her hopes were in vain.

The miles passed quickly; Torlay drove as if he was the original bat out of hell, disregarding speed limits with reckless abandon. Reading the flurry of social media responses, Bridge saw a disturbing trend: the widespread belief that one man alone could somehow cause a spaceship millions of miles away to suddenly go dark, to be the cause of the problems that had beset the mission from the start. The world seemed to unanimously demand his demise.

In moderate traffic, the journey would have taken around two hours, but Torlay's speeding cut it short to a majestic-sounding ninety minutes. Bridge didn't complain; let Torlay deal with the fallout. Her mind was too busy grappling with the safety of the man in the hospital bed and the implications of humanity's collective condemnation.

It was only when she stumbled upon an account on social media that she realised just how grave the situation was. A vindictive, accusatory, fiercely damning post showed a short video of the man in the hospital bed clearly uttering the numbers heard during

IAN D. HALL

the Mars communication failure. The video was undeniable, unmistakably recent. Bridge felt a surge of anger and denial, but also a sense of impending doom. It was her video, the one she had taken in the hospital room as Torlay explained the experiment from the 1980s.

Torlay heard his voice in the background. "What is that? Is that me speaking? Is that my voice?"

"It's a video from the hospital. I recorded him speaking as potential evidence. Somehow, it's appeared on the internet and already garnered a million views. You can't see either of us, but you can hear your voice as you're watching TV in the room. Someone must have hacked my phone and got hold of it."

Torlay was relieved that his face couldn't be seen, giving him plausible deniability. But his relief was short-lived.

"Oh shit. Shit, shit, shit."

Bridge's profanity was sharp and loud enough to momentarily distract Torlay, causing his foot to instinctively hit the brake. Bridge felt the momentum shift and forced herself to roll with the car's movement as Torlay quickly righted the issue and regained control.

"Someone tagged me in the video. They thanked me for helping the cause."

"Shit!" Torlay said, finally understanding the implications. "Who posted it?"

Bridge scrolled back up the screen, away from the influx of hero worship comments directed at her apparent selflessness.

"Someone called Dom."

"Dom? Wasn't there a doctor named Dom in the room?"

"I don't know. I only met two of them, and neither had that name."

As London loomed in the distance, directions to various destinations and markers of historical importance passed by. The undertow of consumerism hung in the air.

"Is that all it says? Dom?" Torlay asked.

"Well, it's capitalised, but yes," Bridge confirmed.

For a mile, they drove in silence. Bridge received several urgent notifications on her phone, and after reading them, she closed her eyes briefly.

Torlay was forced to slow down as the traffic took on a more sedate tortoise-like speed. Inwardly, he cursed. He wanted to get back. His gut was telling him that the day was going to take a really bad turn. *Haven't all the days recently been the same?* he thought crushingly.

The traffic came to a standstill on the Cromwell Road, just outside the Natural History Museum.

Bridge had spent many hours inside the museum in her youth, gaining perspective on her faith. Now, facing middle age, she felt uncertain about her own mind and the world around her.

An advertising board caught her attention, offering a sale with an acronym heading. Despite the looming disaster in space and the likelihood of being set up for failure, she couldn't help but smile at the pun.

Her expression shifted to one of determination as she stared at the board.

Later, Torlay would recall that you could almost hear the cogs turning in her mind, anger pouring like steam from her ears as her demeanour transformed from distraught to disconnected, then to a fiery understanding.

"DOM—it's an acronym. Daughters of Medusa. I've been dragged into their fight as a spokeswoman."

Outside the car, the cacophony of London traffic reached a crescendo, horns blasting, the world demanding action.

Torlay adjusted the volume, missing the simplicity of turning a knob. Cars nowadays had too many buttons and switches, making driving a pain; no wonder Bridge preferred trains and the Tube.

"There's still no sign from NASA that they have re-established contact with the crew of the Mars Mission. However, in a turn of

events that Michelle Lauw, the woman in charge of the project, described as encouraging and hopeful, faint sounds have been heard from inside the capsule. The sounds, expressed as a series of metallic knocks, are faint, but strong, a metallic heartbeat from space... "

Torlay wasn't sure if Bridge had heard the radio update; she was engrossed in furiously texting replies to messages she had received.

"Thankfully, the super hasn't been in touch yet. Perhaps she doesn't follow social media. But this is bad, Torlay. I've been damned by association."

Bridge remained focused on her phone, never looking up once as she spoke. It seemed she didn't expect a response from Torlay; all that mattered was that she cleared her name as quickly as possible.

"Shit!"

Torlay bit his tongue, stopping himself from replying sarcastically. He recognised that Bridge was talking to herself rather than sharing the news with him, as if she were on autopilot, discussing commands and executions like a computer.

"A reporter from the BBC has got hold of my number and wants a quote on why I published the video to the media site!"

Out of the corner of his eye, he watched Bridge type a response to the journalist.

"I've replied that on no account am I available for such a comment until the matter of who accessed my phone has been established."

A ping indicated a reply.

Torlay took matters into his own hands, snatching the phone from Bridge and throwing it onto the back seat of the car. The sound of it bouncing off the seat and into the well beneath his chair gave him immense satisfaction. Before Bridge could respond, he pulled out of his lane, executed a short U-turn, and raced down Queensberry Place towards Queen's Gate and through Onslow Gardens.

Ignoring Bridge's command to slow down and her attempts to get out of the car, Torlay turned up the volume even higher, drowning out the reporter's voice with distortion and the squeal of the car's wheels.

Torlay didn't stop until he reached Chelsea Embankment and pulled into the grounds of the old Chelsea Church, the brakes screaming in pain and horror at the short stopping distance inflicted upon them. A startled blackbird and a sleek ginger cat silently stalking its prey quickly vanished in separate directions as the metal machine left deep tyre marks across the grass.

The fury that had been building up in Bridge finally broke free.

Torlay didn't hear it. He had already left the car, reaching in through the back door to pick up her phone, and started to walk towards the edge of the Embankment. He crossed the road, twirling the keys in his hand as he walked. For anyone who cared to notice, he looked for all the world like a man out for a simple stroll, carefree and untroubled.

His mind, though, was racing like an out-of-control merry-go-round whose operator had slumped over the mechanism that drove it on.

Bridge had changed. She had always been a little brusque, but fair and relaxed when the job was done, with a sense of humour that was sometimes off the wall. She cared deeply. But in the last few days, that caring had diminished. He couldn't put it down to obsession; she had always been single-minded when a case was involved. This was…extreme. It was as if everything that was good about her was slowly being replaced, an addict chasing the next fix. He didn't want to use that word, but her mind had been turned ever since she had been spiked by the hallucinogenic. There was distance in her eyes, as though she had been violated in her mind, and the seed of inner destruction had been planted.

Torlay turned around to face the car and leaned back against the wall that separated the river from the engulfing land. Through

IAN D. HALL

the rush of traffic, he could still see Bridge going ballistic, raging at everyone but no one.

Torlay was frightened.

Deeply and utterly, fiercely terrified. It took strength not to walk away further, to take his phone out of his pocket and call for help, to have several officers come to the rescue.

He understood the implications of her rage, the anger of having her phone ravaged, picked over as a young boy might when he learns of his older sister's more delicate clothing; the sense of having been raided is permanent and forever ingrained.

Men, he thought watching her beat the car's horn with her fists while members of the public looked at her with suspicion and fear as they passed by, *will never truly understand the greater sex. All the burdens we place upon them, and they stand up with strength to deny us what we perceive as victory.* Not for the first time in his life, Torlay damned himself and every other man for the weight they had placed at womankind's door.

He gave it five more minutes, enough time for her to hopefully wear herself out. He didn't know much about psychotherapy, about any type of science-based way to deal with a person who may be losing their mind, but what he did recognise was that unless the person was a complete psychopath, unless their adrenaline was a manufactured high, they eventually had to tire, they had to eventually give in to nature.

Should he have taken the phone from her? He believed it was the right decision. What puzzled him, though, was why she had not got out of the car herself, why she had not just flipped him the finger and walked down Chelsea Embankment towards the nearest Tube station, or even walked back to the station; such surely would have been her determination and fury that she would have route-marched her way back in double quick time.

Avoiding the steady flow of London traffic, Torlay crossed the wide road, walked slowly towards his car and peered inside through the side window.

Bridge was still. She was breathing almost normally from what he could see, and her eyes were shut. They didn't look tight, they weren't screwed up as if he was looking at a young child desperately believing they were foiling their mum by pretending to be asleep.

Torlay waved his hand in front of his superior's face and deduced that she had indeed worn herself out, that she was exhausted. It was only to be expected after the rough battering she had undertaken of late.

He didn't dare delve further; he could only be there for her.

A thought struck the experienced policeman.

He reached into her coat pocket and carefully drew out the journal she had been given earlier, then slowly withdrew himself from the car's interior once more. She shifted slightly as the door caught on the latch, but soon returned to the dreamless sleep that Torlay hoped would snap her out of the malaise, the destruction she was evidently reaping and experiencing in her mind.

He spied a narrow wooden bench underneath the window of the church, settled himself on the rigid slats and began to read the journal.

Chapter Thirty-One

I COULD HAVE KILLED her on any night during the initial run, but opening night made much more of a headline the following day across all the ways that the public now consume and are force-fed their view of the news.

Of course, my hands are clean. My hand at the moment of impact, of collision, is absent of blood.

She arrived at the theatre on the morning of the first rehearsal to applause from a couple of fans who had travelled from Loughborough to see her perform, and the heckles and catcalls of workmen digging up an old sewer pipe. She left this world a star… I suspect it would have been the way she would have wanted it.

I kept my promise. I did meet up with her that morning. I allowed her to apologise, to make, she believed, her peace with me as we drank coffee in a small but expensive coffee shop by Waterloo Bridge. She laid her cards on the table with tears flowing steadily down her unpainted skin, and I listened with a clear conscience.

I walked her back to the apartment rented for her by the studio's head, Linus Rugren, as part of the deal that would see her take the lead in the biggest film of her career. She asked if I wanted to come inside, a hint in her voice of the coy temptress she insisted on playing. I declined, with apparent sadness in my eyes, my throat simulating the catch she would interpret as regret as I bade her good fortune over the coming weeks of rehearsal and the three long months for which she was initially contracted to the theatre and the production.

I left her, insisting it would be good for the future if we weren't seen together, to allow the bitterness of the previous couple of weeks, which had stewed and festered, to dissipate, to heal.

I left her, a wreck of emotion shielded by what I hoped were comforting words.

I received no message in that time from her, but I did see various emails from Rugren, thanking me repeatedly for the commitment she was giving on stage, from the director who told me she was going to wow London with her performance, and one from her mother, sent from an email account belonging to the owner of the home she had been 'imprisoned' within.

I read that email every day until the morning of the opening night.

I can still recall the pleading framed within the sense of hurt she wished to portray as the wronged woman, as the abused mother. I got more than a hint that she was on the verge of the breakdown I long suspected she would have. Her unravelling was as psychologically interesting as it was pathetic. The only difference between mother and daughter was that I believed the mother's spiral into oblivion was authentic.

I never answered that email.

On the day I received it, my inbox full of the usual spam and laced with the occasional enquiry for help for the sick and helpless, I rang Rugren and informed him that his houseguest had got into his email account and sent me a long and aggravating letter, and advised he should immediately deny her of such facility. I also suggested, in a coded delivery that would cast no blame on me, that he should give her the rope with which to hang herself with—a chance to reconcile with her daughter on the night of the performance…if Faith was up to it.

During the weeks of rehearsal, I kept myself busy. My plan was already formulated. I had a working copy of the script, meticulously annotated to indicate where Faith would be on stage at any given moment and where she would stand at the crucial moment in the play's production. Emil Hasda could not have timed it more perfectly.

The day of the opening night, I almost backed out of my plan.

I will admit that as I woke that morning, I had grievous doubts about her death. She was a woman caught in an impossible situation, damned by a mother who abused her, abandoned her and left her to grow into a rotten stump. The flourish of the tree was for all to witness as beauty towering to the heavens, but its roots had a disease not noticed when it was initially planted.

But she had manipulated me. She had brought me shame in my love for her, and I wanted to see those roots wither and die. I wanted the tree to fall.

All day, I wrestled with my mind. I tried to occupy it by seizing upon my suspicions of the woman in the room across the hall and down the narrow passageway from my office. I had long suspected that she had at one time held membership of a terrorist organisation. I tried to derail my wavering conviction by focusing my attention on how I could get the proof I needed to see her removed from the building I paid handsomely to practise in.

When the time came to leave, I did so with my mind still deliberating the question at hand. I am Death incarnate, but do I have the right to seek rebalance by anything other than my will? The walk across the bridge to the northern part of the rat run of London did me no favours, and it wasn't until I stood outside the theatre, watching the procession of the great and the good, the fortunate few who managed to get hold of a ticket via handshakes and promises of backs being scratched at a later date, of favours fulfilled in kind and more than a couple whose access to this prestigious event had been procured by means of force, that my resolve hardened.

Had it been the ordinary public, the people of the city and its far-reaching provinces, then I suspect Faith would be enjoying her reign amongst the galaxy of stars that have us flocking to the cinema to witness them take on roles of such extraordinary worth.

Now she will be played by one of those stars in years to come, her name remembered, her beauty, her unique quality, replaced by another face, a series of masks not quite framing the woman I once loved.

I detest mingling. I find the large crowd filled with pointless chatter to be draining. A football ground or cricket venue I enjoy—the adrenaline, the fear of three points lost or a battering at the hands of a young cricketer who slogs fours and sixes as if it were a simple game. I like that theatre, but a theatre where pretence is king, I find it strenuous, exhausting. How I would have managed if I had been able to carry on playing my desired instrument in the fashionable pursuit of a jazz trio, I don't know, but then I would have been the one on stage, completely absorbed by the music, not by the circumstance of knowing the right person and how they hold their hand out when they want their ring kissed.

Do I sound bitter? Twisted? Viciously hostile to the crowd? I guess I did at the time. They were everything I had come to detest, the undeserving boys' club with time invested and money banked in accounts that were draining the poor.

A thought struck me at that moment, one I will share with you. I wondered if they would be terrorised by the event. Would they go home that night and be silent of what they had witnessed? Or would it be the crowning event of their year, their social calendar filled with days and evenings where they would enlarge upon their view, moving from ten rows back to being one row in front, their mistresses and paramours asking questions over and over again in the hope that it would add to the excitement of the tryst?

I hoped so.

I found my way to the area where the props were kept, the long table clearly marked but unattended as I had hoped, as the director had inadvertently let slip whilst gushing over the work ethic of the cast. I switched the gun that was to be used for the play's climactic scene and left without anybody seeing me.

I returned to the auditorium having not been missed, except for by the studio head and his plus-one for the night, the redoubtable and grossly indescribable Doreen Tuttle.

He clasped me by the hands, his fingers slippery, sticky, oozing sweat from nerves that he was desperate to conceal but failed to, the secreted bodily fluids transferring from his palm to mine. I felt sick but had no choice but to shake his hand as several people were looking our way.

Then he introduced me to Faith's mother. I was not overwhelmed or intrigued by her. She had the repugnant air of the intellectually stretched, a fame seeker, a person to whom life had been kind by not giving them a personality or indeed a single interesting story to tell. She was a coal pit devoid of light and a canary.

I was thankful that Faith had put aside a ticket for me a couple of rows in front and ten seats apart from this tedious infection. When the time came, I wanted to see her face. I realised that was as much about revenge and anger at Faith as it was humiliation and upset for her mother.

The cheer that erupted from the stalls and the balcony seats when Faith walked on stage to deliver her opening monologue to the assembled theatre crowd was…deserved.

She sparkled with intensity, and she had the sense to let the audience simmer down of their own accord before she began the speech that would set the scene for the play.

The performance proceeded with charm and style. If I were a reviewer, I would have given it five stars. But what do I know about such things? I don't have the concentration required to fawn over trivialities such as a director's choices of background music.

The two-hour play was without an interval. Apparently, it enhanced the climax of the production, to keep the audience on edge right until the last possible minute, the urgency amplified by the silent contest for who could hold their bladder the longest.

Having foreseen this eventuality, I made sure I had visited the toilet only minutes before and not touched a drop of the free champagne on offer—an offer I was pleased to see Doreen Tuttle had not passed up, taking the glass I had politely refused, and another for good measure, from the silver platter carried by the young waitress.

In her first and last performance on the theatre's stage, I have to tell you that Faith was magical. She carried the role with stunning application. At one point, when she discovered the plan of the male protagonist in which she was to have accidentally killed him, she screamed and yelled with such ferocity that I could scarcely believe it was the same woman who had been dealt a hand of ignorance. Then I realised: she had been playing the part all her life. That scream, the sense of injustice, she had performed it in front of me many times over.

The moments ticked by.

I could see people starting to squirm in their seats. I sneaked a peek behind me and saw that Doreen Tuttle was in a state of anxiety. To leave now would mean she missed the extraordinary ending and would be seen to have left as her daughter's big scene came fruition. Nobody knew who she was yet, but they would know before the curtain dropped on the call for a second bow.

Then it came.

The climax of the play was the death of the actor, the hero of the tale. And so, it was set to be. All the while he had carried his own weapon, it was an allusion that only he could take his life. But just as he shot himself, his mistress was meant to have killed him, to have murdered him in the hope that she would be free of his madness.

Before the performance, I had spoken to Linus Rugren about the twist at the end, noticing Doreen Tuttle greedily eating up my words.

The studio head roared with laughter. It was fitting, he insisted, that the lover should also die. Robbed of that which had driven her, she snapped, lost her mind at the sense of injustice, lifted her gun to her head and...nothing. The bullet would not fire. Only a voice in the crowd telling her to have another go, to teach him a lesson, would push her over the edge and see the curtain come down as the shot was fired.

The reveal was that she wasn't dead; she had just put another bullet in the dead man's body.

So greedily had Doreen eaten up this information gifted by Rugren, so obsessed was she with being part of her daughter's life, she was willing to be the unknowing aide in the actor's most memorable scene in her career.

I could see in the semi-darkness the excitement on Doreen Tuttle's grotesque face. She could not help herself, and before the first missed shot was supposed to take place, she sprang from her seat and yelled, "Try again. Have another shot."

The fact that she spoiled the ending was too much for some, who openly booed her. However, her daughter, Faith, looked down upon the crowd in the stalls and took pity on the woman who had abandoned her and smiled for the audience. For a split second, she kept her finger on the trigger and poised; the sound effect of the shot would have echoed around the theatre, and the curtain would have come down. Just for a second, she stuck to the script, then in a bid of knowing reconciliation, she assumed the part she had been born to play, and in a flash of powder, she was dead, shot by her own need for love.

The shock hit the audience as one. No one moved, no one screamed. It was as if Time had stood still; not a single breath could be felt wavering in the air.

Then, as if by design, Doreen Tuttle, inevitably, screamed for her child. She bulldozed through the people in her way. Pandemonium ensued, as the curtain wouldn't come down, and the efforts of the staff who tried to get audience members to calmly leave the venue were overshadowed by the consuming mass of leavers, the droves of people who could not face the tragedy that had unfolded right before their eyes.

Doreen Tuttle made it to the centre aisle, punching a woman in the face as she went, biting down on the hand of a man who dared to reason with her, blood spurting as she ripped the top layer of flesh in a carnivorous act worthy of a medieval banquet.

In amongst the carnage and panic, my attention had been on Doreen Tuttle and her now-dead daughter. I bowed my head, fully understanding my part in her death, but I was not the one who pulled the trigger. I had laid the groundwork, prepared and directed the scene, but I was not the one who gave the execution order. As I lifted my head once more after my silent prayer, I noticed Linus Rugren in his chair, head buried in his hands, sobbing gently.

I wasn't sure if he was genuinely upset. I hoped he was moved by the death of the woman who, in various interviews over the days that followed, he called the greatest actress he had worked with. Or was he simply crying over how much money he would lose as the personal disaster turned into a financial quagmire of litigation and insurance?

I went to pick up my coat. The scene had been set and Death had called *Action!* I could do nothing more. Except, my coat, which I had placed on the back of my seat, was draped over the seat behind, all folded, neat and tidy other than a small piece of paper poking out of one of the pockets.

I believed I had been unseen when I left with the dummy gun hidden away. The note suggested otherwise.

***

Torlay breathed out and cracked his neck. He had been so engrossed in reading that he hadn't noticed the warning signs of the early stages of crepitus he had been warned of, aggravating his neck.

Was it all from this?

Every action since had been because he killed the woman, and someone had taken great pains to exact revenge on him, the journal acting as a conduit for retaliation. *Why not just inform the police if you had this in your possession? Why not let the man in the hospital bed face justice? Because it was the person who attempted to kill him who stole the journal.*

Torlay groaned. They missed an opportunity at the facility. They should have read it immediately and asked the secretary and staff where it had come from.

We— He stopped his thinking there. Bridge. He had to wake her up. He looked down at his watch and was surprised to note that an hour had passed since he started reading. Somewhere, time had been stolen.

He looked to his car and saw that the passenger door was open. He stood up and walked over, tentatively calling out to Bridge by name and then rank.

She was gone. There was no sign of her at all.

He went to pull out his phone and picked up Bridge's instead. The notifications LED was flashing impatiently, missed calls by the dozen, unread texts demanding to be answered. He felt his own phone vibrate and, fumbling it when he saw the name on the screen, answered.

"Superintendent. I think we have a problem. Bridge is missing. I think she may be unstable and out to cause someone great harm."

Chapter Thirty-Two

UNBEKNOWNST TO INGRID Bridge, her name was broadcast across every available police frequency within minutes of Torlay speaking to Superintendent Lenton. It was only a matter of time before Lenton issued the command to make the situation public, to inform Londoners that an officer of the law had been subjected to great emotional stress and was to be considered dangerous, and that nobody must approach her.

She had woken from her stupor-like state, induced by a manic episode she barely remembered, and through hazy, fog-filled eyes, she saw the figure of a man sitting in the near distance. He was blurred, indistinct, and she was worried about being close to another human being when she had no idea what had happened to her.

Her mind questioned if she was experiencing the aftereffects of a date rape drug, while her heart suggested otherwise; at least, not in the conventional sense. She was certain, though, that the man seated not far from her, on a bench—or what she thought was a bench—as she rubbed her eyes wildly in the hope that the heavy blur would fade, posed no threat to her. But that didn't mean she had to stop and find out if she would be contradicted.

Unconsciously, she slipped into survival mode, into the police handbook that she once knew word for word, and slowly took stock of her surroundings. She remained perfectly still, her nearsight refocusing to the point where she could see she was in a car and that she was not restricted by the seat belt. She reasoned she was not a prisoner, not physically so anyway, but the relentless,

IAN D. HALL

stabbing ache in the back of her head told her she had again been mentally abused.

Ingrid Bridge knew who she was, but her raison d'être eluded her.

She groped in the darkness, avoiding the punishing white floodlight that the headache emitted, as though she were a prisoner on the run.

Bridge had once seen several aerial shots of people walking across Battersea Bridge Road when studying the local area south of the river for a raid on a brothel. She remarked at the time that the shadows caught in the picture reminded her of those seen in silhouetted black and white after the destruction of Nagasaki and Hiroshima—ghosts caught in the echo of a blast, the remainders of life when flesh and bones had been stripped away by the blinding, searing heat.

Consciously, she felt the memory burn—a world at war and London its sacrifice—as she part-marched, part-staggered towards the south side of the river, a place she only knew as home.

From streetlight to streetlight, she faded in and out of her mind, barely grasping reality, holding on by the tips of her bitten fingernails to the vestiges of her own personality. The bomb, the big one that Londoners had feared since the end of World War Two—the one explosion that would put all others, be it from the IRA, from cults or groups with agendas so varied that the public didn't know half of them existed, let alone the threat they posed to the capital—was falling directly above her. If she looked up, she would see the image of it speeding through the air, plunging to its detonation point...her mind.

If she looked behind her, she would have observed her shadow lengthening, gaining in width, appearing twice her size—the silhouette of her body merging impossibly with that of the man in a hospital bed just a few short miles away.

The shadow loomed heavy in her heart. Her eyes were blurred but focused on the next footfall, of placing one foot in front of the other.

Where's Torlay? She had worked alongside him for years. On occasion, he was the best man for the job; on others, he exasperated her with his refusal to accept the promotion she had recommended him for. What was she doing in the car, *his* car, and where was he when she came to? It crossed her mind that he was the blurred figure sitting on the bench, but was it really him? Her mind was in such chaos that if she closed her eyes to think, all she saw were the demons that lived in the darkness—the coloured dragons of her childhood now turned brittle grey and seasoned burnt black, the roses she once stopped and adored now withered, and the dream, the beauty that would occasionally raise her spirits, in tatters in the shadows that fed the shade behind her.

In London, as in all large cities, it is possible to become lost in the mayhem of the loud and the shadows. Bridge felt a primal urge to disappear; she wanted to feel the instant flare of the bomb rip her apart as the headache grew, as…

…he was there.

Bridge felt his presence like a gunshot to the head. She fell against the brickwork of the bridge, the instant pain in her shoulder threatening to destabilise her completely.

Pulling herself up off the floor, arm throbbing from the tumble, Bridge heard the man in her head speak to her.

"Death always needs an apprentice, Ingrid."

She staggered onwards, across the bridge, and struggled heroically all the way down the southern portion of the Battersea Bridge Road until she turned off onto Parkgate Road and towards Carriage Drive North, where the last thoughts that were uniquely hers pointed her directed her towards the small pagoda on the other side of the trees where she could rest and let the Thames' water soothe her soul.

"Ingrid?"

Ian D. Hall

Bridge stumbled but held her pace and momentum. She was as feral as she was human and snarled in her head at the intrusion.

"Ingrid. Don't ignore me. I know you can hear me. You're coming to the hospital. The desire to confront me is overwhelming you, but you need to save me, not kill me. There is a woman speaking privately to the lead doctors. She wants them to turn off the machines."

Bridge heard but refused once more to acknowledge him with more than a savage snarl.

For the next ten minutes, police sirens wailed in the distance but the voice stayed quiet, allowing her to focus required to avoid the suspicious eyes of strangers and find shelter in the pagoda.

***

Alice Sidney looked down at the figure in the hospital bed and decided that the man had to die.

When he was younger, he was no threat; he was a victim of circumstance and nothing more. His aunt, that harridan of a woman who made the young boy's life a misery, compounded it by making sure the home he had lived in was left to the church. To Alice's mind, it was out of spite, a reflex long planned in the form of malice, that she had been lumbered with a child fortunate not to be born as feeble as his father but nonetheless the product of a nasty affair between siblings.

Alice had played out in her mind many times the moment that must have convinced the aunt to give her money to the church rather than ensure what had been designed by law could be circumvented, could be abused. It must have been ordered by the grandfather the young boy had never known, yet in the last couple of weeks, he had begun to exhibit the latent tendencies he had inherited from the man.

Alice Sidney regretted not giving all the relevant information to the detective, the true nature of the horror that stalked the boy's family. However, if what she was hearing was true, then perhaps it was fortuitous she had not freely given all that was in the substantive file that accompanied the family headed by a monster. If Bridge were to survive, she deserved to know.

**

Professor Seward was lost in thought as he sat unnoticed in the carriage. The train rolled gently past Hemel Hempstead, the Buckinghamshire town imploring him not to travel onwards, to remove himself from the situation, head back to Perchester and lock himself in his study, type the letter explaining his part in the awful circumstances surrounding the case and do the honourable thing.

His father had taken the sword during a house raid in Belfast and omitted to declare it, instead bringing it back with him to the family home in Southampton, where it had remained, encased in its glass tomb, never handled but admired by the patriarch for the rest of his days. Not even his wife's insistence that it needed to be out of the children's reach had deterred him from displaying the weapon for all to see.

Fifty years after it was taken from its rightful place, forever taunting the wielder with the power it endowed upon them and the vulnerability it could instil in whoever stood before its quivering tip, the sword was bequeathed to Seward. The only reason he stayed on the train was that this implement, which could have taken his life ergo saving him from being the second director of the facility to be unceremoniously ousted from that prestigious post, was no longer in his possession.

The problem he had to suddenly deal with, after the detective's visit, had been fabricated…but not by him.

He had been told that Alexander was found in a state of extreme upset and had locked himself in the bathing room, threatening to set fire to the expensive equipment within. For fifteen minutes, the aged professor stood outside the room, which acted as a sensory deprivation chamber, imploring the disturbed man to open the door. Finally, when he reached the conclusion that the danger required a more direct form of action, he had one of the larger, more muscular porters kick the heavy door down, only to find that he had been duped, made to look like a fool. He had been negotiating with an empty room.

Those fifteen minutes were more than enough time for the patient to go into the unlocked study, steal the sword in its case and leave the premises. It was a further fifteen minutes before they found Seward's secretary, her throat cut, her body bundled into the cupboard behind her desk.

The CCTV had captured it all. Not three minutes after the detective and her officer departed, another vehicle rolled up the gravel path, and Seward had instantly recognised the owner: the wife of the florist. She came to a quiet stop beside the steps that led to the front door, and Alexander and an unknown woman carried the glass case containing Seward's father's stolen bounty to the back of the van. Slowly, with precision, they climbed into the space where flowers and potted plants would normally have been, the lingering scents of the blooms replaced by the stench of treachery.

Seward had rewound the digital picture a few frames and then pressed pause on the clearest view of the woman aiding the patient. And again. And again. If he hadn't known better, he would have said she was his secretary, but his secretary was dead in the cupboard that held her personal possessions, squeezed in so tight it would take a herculean effort to get her stiff body into some sort of shape for burial.

It was remarkable; the likeness was damning.

The train meandered its way through the English countryside, and for every mile, the professor apologised under his breath for the death of his secretary and prayed that he could stop Alexander Peros from making the biggest mistake of his life.

***

Portia Cullise removed the wig that had given her the appearance of the fallen secretary. She and Pero's father had been cramped together with the sword in the glass case between them since they climbed into the florist's van together. They had not been able to stretch their legs or transfer to her car, which had been parked on Market Square while the theft had taken place.

Donna Glosh had seen the detective leaving her shop and had hung back on the corner where she was sure her van would not be immediately seen. When Portia asked what was going on, Donna immediately shushed her and watched keenly the detective's movements. Such were the resources of The Daughters of Gorgon that she had been informed that the police officers were in the area; it was Portia who had given the journal to the detective in the facility, not the old professor's secretary. It had been a close call, and Portia was still riding the high from killing the secretary and taking her place mere seconds before the Ingrid Bridge and the professor walked out of his study.

The detective's subordinate took himself off towards the lonely fast-food franchise, one of the few remaining of its kind in the country, and the florist found herself willing the woman to follow suit.

Instead, Bridge walked in the opposite direction, sat down on the square's only bench, and started to read the journal Portia had given her.

Donna had silently fumed when Portia regaled her with a broad smile on her sickly white face of how she had pulled the detective further into the conspiracy by giving her the journal that had been saved by the Daughters. It had not been part of the plan, it was a mistake, yet Portia was unrepentant.

Alexander, who had been silent throughout, asked with agitation in his voice what they should do. Donna offered him a watery smile and told him not to worry. Then she turned the ignition and drove slowly, keeping an eye on the detective in her side-view mirror as she parked in front of her shop and told her two passengers to keep their heads down and stay quiet. With a look in the direction of the fast-food restaurant and back towards the detective, she strolled into her shop as if she didn't have a care in the world.

There had been many times in her married life when Donna had secretly wished she could have killed her husband, but lack of opportunity and momentary weakness had always stopped her.

Terry Glosh's back was turned to his wife as she entered the shop. He looked up quickly and saw her in the mirror and smiled. It wasn't the greeting of a loving husband, just someone pleased to see their partner return so they could share in the closing up of a shop, the dull deeds of cleaning up the day's mess and taking a note of the following day's orders, a precursor to a night where they would go their separate ways; Donna to her secret life as a Daughter of Gorgon, and Terry... She had often thought he had a male love on the side; in truth, he kept a young sixteen-year-old girl fresh out of school in a position that would have sickened Donna to her soul.

She would have to drive them to London; she was now completely immersed in the organisation. Her great-grandmother would have been proud of her. The thoughts of blowing up pillar boxes as part of a different struggle had been an inspiration to the young and impressionable Donna.

It's time to terminate the partnership.

Terry returned his eyes to the money in the till. The takings were steady, not life-changing, but enough that day to squirrel away some money in the hope of having fun the next weekend his bullish wife was away at one of her seminars.

He never saw her close the door, turn the latch and turn the open sign over to closed. He never imagined that she would pick up the long-bladed secateurs in anger and then come up behind him and plunge the steel into the back of his neck.

***

Ingrid Bridge huddled herself against the encroaching dark and the sound of rain that started to hammer on the roof of the pagoda. She felt completely devoid of humanity, but she somehow knew that the players in the final part of the crime were almost in place; it was time to make her move.

Chapter Thirty-Three

CAPTAIN LICETT NYHOLM'S crew were almost all dead. The explosion had ripped the ship apart. Communication between Earth and the ship was lost. Only the sound of twisting metal and the hammering of Science Officer Jerome Brassington was enough to convince her that she had not joined her fellow astronauts in Death's final embrace, forever doomed to wander the stars alone, for why would anyone follow in the footsteps of the damned?

Flight Engineer Thomskilyvan had died first. An accident, so they thought, a painful blow to the mission. The misfortune had been felt by all, Nyholm had believed, but as the days wound themselves onwards, as another member of the team was lost in tragedy, she began to understand that this was going to be the largest disaster faced by humanity in space.

Nyholm had grown up on tales of exploration and calamity. Her father had worked on the project that led to the space shuttle disaster that saw the space exploration programme shelved for a decade. Although a mid-level technician, Nyholm's father had taken the accident personally and had crawled into a hole of conspiracy, never fully accepting the official report that absolved all but a few of the ground crew and the technicians and mathematicians safely tucked away in their offices and workstations.

The day her father died, he had received a letter from England and flown into a rage nothing like Nyholm had ever seen from him before. It was the breaking point of the depression that had hung over him for the majority of her life, causing him to trash his study with the strength of the possessed. Everything he had so carefully collected, his prizes, his pictures, his intellectual property, his computer, his notes, the accolades of a life spent at the sharp end of exploration, the records he had collected and preserved, all destroyed and then set on fire, save one, which played loudly, joining in the cacophony until it started to melt, to distort. It was misfortune that saw the door to the study become double locked. It was tragedy that his rage, suddenly rampant after many years of docile apathy, triggered a cardiac event. It was catastrophe that Nyholm lost her father as the flames surrounded him and burnt him to death as his heart faded out.

Exploration and calamity, as far as Nyholm understood, went hand in hand, but somewhere in between, held in the hands of the brave and inquisitive, of the courageous and the sometimes devil-may-care, stood illumination. The human spirit that craved to know what lay beyond the next hill, what was beyond the sunrise.

The mission had been kept top secret right up until the launch. The powers that be had not wanted any fanfare until the last possible moment. The mission's success was paramount. It must not be sidelined and diverted by the media circus. Humankind's unnerving attachment to social media could only lead to threats, divisions of opinion, and worse, the extremely high probability of sabotage and terrorism.

Nyholm listened to her science officer's hammering. He was the only one who could have killed all the others, and eventually, unless she pressed the button that would set in motion the final countdown of her life, a brief blip in the history of the universe, then he would kill her.

Brassington had upset the order. The crew had been handpicked with her at the helm, but when Kenyan born Jack Kiplagat had to be pulled off the mission, his replacement proved to be the reason why her own personal mission would fail.

Her hand hovered above the kill switch. All communication was lost, so why was she still listening to him hammering away?

Ian D. Hall

There was a pattern, she realised. He was sending a signal to Earth. Well, if anyone was listening, at least would have an answer to why the ship suddenly exploded. The back end had sheared off, and only quick thinking saved the portion she and her science officer now occupied from following the metal screams silently littering space.

The letter had been lost, ashes in her father's charred hand, but no matter. Nyholm had heard the contents through the door as her father shouted them out in anger, repeating the most salient, damning parts. The accusations of a cover-up, the external force behind the event that the government was aware of but had chosen to ignore.

Exploration and calamity.

She had devoured it all during the course of her life, of her career. She had spent every waking hour digesting the malfunctions and failures; every possible action that might see a mission fail and how to react when the possibility arose.

Whilst she initially studied the historic—the sinking of *The Mary Rose*, the senseless tragedy of the *Hindenburg* disaster, the locomotion derailment at Avoncross Station in 1906, the R101 disaster—she eventually began in earnest the analysis of all that had taken place since the middle of the 1980s.

The list was endless, scattered, never a pattern except for human incompetence or hubris, Chernobyl, the Sellig catastrophe, Durban Range oil spill, and then those closer to London, those that seemed to circle the city and strike outwards. The Peckham Vale Tube disaster, the digital attack on the stock exchange that led to 100,000 people losing their jobs within a month as the market and banks foreclosed on businesses countrywide, the sinking of *Black Rose* in the Thames, which closed the seaway for six months...

So many disasters, so much bad blood and ill thought afterwards.

As if the world was fighting against a malignancy in its midst.

And it was losing.

The hammering continued.

Nyholm moved her fingers hesitantly away from the kill switch and towards the last remaining intercom button on the bedraggled floating corpse of the spaceship.

It was all planned. This was to give humanity the wake-up call it needed, their long exile, never to return, would be the moment when the people of Earth would see what came of exploration. Then she found him.

It was by a series of accidents that Nyholm came face-to-face with the man who had sent her father the letter that caused his rage and the subsequent fire that burned down the family home in Gothenburg. He had come recommended by a friend, a lover, concerned about the punishment Nyholm was heaping on herself as the secret mission became a reality; no longer a pipe dream, but a chance to alter the course of human history.

In between courses and schedules before the final weeks when the crew had to be isolated from the world, Nyholm left her London flat daily to seek counsel from the man. She had lived in the city off and on for five years, seeking the epicentre of the quake of destruction, what she had come to believe was man-made demolition, the aftereffects of a group of people hell-bent on taking the world apart one constructed idea at a time.

That epicentre hit her like a tidal wave as soon as she stepped into his office for the first time. It was in the form of music that played gently, slowly, and then with gusto and determination, it broke out into the realm of the free-form jazz piece she had heard through the double-locked door of her childhood home.

"I looked you up. I saw who your father was, and I have to say, it is an honour to have you in my consulting room, Licett... daughter of Melker."

That brief introduction echoed around her even now, in space, leaning against the metal panels of a dying craft. Those words changed her outlook, and she should have been mad. She should have ranted and raged as he confessed to having written to her father in the days leading up to his death. Instead, something different took hold of her soul, and she listened more than she talked.

Every day for a month, for three hours she sat in the man's office and heard him speak of things that should not be. Each night, she would log them and study them, looking for the loophole, a way in which she could bring to attention the ideology the man was espousing. She never found one.

Humanity's place in the stars—was it worth the risk? Did we have the right, the sense of humility to preserve what we found in our cosmic backyard? Or would we treat it as though it was an extension of Earth, litter it with our anxieties, abuse it with our confidence and conviction?

By the time Nyholm left the country, her mind had been changed. It was not what he said, but the way he said it.

***

On the other side of the door, Jerome Brassington kept hammering out the message in the vain hope that someone on Earth would hear the strangulated cries of a man driven mad during the time of the flight. The rhythm was reassuring. What he wanted, though, was reaction. Not only from Earth. But from the woman on the other side of the hatchway.

Jerome Brassington had been a last-minute replacement, but not in the way that the rest of the crew imagined. Jack Kiplagat had been hospitalised, but the truth was more disturbing.

Jerome had been fully briefed on how to handle the crew's possible suspicions; his handler had given him every manoeuvre that they might make to cancel the flight, from citing security protocol to the fact that Kiplagat was an indispensable, irreplaceable part of the team. They could wait; give it a month and their colleague would be fit again by then.

The truth was that Jack Kiplagat would never be in shape for such an arduous, mentally challenging journey across space, for Jack Kiplagat was dead, tortured by what some would call extreme measures but what those in the shadows would describe as a judgement call.

Jack Kiplagat had been one of the top-rated astronauts available to Nyholm. They shared common interests; she was in awe of his unflappability in the face of complex questions; in short, he was perfect for the job.

What Nyholm was unaware of was his weakness. He was calm under pressure, but he could talk once the drink started flowing. He had turned his back on his parents' strict upbringing, the religious dominance that had been drummed into him, forced upon him as a child. His first taste of alcohol had lifted the veil from his eyes and installed in him the confidence with which to disagree with them about science and indoctrination.

Like most confidences in life, it was a cover for what had truly ailed him: that of being a rat when it came to secrets.

Ply him with enough drink and those secrets poured out of him like water from a tap. Those secrets were the uninvited guests in his life, the reason he died in agony, still swearing to anyone who would listen that he could be trusted to see the mission through. They hadn't believed him.

More importantly, a well-known doctor hadn't believed him, and in his report, he made it abundantly clear that the thirty-six-year-old Kenyan, who ran away from home at sixteen and became an asylum seeker, finally settling in the United States and excelling in science and sport, had been tipped and groomed to go a long way, but nobody told his tongue that.

Having been warned several times, his inclusion in Nyholm's team on her insistence had depended on his conduct going forward. But one night in a bar in one of Dallas's more conservative, Christian, areas, he overstepped the mark. Before he made it back to his hotel, he was picked up by three men in dark suits and showed what happened to those who messed with their beliefs.

That's where Jerome Brassington stepped in. Installed as the replacement, eased in without headline or front-page news, he walked the tightrope of suspicion and mistrust for several weeks by fulfilling every requirement of the pre-mission status. It was two hundred and ninety days before his cover slipped, a throwaway remark while working with Flight Engineer Thomskilyvan on a simple overhaul and diagnostic check that led to the man's death.

In the ensuing days, he walked a tightrope, a hot, burning with accusation and allegation sliver of steel. The voices he had kept under control, the suffering he had endured through the loneliness of the expedition, was terrifying, but at least they came from his own mind.

Not so with the decorated captain, the woman behind the mission, who now was all that was left of the crew and would be labelled heroic whatever the outcome…if his message wasn't picked up.

***

Licett Nyholm had not used Morse Code in years, but as she finally began to understand the message being hammered out, she realised she had no choice but to complete her mission: to blow what remained of the ship to pieces.

The hammering continued; she bowed her head in silent prayer and pressed the button that would end it all.

Somewhere in space, the transmission suddenly stopped. The explosion was picked up by satellites a few minutes later and relayed to Earth. For a short while, Nyholm was proclaimed a hero.

In a hospital bed in South London, a man's eyes opened, and he started talking. He was still in a coma, but his brain function had become alert, receiving a message, which he repeated and which, once translated, would make the whole world think again.

"•—•• •• —•—• • — — / •••• •— ••• / —•— •• •—•• •—•• •
—•• / ••— ••• / •— •—•• •—•• / ••• •••• • / •• ••• / —••• •
•••• •• —• —•• / ••• •— —••• ——— — •— ——• • / •—• • •——• •
•— — / •—•• •• —•—• • — — / •• ••• / — •••• • / —•— •• •—••
•—•• • •—•"

Ian D. Hall

Chapter Thirty-Four

THE POLICE CANNOT be everywhere.

Bridge understood that in every fibre of her being. Whilst it drove her mad to have to explain to members of the public who had genuine concerns about how their local area always seemed blighted by antisocial behaviour, a police officer could not be in all places; crime just moves on. Sometimes you get lucky; you get to solve a crime that has hung over you, and the world takes on a hue of colour that for a while even the inanest complaint by a serial nit-picker can be looked upon as being solvable.

Thankfully, the night she managed to get into the hospital undetected by the local police and those who had been drafted in from further afield was not a night when crimes of high value and equally low importance would be solved.

Within the hour, Bridge knew another crime would be added to the daily reports, and if she didn't succeed, then by the end of the night, something else would have taken place and a lot of people would be hurt, would lose their lives…What was better? One death but her soul lost, or a dozen, a hundred, maybe a million deaths caused by the mind of an ego out of control? A mind that cut short a life just by introduction.

Bridge had seen it all, had heard every whisper, every hiss that the snake in her mind conveyed. She had walked slowly, almost dragging her feet along the paths and roads that led back to the hospital, and there she waited beside a couple of bushes, crouched down unseen, until the side door opened and the security guard she had met days earlier took a cigarette break and left the door open.

It was all Bridge needed. With every muscle burning, every sinew taut, she sidled up to the door, taking care not to alert the kindly guard who, unfortunately, would receive a disciplinary for his troubles when the hospital bosses worked out how Bridge had managed to gain entry.

The darkness that had settled around her as she sat in the pagoda had also brought rain. The ground on which the hospital sat was drenched by the downpour, making her tracks easy to follow, the muddy tread of her boots transferring to the vinyl floor of the corridor leading to the stairs and deeper into the bowels of the stark, white orifice.

The guard would have had no problem tracing her route. Bridge was physically and mentally drained; he would have caught up with her, no doubt overpowered her, and the threat of dismissal would have vanished into the ether as it was announced the next day on breakfast television that the errant detective had been apprehended…had he been alive to do so.

A figure stalked the detective through the passages, up the back stairs, past the nurses and janitors who worked tirelessly and without thanks. The figure left its own mark on the floors as drops of blood ran cleanly off the weapon it had used without mercy on the unsuspecting guard. He was dead before his body hit the ground; his head followed moments later.

Bridge felt the players starting to merge, to come together: the calculating innocent, the duped professional, the shadow in the midst, the woman pulling the strings of them all, the dying spider in the middle of the web, and then herself, the one who—

She felt them because he felt them. She understood his pain, his fear, his strength, his temptations, his belief.

She was the one to whom the baton of influence had been passed.

She rummaged in his mind as he guided her. He didn't try to fight her as she searched his memories, and then, as she reached the set of stairs she was looking for, she felt a blow against her mind from the inside, a punch of mental force that was the defence of a dark secret, the reason for it all.

She pushed on against the pain, even though it left her giddy, breathless, more nauseated than she had ever felt in her life.

You never believed you had any power except that of being able to convince people—your victims, your followers, those whom you could manipulate. It was fantasy, it was an illusion, a childish dream. What was it that stopped you for a few years? If you were truly exceptional, why wait to control a conversation, to have your way with any woman you wanted? You could have made them all believe that they chose the outcome, that the doubt in their head was purely down to their skittishness, their disgust at the ease of their wanton sex...

Bridge climbed the steps as if programmed, as if she had no other choice but to follow the patterns and commands encoded into her robot brain. The slave took them one step at a time, each counting upwards past pipes that carried waste and water combined, from the bowels of the Earth to the quagmire on the top floor. The shit ran downwards just the same.

The trouble was you convinced yourself. All those meticulous notes and detailed observations—it was circumstance, it was conditioning—right up until you were hit on the temple for a second time in the same place and the pressure of it unlocked your full potential. There was a latency there, wasn't there? Something that resonated in your mind when the wooden boomerang hit you with such force, but it wasn't truly unlocked until the assailant smashed you in the head.

The assailant, the willing assassin... I forgot your part in this cruelty of my mind.

The thing is, I was under the impression he'd been expecting you. You were the guest for which the second glass had been set, and yet as you stood behind him, you set in motion all that has happened over the last couple of weeks. *You didn't kill him, but you were the catalyst of my torment. All it took was a swing of an arm, a hand holding an item of weight, and the clock reset, knocking the final part into place so that the bomb in his mind would go off.*

What pushed you to kill him now? I know you are there, skulking around in the hospital, following me...You can't hear me, we are not bonded in that way, but I can hear your heart beating wildly. You don't want to do this, but revenge is a powerful force...I should know. I feel the urge to destroy him once and for all. For even if he wasn't Death as he so poetically wrote in his journals, he has become something else—someone who can push another into doing his will. I imagine it is only a certain distance for now, but what if...

What if he can manipulate a person, a group of people beyond, say, a mile radius?

What if...we said five miles? Ten? Fifty miles?

What if we conjectured that it would, in time, be possible for him to project his thoughts sixty-two miles away? A hundred, a thousand...

The stronger his mind grows, the more adaptable and adept he becomes at flexing his will. Soon, he would influence everyone, enslave us all, steal our free for every major and insignificant decision. From the coffee and pie stall around the corner from Waterloo Station across the dirty old river to Parliament, from deep underground where a train driver going at fifteen miles an hour suddenly feels overwhelmed with a destructive thought and ploughs into a station at twenty-five, thirty-five, fifty miles an hour. From deep underground to space, no one will be sa—

Bridge stopped climbing. This state of reasoning she was using suddenly gave her the final insight to the problem at hand.

Oh, my God, he already does have that range. The mission, Mars, it's going to end in disaster. He's inside the heads of the crew. Not directly, not across the millions of miles, but I bet anything that his list of clients includes at least one person on that ship.

It was at that moment she felt the stranger who was following her fade away. Intuition told her he was still stalking in the shadows but had instinctively hidden himself. Surely, he couldn't have known she had been…what? *Infected* was the only reasonable word she could conceive.

The clarity was bond breaking. She felt the revelation of the word untie her, unshackle her. She was still enthralled, but something in that moment had altered the dynamic.

Where are you?

And there he was, and he was blind without her.

Bridge. Don't you abandon me. I…I…

Bridge screamed, but not out of fear; out of fury and freedom.

"What? Come on don't be shy now, after you've been groping my mind all this time, your inky, devil-like touch fondling my psyche, what is it you want, you ego-driven man?"

For a moment, there was silence. The hospital that had been so full of noise, of boilers belching tunelessly, the clanking of pipes and the echoes of doctors' orders. And in that single, perfect moment, the voice spoke out with a tremble.

I'm afraid of the dark, Bridge.

Bridge smiled to herself.

If there had been a mirror in front of her, she would have not recognised her appearance. It was a smile driven by exploitation, the power of forgery of a human conscience being replaced by a darker, more insidious heart. She was Death's apprentice no more.

She climbed up one more flight of stairs and came to the door that led to the ward where the man was being cared for.

Lights started to flash and growl with electricity surges; machines grew tiresome as she took a tentative step into the world as herself for the final time.

All the pieces fitted.

The Daughters of Gorgon, all smoke and mirrors designed to frighten the citizens into giving people what they wanted: autonomy, sovereignty, authority to bring a man to justice. It was just as much a manipulation as every other group on the planet;

the only difference was that two of the women involved had wildly differing agendas. One wanted the death of the men she blamed for her father's mental condition, the other wanted all men dead, and those women who stood in her way would be tried in absentia and killed for the traitors to their sex that they were.

If Bridge was able to feel any kind of empathy or sympathy at that moment, she would have shuddered as she realised that Portia Cullise had been the brains behind the bombing at Tottenham. She had killed the mobile food van owner. All the information had been there the whole time; it was just that Bridge had been blinded by the infection that had bedded in the moment she took an interest in the attempted murder of a nondescript man.

The corridor was unnaturally empty.

A tannoy announcement broke her silent recriminations and reveals.

She immediately recognised the voice.

"Bridge. Ingrid. This is Torlay. You have a man in the building wielding a sword. He has killed two people already, but we can't see him. We're going to shut off all but vital power. You will be in the dark, but so will he. We have in custody two women. One is the owner of the gallery in Whitechapel, the other is the wife of the florist we met earlier today. It seems the wife did him in before driving Portia and the man to London."

Silence reigned again, and the power, as good as Torlay's word, was stripped of all but the most essential duties to life and limb.

Bridge knew the playbook; they would come after the man with every possible reason to take him down, fully endorsed by their superintendent and with the backing of the intelligence services.

"Bridge, if you can hear me, please understand. If we get the chance to take you down as well, if you do anything stupid, reckless… if you kill anyone, you will be shot. Last thing, we have Alice Sidney and the professor with us."

It amused Bridge that Torlay had not given her the sentimental signal of 'Good Luck'.

She was being told to stand down.

She inwardly scoffed at the suggestion.

I loathe you.

That was her own inner voice, and it made her quickly ashamed to have given it room, for she knew there was no reason to be anything but thankful to Torlay, yet those three small words must have come from somewhere.

Was she as free as she thought?

She continued onwards. Empty spaces greeted her at every step. She smiled grimly as she thought of the police station during the night shift, the eeriness of the stone walls that whispered the crimes of all who had inhabited the Victorian cells, that had granted refuge to so many during the Blitz, that held the memories of some of South London's most notorious criminals who could have burned down the building at any point but saw the investigations into their empires as playing a game. She felt their every stare and confession as she walked through the building.

Nothing, though, felt more desolate than a near-empty hospital floor.

Bridge didn't dwell on it for long. There was little point in wondering how the staff had emptied this particular level. It was only when she allowed herself to look out of the corner of her eye, to see beyond the narrow view, that she saw the occasional figure sitting statue-still, their patients unable to be moved. These were the ones who were close to dying and the nurses who refused to let their patient face their last moments on Earth alone.

Several women sat in the darkness, holding the hands of the patiently departed, as she trod between them.

Finally, Bridge came to the room.

Even in the dark, she saw the man she had been warned of. A small sliver of light came from the array of machines, the blinking pulses that suggested life was possible even in the joyless soul of a coma.

By his side was another man. They had never been formally introduced, only exchanging a glance where she had noticed the scar on his head, but she knew exactly who he was: Alexander Peros, holding the sword against the neck of his tormentor.

Chapter Thirty-Five

BRIDGE WAS GLAD that the man who had caused so much trouble for her and others was oblivious to his fate.

Peros was sweating, beads of perspiration running down his face and falling to the linoleum floor. Bridge nodded to show she understood his intention. Slowly, she raised her right hand, her open palm imploring the man to listen to her. He didn't react in the way she hoped, but neither did he push the sword harder against the skin. The blade hovered and then moved up over the chin, past the nose and the open but motionless eyes, until it came to the middle of the forehead.

Bridge could see the madness in his eyes. She could feel the terror oozing out of the pores of his body. The smell was nauseating, sickly. This was a man teetering on the edge. It was hard not to feel pity for him, but she could not allow him to kill his oppressor. What had he done except look at him wrongly, send flowers every week by way of apology? It would not even get to trial, not in this case anyway. The two people he had killed, according to Torlay, that was a different matter, but he was undoubtedly mad and would be permanently removed from society, but if he made a move to kill his psychological aggressor, he would be scarred mentally in such a way that he would be better off dead.

Down the hallway, the sound of soft footsteps carried in the air.

They were coming.

The soldiers of Death.

Bridge, still holding her hand out with her palm showing, took a step closer to Peros. He flinched but stood his ground.

"What is he to you?"

The question caught Bridge off guard. She felt her mouth quickly go dry, gallons of sand drowning her voice, catching at the back of her throat. She sucked at her cheeks to release enough saliva to clear the words and give them an escape route, to give Peros the safety net he was going to need in less than a minute.

"He is a person of interest, a man who has caused others to do inexcusable things, to cause harm to innocent people like you, Alexander."

"You know my name?" His hand slightly wavered as he asked the question, a hint of surprise on his tongue. From experience, Bridge knew she had made a connection. It never failed: use a name the person responds to, to show them you care at least enough to call them by a first name. Never use a surname on its own; for some, the trauma of the institution is enough to set them off.

Footsteps, closer now. Could the man hear them?

"Look, Alexander—may I call you that, or do you prefer Alex?"

The ghost of a smile appeared on his lips. "Alexander is fine, thank you."

"Alexander, I know the pain you have been in. Trust me, I know. He is in my head too. His voice, his manipulation, his accent, certain words that trigger a response—I hear them as well."

If the light had been sufficient, Bridge would have seen a couple of tears flow and battle it out against the sweat still dripping down the man's forehead.

"You do?"

The words were spoken in anguish, expressing grief for what he had endured since that day when he laughed at the boy who had been hit with the boomerang. What he saw in those eyes at that moment, Bridge would never know, but she felt the distress in those two small, meaningful words.

"I do," she confirmed. Two more words, the shortest phrase of all, yet one which showed solidarity, a profound statement of mutual understanding. A vow.

"Please, Alexander, put down the sword. There are men coming with orders to take you down. Do you understand what I'm saying?"

Watching someone mentally go through their options can be disquieting. Bridge had seen such a look before on a man holding a woman hostage in a Post Office robbery that had gone terribly wrong. The perpetrator had been a model citizen, the type who never made waves, quite content with his lot in life, money dutifully saved, a wife who respected him, three children who adored him, never gambled, barely drank, enjoyed a cigar at Christmas, popular, and all the other clichés one might throw at someone when they have walked through life without causing a scar on someone else's heart.

Then his middle daughter was abducted as she walked home from school one fine June day; she never returned home.

For a week, the press were all over it—no surprise there. She was a small, blonde child, and the journalists who picked up on the story made a fuss of her smile, her loving attitude. Then they decided that the father, even though he was with his eldest child at an emergency dentist appointment at the time the incident occurred, was responsible.

It only takes a word in the right ear, an opinion piece by a person with a dirty, suspicious mind, to start the ball rolling and destroy another's life.

The press found out there was a fifteen-minute window in which the loving father was not on the premises of the dental practice, and for two weeks, he became suspect number one. The inhabitants of social media, the trolls, the ones who mean well but cannot but spread idle gossip, the seekers of damnation and those who bring down wrath to make up for their own dark hearts and boring lives—they destroyed him.

His daughter's body turned up in a breaker's yard stuffed in the boot of a car that belonged to a known paedophile. He confessed immediately, but the man's mind was broken. He had lost his daughter, and whilst his wife and two other daughters stood by and in front of him, pleading for the press and the public to leave him alone, he was already damned.

As Bridge looked into his eyes that day in the Post Office, as she tried to calm him down while he slipped further into madness, he told her that all he had done was slip out for a moment to think. If there had been a camera in the alleyway where he stood, fretting and agonising over the poor state of oral health that his daughter had kept from him, then the weeks of torture would have never happened. Bridge asked him to put down the gun, promised she would make sure the courts treated him with understanding, that he would receive help, just to let the woman he had in his arms go. He wavered, and she could see the cogs whirring behind his eyes, shortening his options to what Bridge hoped would be the right one.

He let her go.

And then he put the gun against his temple and fired.

The memory had haunted Bridge ever since. It was one of her first situations where she was the lead officer.

That same haunted stare that the bereaved man had etched deeply on his face as he lifted the gun to his head, was now appearing on the man holding the sword over his intended victim.

Bridge understood the reason for the man's sudden change. It was his perception that she had lied to him; Bridge didn't need to turn around to know there were two armed officers behind her. Peros' face told her all she needed to know.

"Alexander, listen to me. I am on your side. I know what you've been through, I can help. I promise to do all I can. But first you need to put the sword down on the floor and then put your hands on your head. It is important. Do not attempt to raise the sword, do not wave it around. I know you want revenge. I know this man is the cause of your pain, but please, let me help you get out of here alive."

The wavering face, the mind processing its options… The irresistible draw of déjà vu reared its head and laughed at Bridge.

It was over quickly.

The decision was taken.

Yet the domino effect of Alexander Peros' final moments was put into motion by the man in the coma lifting his left hand and grasping the wrist of the man who had once tried to take his life and was on the verge of making a second attempt.

Bridge was sure that what had just occurred had not been witnessed by the officers behind her. Despite them wearing the required night vision goggles, the darkness had obscured the disturbing scene. Was it the last vestige of consciousness? Was she hallucinating? She had, after all, not long ago been hospitalised herself. Was it the painkillers she had been prescribed? The knocks she had taken when she refused to stay in on the advice of the doctors? It no longer mattered, for as the grip tightened, behind her she felt the officers take three steps back and then throw the stun grenades directly into the room.

The detective turned in mid-plea to stop their action, and as she turned, the man in the bed was able to bring down the sword across his neck, killing himself with such force that it virtually decapitated him in a single stroke. The thunder flash of the grenades seared their cold, white heat onto the detective's retinas. Blinded, she fell to floor screaming in agony, only partially aware of the three bullets that took the life of Alexander Peros.

***

Outside in the cold night air, Torlay received word that the suspect was down. He understood the message, and as Professor Seward lowered his head in sadness of a patient lost, he asked with concern on Bridge's condition.

There was radio silence, agonising, unbearable, excruciating silence that reminded Torlay of the desolation felt by the journalist as he looked upon the world overrun by the corpses of dead Martians.

"Detective Inspector Bridge is down. She is alive. She caught the full flash of the stun grenades. I think…I think she's blind."

Epilogue

P ROFESSOR SEWARD SAT back in his chair and studied his patient.

The detective's sight had not returned, and the trauma of the experience, the intensity of the weeks leading up to the moment when she was robbed of one of her senses, had led to her breakdown.

The collapse was expected, at least by Seward, who had himself been driven to the brink of madness as he sought to clear his name with the committee that had been set up to fully investigate the facility, Seward's part in the death of a man in his care, the murder of his secretary by the art gallery, what the facility had been used for after the fire that destroyed it in the mid-1980s and, years before that the murder of a drug addict by an Afghan terrorist and drug lord.

Bridge's condition had initially been diagnosed as psycho-somatic, the mind blocking out what it never wanted to visualise again, but subsequent tests had shown the back of retina in both eyes had burnt out, as if she had stared directly into the blazing sun for several minutes. Legally, she was now blind, but at least for now she was safe from the demons that had plagued her after the horrific events in the hospital.

Seward had spoken to her on numerous occasions after she had been carried by two doctors to a secure room, screaming that it was the devil, not Death, whom they should fear. The devil was still out there and coming for them all.

He tapped the desk absent-mindedly, paying little heed to the paper that showed the headline:

NASA Investigation Finds Captain Licett Nyholm
Guilty of Sabotage

Drusilla Pero, Portia Cullise, and the disgraced police officer were all found guilty of various murders, of sponsoring terrorism, and were now in jail, far from the prying eyes of those who smelled a story that had much more to tell.

None of this mattered to Seward. His focus was on the woman in front of him. She was calm, erudite, passionate. She still had nightmares that she couldn't express, but on a day-to-day basis, she was well enough to return home—with help. Her friends Torlay and Beaumont had already guaranteed their unwavering support, and Nico's family had said she could live with them for as long as she needed.

"Ingrid?" He spoke to her softly but with intent.

"Yes, Professor? I'm sorry, I was miles away, I was listening to you tap your desk. It sounded…I thought it was recognisable."

"That's okay, Ingrid. I asked you if you feel you are able to go home with the support that has been promised. There will be an adjustment, of course, and I'd like to meet with you once a week for the foreseeable future. In time, we can reduce that to once a month, and then only when you need to talk to me. Do you see any problems with that?"

Bridge smiled broadly, her dark glasses rising as the smile reached the creases and scar tissue.

"Professor Seward, all is well, and I assure you. I can see no problem at all. But don't think for a minute that because I am blind, I cannot see at all."

Acknowledgements

I, Death came from a love of the science fiction/horror films that, when watched in isolation, are often viewed by the critic as having nothing to offer the audience except an hour and a half's distraction.

One of those films, *The Medusa Touch*—which came on the back of the outstanding *Equus* and starred the great Richard Burton, the powerful performer Lee Remick, and Jeremy Brett—gave me a shiver of fear the first time I saw it on television sometime in the early 1980s.

Written by the superb Peter Van Greenaway and released fifty years ago, it is a tale that, like films such as *The Andromeda Strain*, *Logan's Run*, and the sequels to the mighty *Planet Of The Apes*, transfixed my young mind with the seemingly implausible and unlimited ways we can be pushed to our limits by that which we do not accept as a truth of horror.

The cinematic adaptation of Peter Van Greenaway's novel inspired me to revisit the idea of a person being able to cause harm to another human being by thought alone and how that could be deemed fantastic, yet the delusion of it is more accepted. In that kernel, that drop of realisation, I found my next novel, *I, Death*, to be one of exciting possibilities.

I decided early on, as far back as writing the ending of *Colony*, that this book would be part of the world in which the city of Avoncross features—not as a sequel to *Underneath* or *Colony*, but a side view of the world around the events that have already been established.

I hope this gives the reader an even greater awareness of the idea of what a place—a city, town, village—can create in its midst; the horrors that can be spawned and birthed there.

I owe huge thanks to various people for their continued support while I was writing, not least my mum, Julie Hall, who has been dealing with the failing presence of health of my father as he deals with the continuing battle of Alzheimer's, my cousin Bryan, who has been a brother to me for fifty years, friends such as Justin Brown, from my school days at Bicester School, and musician Mark Luker, who allowed me to send finished ideas to them to safeguard.

I also want to thank those who gave me their support in raising money towards the audio adaptation of *Underneath*, and to the actor Paul Duckworth, who has been instrumental in bringing the words to life.

As ever, none of this would be possible without the wonderful belief of two important women: my publisher Debbie McGowan, who has once more taken me to places I could never believe would be open to me, and my supportive and tremendous wife, Judith.

I am always thankful to these two women, without whom in reality I would never have been given the voice that I dedicate to the books of James Herbert, and to those friends who have lost and lost during their lives.

Thank you again for taking me into your nightmares. I hope I have found a place in your dreams.

Ian D. Hall 2024

About the Author

Having been found on a 'Co-op' shelf in Stirchley, Birmingham by a Cornish woman and a man of dubious footballing taste, Ian grew up in neighbouring Selly Park and Bicester in Oxfordshire. After travelling far and wide, he now considers Liverpool to be his home.

Ian was educated at Moor Green School, Bicester Senior School, and the University of Liverpool, where he gained a 2:1 (BA Hons) in English Literature.

He now reviews and publishes daily on the music, theatre and culture within Merseyside.

Please visit www.liverpoolsoundandvision.co.uk

By the Author

Poetry

Black Book

Tales from the Adanac House

Four in the Morning, Pavement Blues

Writing Out of Earshot

Novels

The Death of Poetry

Dark Chrysalis

Ghost Apples

Underneath

Colony

I, Death

Sound and Vision

A Trip to a Festival (Me, Myself... Only)

Listening Out of Earshot:
A collection of words and music from the friends of Ian D. Hall

Beaten Track Publishing

For more titles from Beaten Track Publishing,
please visit our website:

https://www.beatentrackpublishing.com

Thanks for reading!

www.ingramcontent.com/pod-product-compliance
Lightning Source LLC
Chambersburg PA
CBHW021520240626
47154CB00002B/718